Cadillac Orpheus

A NOVEL

Solon Timothy Woodward

Free Press

New York   London   Toronto   Sydney

FREE PRESS

A Division of Simon & Schuster, Inc.
1230 Avenue of the Americas
New York, NY 10020

First Free Press hardcover edition January 2008

FREE PRESS and colophon are trademarks of Simon & Schuster, Inc.

For information about special discounts for bulk purchases,
please contact Simon & Schuster Special Sales at 1-800-456-6798 or
business@simonandschuster.com

Book design by Ellen R. Sasahara

Manufactured in the United States of America

1   3   5   7   9   10   8   6   4   2

Library of Congress Cataloging-in-Publication Data

Woodward, Solon Timothy.
Cadillac Orpheus : a novel / Solon Timothy Woodward.—1st Free Press
hardcover ed.
p.   cm.
1. African Americans—Fiction.   2. African American families—
Fiction.   I. Title.
PS3623.O687C33   2008
813'.6—dc22
                            2007023473

ISBN-13: 978-1-4165-4930-7
ISBN-10:   1-4165-4930-7

For Ev

And nothing remained but to sink back into the pillows, tired from the disappointment, breath-robbed and voiceless, whispering: "No more sleep." Yet now for the third time, as if in succor, came an astonishing reply: "No one has been so watchfully awake as you, my Father; rest now, for rest is due you, my Father, rest and watch no more." His eyelids closed softly upon being called father, which was like a gift, like a reward for his self-abnegation, a dispensation for his vigilance . . ."

—HERMAN BROCH, *The Death of Virgil*

Expelled from Paradise,
that will be our paradise.

—WILLIAM LOGAN, *"Van Gogh in the Pulpit"*

Acknowledgments

I am very grateful to Amber Qureshi, my editor; Alex Glass, my agent—who believed in me before the first word was written; and John Casey, a gracious mentor throughout the years.

Cadillac Orpheus

What he would suddenly remember was how dry her lips had been—his mother's—as if she had had a fever: such crinkled, pinkish hulls. As if instead of flesh the glassine panel of an envelope had brushed his forehead. This was what came to him in watching his father's face, his mouth. The boy was seven or eight. He had not anticipated his father's crying, no boy expects to see his father weep; he tried to focus on his father's hands massaging the steering wheel—but the boy found himself, instead, tracking where the tears and sweat gathered in his father's mustache. The boy's cousin was in the backseat, asleep through it all. The revolving light of the sheriff's sedan pulsed through the interior of the car—his father's car, as his father emphatically reminded his mother as she pushed the boy about the house to gather his belongings (pea coat, toothbrush, boomerang, a puppet: the boy's hands found these things automatically). When his mother came to the car, carrying the green and tan valise that was hers in miniature, his father twisted it from her and threw it onto the carport.—*Jack-shit from you. I can buy him whatever the fuck you've got in that suitcase!* That was when his mother kissed him, quickly, furtively. Her lips were parched: she had stopped crying a while back; she was exhausted. *You're just too fuckin' drunk to care. Ain't that right?* his father heckled.

I

The sheriff had not anticipated confronting a grown, colored man crying at the steering wheel. A woman, yes—that could be foreseen, even expected: fear, maybe manipulation. Who knows! If he had been privy to the emotions over the past twenty-four hours, traveling with two young boys, fatigue, maybe. But what the officer would not know was that his father had actually been cheerful up until the moment they'd been stopped. They had been lost for a few hours on access roads and traces spidering through the Tennessee backcountry. *We're meandering!* his father said, turning the steering wheel to and fro like a child playing at driving, the car zigzagging across the red baked clay. *We're goddam meandering!* his father shouted at the windshield. The boy flinched at his father's voice. The glass was a mire of sodden leaves and cicadas and other brown debris—but there would be the brief tags of emerald luminescence from the fireflies, which the boy welcomed, withdrawing from his father (and the parched lips of his mother) to the gray night foliage and verdant memory.

His cousin had been asleep through all 476 miles from Georgia to their present location. Paul had slept through the leaf-stripping rain; through the stultifying noon heat; through the boom and scribble of the lightning cascades (whose glare the boy found frustrating—like the fireflies, only a hiccup: a hesitant glimpse of the surrounding orchards and hills.)

But his cousin: sleep was where he primarily resided. Paul seemed to sleep through his childhood, through natural disasters, family upheavals. Most impressive, Paul had slept through The Rabies Child incident.

It had been a neighbor's mongrel, one late spring, just above the Florida panhandle.

Only when the girl was slavering, flailing in rictus, did someone connect the immured bats, the dog, and the girl. The girl was a younger sister to Paul. She was only nine and, sick, began barking:

2

the slightest noise, a pulse of wind, a bad smell, would bring on a laryngeal spasm, then a choking squeal. She became haunted, snapping. She died in fever, recoiling at the slosh of a washbasin.

It's that fuckin' dog, one of the uncles, Simon, suddenly recounted. He told the other brothers (eight of them in all) of seeing the dog jogging and whimpering past him down the trace with a wreath of four or five fluttering bats dangling from her neck, an embedded necklace. Simon and a buddy were drinking in the cab of his truck, laughing at the bitch's misery as she went by. Then it came together: the bite, the girl's seeping wound, the strange sickness of the girl. And then—the cur yowling, trapped in the neighbor's barn, shot. The eight Toak brothers convened at the house of her father, Pritchett, where it was decided that he should seek justice in the death of his daughter through the death of the owner of the dog. So they equipped him with a rifle and a Luger, their souvenir from the war. *Lemme come wit you, Pree. No tellin',* the oldest Toak volunteered. Pritchett nodded in the affirmative. Paul was no more than half awake on the couch. Blinking, stultified, he sleepwalked through the commotion to the kitchen, where he sucked down a concoction of cornbread and buttermilk, bobbing his head in tempo to the course of the discussion. Then Paul staggered back to his corner of the couch (the glaucous-eyed, cataract-beset grandfather occupying the other) and curled up. The two Toaks hurtled from the family's luctual chorus (the boy's father the loudest) over three miles of paltry tobacco land, swamp bush, and pitch, and murdered the owner of the dog along with his family (a wife, four children.) His cousin slept on. *All them Toaks a devil's piece of work,* the boy's mother said. Soon after, the perpetrators of the bad acts were two of the thirty-nine Negroes lynched that summer.

License and registration. The sheriff was perplexed and bemused. The boy from fear began to cry. His cousin, either coming to surface from sleep or in sleep, began blubbering as well. *Jeez Gawd the Almighty,* the sheriff shook his head, *My luck. A carload of wailing nigras.*

3

Everything that is sclerosed into memory may still be betrayed by willed nostalgia. The boy's eyes moved from his father's mouth to his hand: the falsely benign hand against the rocker panel. Years later he would try to see it (the hand) as something separate from his father, or maybe an aberrant tic; alternatively, he would tell himself that his father had no choice, that all was done in an effort to rescue them.

The hand pounced upon the sheriff's tie and jerked his brow against the doorframe before thudding the head onto the steering wheel. What the boy would remember was the tail end of what the sheriff said starting with, *Jeezgawd*—the first thing said he couldn't recall in part because of his father shouting. The sheriff in memory was younger than his father. And the boy thought he could remember the last thing said by the sheriff, *Ohjeezgawd*.

But what was the first thing? It bothered him, because he could not remember. Maybe, *Help,* he said, or, *No! Stop!* Maybe it was the backward plea to Jesus.

What's wrong with you? What's wrong with you, man? his father shouted. The officer yelped, his body contorted in the window. His head was almost in his father's lap. The curious thing—no, the frightening thing—was that his father was engaged in a monologue. Long afterward, the boy could see his father (this alchemy of thought and memory) pummeling the officer repeatedly in the face, all the while talking to himself, his father's face still damp (the boy saw this between the shadows cast by the blue revolving light) from his tears and sweat. At that point it was as if the boy, and the man the boy was to become, sat together watching (the boy on the man's lap, say) and together came to the realization—My father. My father is not good. But it was the boy by himself who was frightened as his father's hands consumed the sheriff's features.

In the end it was his cousin who tried to stop it. He reached over the back of the seat and, with his child's strength, grabbed the thrashing arm and pulled; when that did not work his cousin deliberately scratched him: parallel tracks of black streaks beginning at his father's wrists, deepening into a single welt.

His father had the man's head between the spokes of the steering wheel. A grotesque sculpture: John the Baptist's head before Salome. He gouged one eye repeatedly and pried at the other, all the while chittering over the officer's pleas.

Then his father pried back the lid of the man's left eye, the relatively good eye, and addressed the man in an unintelligible murmur that the boy could not hear.

What did the old man say exactly? The boy—Feddy—as a man conjectured it was about blindness, possibly blindness and sleep, for his father on occasion in later years would ramble on about the sleep of the blind, speaking of *his* father's blindness. The boy questioned his father well into adulthood, trying to get him to recount what had happened that night—but his father construed the query as a prompt for anecdotes of his youth and survival, which he turned into forums for wheedling, intimidation, and braggadocio. He would wax pensive, once actually expressing a kind of remorse for *not* killing the officer, drawing the analogy: *A sandwich fuck. Like having one woman underneath you but fantasizing about the one you really want.*

I should kill your motherfuckin' ass but I've got children in the car, his father said. He then adjusted a new cigarette, plucking a fleck of tobacco from his tongue. The spavined man moaned in response and the boy watched as his father placed his hand on the man's crown, and in an inverted obstetrics, pushed. His father then stepped from the car, grappled the man by the collar and seat of his pants and threw him into a selvage of laurel and scrub. *You don't know me,* his father said. *And you're goddam blind now. But let me tell you—some goddam nigger did this. Heh. Remember—and you shouldn't have any trouble now going to sleep. Heh.*

The boy made himself believe that this was what he heard. What he remembered.

The boy would definitely remember that the wind that night was festive, with scraps of scudding clouds and whirling snarls of black skittering things.

It would only be as a man that he could say to himself it was like checking a stage clock during a play (a revelation that occurred while watching his son's Halloween performance): inadvertently you chase the minute hand for time. You, in your near-adult fears and concerns, near-adult worries, turn to that parent as a child—glance at the clock. Because you forget. You forget that he or she can provide neither the succor nor the ballast you desire and need. And then you sheepishly remember that neither real time nor the time of the play moves the clock, that the clock and that parent are in a place outside of time, both chronometric and human.

Book One

I

The complete destruction by fire of Ardath Cremations, Inc. (listed in the phone book between Credit and Cruises, "The Dignified Alternative . . . Save Your Money for Somebody You Love"), was singularly the result of recalcitrance. James Ardath, in contrast to first cousins of the same surname who owned a chain of mortuaries throughout northern Georgia and Alabama, had had a three-man operation on the north side of town that, for the past ten to fifteen years, was considered a blight on the black community. Several organizations tried, unsuccessfully, to have the area rezoned and the crematorium removed. The business was on the edge of a semicommercial center where, just before the crematorium, a used-tire lot and the now defunct Sha-Na-Na Burgers (with its boarded windows and decapitated car speakers) gave way to a Crayola box of red, yellow, and green clapboard houses. Behind the site was an anemic cluster of pines. Arsonists had tried to burn down the business twice before, so it was a complete surprise when it came out that the fire was from natural causes.

"You don't burn four hundred and twenty-six pounds of fat. That's just plain suet," Seth Burnett said. He had, at one time, worked for the assistant medical examiner of the county. "It's like lighting a keg of dynamite. But who's gonna listen to me?" He had repeated this insight to various television reporters as they arrived throughout the fire. In fact, there was Seth in miniature on the bar television repeating word for word the same explanation. This wasn't done without self-interest. Seth positioned himself for each local-news program strategically alongside his van, DISAST-PRO: SON-SHINE INDUSTRIAL SPECIALTY CLEANERS FOR OFFENSIVE SPECTACLES, just for the interviews. Burnett and Sons had recently begun scouring and sterilizing residential and commercial sites in the wake of all manner of catastrophes. They lived a block or so from the crematorium; Seth had been one of the few people in the neighborhood who would have anything to do with the Ardaths. "I tole him. The Lawtons tole him." Lawton Mortuary had turned down the body for cremation, gently recommending standard burial, given full assessment of the bulk. "I tole him, I said, 'Mr. James, with all that fat, Mr. Smullian's gonna blaze hotter than a comet. You ain't gonna be able to control that burn, not with the kiln you've got.' What'd he do?" James had dutifully nodded in agreement and with the help of his two assistants loaded the remains onto the pyre. Soon thereafter the owner of the used-tire lot was seen zigzagging through the rows of tires that bordered the blaze, arms flailing in wide ovals and figure eights, spraying the tires with a puny arc of water from a garden hose.

"You don't burn four hundred and twenty-six pounds of fat," Seth repeated to his friends at He Ain't Here. The He Ain't Here Lounge was a bar with a sign and no other distinguishing exterior features excepting the paint job, which was a Mardi Gras explosion of purple, green, and yellow. It was a shotgun shack with skeletal dangling lights and leathery wood floors that would, at certain key points, buckle and whine with walking weight. The canteen doors were always propped open with cinder blocks (even on a rainy day, as today was), and directly to the left was a small stage that, in the past, precariously bounced and shook under whatever acts Leon, the proprietor, was able to wheedle and snag for a weekend. Changing tastes, however, had led to Leon's recent experiments with open-mike night and hip-hop DJs to attract younger crowds, whom he secretly hated.

"... I mean a real high combustion point. You double the amount of fat, you quadruple the heat. Next thing you know you've got hell's fire in the kitchen." Seth looked about the table from Feddy to Melan to Ce-Ce and back to Feddy.

"I bet that's what's behind those folks just catching fire, that spontaneous combustion. It's the curse of the supersized," Feddy said, nudging Ce-Ce. "Fat people, Seth. I'm telling you, you best stop stroking those big girls. You've got to leave that honey, Rene, alone! One day, the two of you'll be squeezing each other, all lovey-dovey, and then you'll start sniffing. 'Smoke?' you'll say, though you know how that chick likes her barbeque and you'll be thinking it's some of that sauce she dabs behind her ears for perfume—next thing you know we'll be throwing dirt and passing the collection plate."

"Here I am trying to talk to you folks serious and you start sounding stupid," Seth muttered.

"All right, man. I apologize deeply. I'm sorry," Feddy said. He waved the waitress over. "Chicken livers and potato salad, soul eyes. And a bottle of hot sauce?" After he was sure she was headed in the right direction (the kitchen) and not back to the magazine waiting at the bar, Feddy Toak returned his full attention to Seth Burnett. He loved the man. They had grown up together, meeting over thirty years ago—around the age of twelve—in a schoolyard fight. Since childhood Seth was one to get a hair up his butt for any reason he could muster. "I finally figured it out, Seth. I figured out why you're so goddam sensitive and I'm going to explain it to you. You know why? It's called weaning. You came off the titty too soon." Feddy had presented this insight a few months ago while they were all sitting around watching the Super Bowl; Seth ended up not speaking to him for a good three weeks.

Swaying at the bar's back entrance was Seth's oldest daughter, Bethena. Reverend Seth Burnett, in addition to being pastor of the Hope and Savior Christian Faith Church, owner and operator of Sonshine Industrial Cleaners, and nighttime janitorial supervisor at Diglot's Bakery, had been married twice, divorced twice. He had two families now under his watch; a total of nine children. Bethena was his special child. The two-year-old moved in tandem with her mother while a glair of snot bivalved from the child's nostril. Bethena was visibly pregnant again. Seth explained to people, meeting her for the first time, that Bethena had been dropped headfirst at the age of two. "Deddy! Deddy!" she whispered loudly from the doorway. She wouldn't enter because, she complained, people looked at her funny. (The fact of the matter was that her head was unnaturally flat. "You could park a dinner tray while getting a blow job," Melan ruminated to Feddy from his convertible one summer day as she lurched down the street in her halter top.)

"Bet, girl, what do you want?"

She looked down, raking a foot across the gravel. "I need to talk to you about somethin'."

"Well, go home and call me later."

"But it's important."

"What'd I say?"

Bethena stomped off, forgetting her daughter, who stood glued to the doorsill.

Seth sighed. "Go on, Bochelle." The little girl skittered away.

"That whole thing's a mess—not just the fire but the nuns and all," Ce-Ce hesitantly contributed. Ce-Ce was still considered Melan's new girlfriend (exquisitely lustered and deep complected—"Moves like black honey," he'd sigh to Feddy). She had moved to town from Cheyenne, Wyoming, a few months ago, stumbling into the He Ain't Here through her job as an insurance adjuster trainee. There she latched on to Melan. Melan worked for the Port Authority in some undefined role that allowed him to oversee the comings and goings of the dock. Melan eventually got Ce-Ce hired as an assistant. And it was Melan who got Feddy his current job supervising loading. As to Ce-Ce—she was a good twenty years younger than Melan (who was forty-six). Feddy figured that as a kid Ce-Ce (actually, Cedera: she confessed to Feddy that she'd given herself the nickname after leaving Georgia) kept looking for ways to fit in with children her own age but couldn't. She probably irritated them—Feddy saw her as the type who was always seeking grown-up approval. He could tell that she had resigned herself early to the company and condescension of adults—deferring, teasing, and seductive—but always halfway, tentative. Subsequently there was an undercurrent of resentment that on rare occasions came off as a priggishness.

"Yeah, but those were some tough old nuns," Melan said, stealing a chicken liver from Feddy. Seth tried to follow but was too slow and a butter knife rapped his knuckles.

"You all got jobs. Order your own plates," Feddy snarled.

"And I mean those were some *old* black women!" Melan continued. "Hell, Sister Mildred and Sister Lawrence looked all of ninety back when I was in school! You all were probably the last ones to see them gussied up and pretty in their horse and buggy, though," Melan said, blithely taking the remaining half of the Parker roll from Feddy's plate while Feddy was distracted, trying again to flag down the waitress.

"Rev . . ." Melan crooked his finger, motioning to Seth.

Seth, padding his sweat-dappled forehead with a gray handkerchief, leaned forward.

"Seth, man, you got to let me in on one thing. This television business—some acting bug, I guess—this is a family trait, right?" He pointed at Seth's oldest boy, Bayonne, who was now on the news in clown dress with a multicolored wig. Bayonne was pantomiming a knife fight with a similarly dressed young man; all this was incorporated into a breakdance routine. "Mind, I get you two confused," Melan said.

Seth ignored him. "Said when they picked 'em up it was like lifting Styrofoam. So light."

"It's a miracle they ain't all dead, all I can say," Feddy said.

Suicide by asphyxiation: Smullian had let a car engine run in his garage. Four retired Oblate nuns—Sisters of Mercy, Negro women from an order founded back in the 1920s—had lived in a Moncrieff Street apartment atop Smullian's garage. The carbon monoxide that killed him unfortunately drifted upward. Two died in their sleep; two were hospitalized at county. The two remaining now hobbled about town, one in a warp-wheeled flea-market chair while the other, tottering, pushed.

"Myself, I think it's kinda pitiful. I saw those two old women at some used-car lot off Philips," Ce-Ce said.

"You telling me somebody's gonna sell Methuselah's aunties a car? And where did they get the money?" Seth asked.

"Come on, now. The family paid a little money to keep all this from going legal," Melan said.

"You can't sue a dead man."

"Nope, but you can hit the estate." Melan stretched and leaned back in his chair, knocking over an iced tea. A small stream ran into Seth's lap. "Man!—" he started but then got up and headed to the restroom.

Speculation had it that Bayonne had been in the car with Smullian. Melan unsnapped his olive-green summer issue. He'd been in Desert Storm as a reservist and he liked wearing the fatigue jacket as a reminder. Melan rubbed his chin, shaking his head in wonder. "Nearly five hundred pounds? Look, Feddy, it ain't that he's gay. And it ain't because the guy was white. Nowadays it's a man's own business what he does and who he does it with, but, come on. Bayonne's not bad-looking. What in the world did he want with Free Willy?"

Feddy hadn't told Seth and certainly wasn't going to tell Melan what the kid had told him. Feddy happened to be sitting across from Bayonne at Peebo's Cafeteria off Taylor. Disast-Pro Sonshine Industrial Specialty Cleaners had been hired to clean up the apartment, which Bayonne, under much duress, had been made to assist. "It wasn't too bad," he said between slurps of Mountain Dew, "They gonna move back. The two that's not dead, that is. Somebody shitted all over the place, though." Bayonne then suddenly recounted how he and Smullian had a suicide pact, each vowing to be steadfast and holding the other's hand to the end. But the car was to have been stuck back in the scrub pine on Smullian's property just at the Georgia–Florida state line. Smullian changed his mind. "By the time they would have found us I'd have been a gooey mess," Smullian had joked. "This is much neater."

"So you sat there next to the guy while he choked to death," Feddy prodded.

"Naw, I was coughing too much. And Big Boy was vomicking. I got the hell out."

Seth's attempt at rinsing out the stain resulted in a wet spot extending from his crotch to his knee. Feddy grinned. "Seth, all this talking about death and such got me thinking. I've decided that when you kick, we're gonna have to look to something special for you."

Seth raised an eyebrow and guardedly glanced over at Feddy. "What's that?"

"A fitting memorial. Something that when you die, people will look up and say, 'Damn, that *is* Seth Burnett.' We might as well start thinking of those things now, you know, with your bad kidneys and all." Seth, already on a diuretic, had recently been told that he had an enlarged prostate, too. The result was that he was constantly running to pee, as he'd done a half a dozen times already.

"Kiss my ass," Seth said.

"But," Feddy continued, "I'd like it to be something that captures the prime Seth, the real you. And with that being the goal, I'd like to nominate your little sanitary-napkin belt. Have it bronzed, spotlighted up there above Leon—"

To their generation, in their neighborhood, the story of Seth and his sanitary belt had become a staple anecdote at company picnics and church reunions. Even as a young man, Seth would bludgeon co-workers at the paper mill with his detailed medical histories. These included recent remedies and the fleeting successes of cures. One day he was left in a miserable state after an improvised treatment for hemorrhoids involving rubber bands and witch hazel. Seth ended up borrowing his wife's sanitary belt, wearing it backward. This was fine at home. However, familiarity led to a certain degree of absentmindedness and the next thing he knew he was standing in the locker room at shift change—naked except for the backward napkin. A week later Seth quit his position at the paper mill. People for years would harass him, sending him, for example, a gift-wrapped box of Kotex at Christmas; another time a hot water bottle with an old-fashion douching tube hung from the rearview mirror of his Thunderbird.

Seth endured the first wave of yelps and guffaws. But when Feddy then proceeded to elaborate on other mementos people had given Seth over the years (at this point he was describing the large Costco box of feminine hygiene spray), Seth decided his limit had been met. He reached for his beige umbrella, tapping the floor twice before using it to push off from the chair. Seth then did a little doggy shake as his exiting flourish and, with his head held up, strode to the canteen door.

The wind seemed to be lying in wait for Seth, for it suddenly gusted in a light rain at the precise moment he opened his umbrella. The apparatus proceeded to bloom from his hand and cartwheel into the field across from the freeway entrance. Seth unthinkingly fluttered toward his umbrella for a few steps in the rain before stepping into a small depression in the yard. He stood for several seconds in the ankle-deep water. He then heaved a sigh and sloshed to his car.

From inside He Ain't Here, the table witnessing the spectacle had grown quiet. They silently watched Seth's burgundy Thunderbird do a U-turn and sizzle past, in a direction opposite the freeway.

Melan finally stood up and stretched. He then headed to the private toilet in the hall beside the kitchen. "That, gentlemen—and lady" (since his back was to them, a flourished hand gesture for Ce-Ce), "is the most perfect example of God pissing on you that you'll ever see."

"Tell me something, chief," Melan said as he plopped down after he returned, snatching the remnant remaining on Feddy's plate, some piece of fried batter. "There's something I've always been a little curious about. Since you and Seth seem to be the authorities on the subject—do they burn up that coffin when you get cremated?"

It was Feddy's turn to sigh. Though he worked for Melan down at the docks, his old job—at the county hospital, where he had worked as a hospital diener—would be the role that continued to define his life: there was something about seamy jobs that caught people up like bad smells.

"No, man. It's like at the Y. They give you a locker with a number, then you strip down to your skivvies and they put you in a duffel bag."

"Naw, naw, man—I'm serious. Look, you shell out, what—two, three grand for a coffin—to have it go up in smoke? That, to me, don't make any sense."

A predatory behemoth of a car—a gold Cadillac Seville—slowly rolled past the opened doors of the bar with a toot. Even though Feddy knew the driver couldn't see beyond the darkness of the doorway, he gave a perfunctory wave. The car he knew. It belonged to his old man.

"You're right, Melan," Feddy continued. "But I'm gonna let you in on a little trade secret. What they do is that they usually put Mr. or Mrs. Jones in a cardboard box and leave it at that. Sometimes, for sentimental reasons, they'll prop the old guy or gal up in a lawn chair so as to let folks exit at their most comfortable. Let you glide on out."

"Well, baby, when you finally kick, remember—I've got you. I've got your back. I'll have you sitting tight with your legs all up and a forty-ounce in your lap."

Leon, who until then had seemed to be engrossed in surfing between *Judge Judy* and *The Bold and the Beautiful,* suddenly chimed in, "For y'all's buddy—I recommend a damn Port-O-Potty."

The city's jail occupied what was now considered prime real estate. It dwarfed the peeling clapboard businesses and residences dotting the river. When it was initially built in the early 1980s, the city shared the disdain that most small cities had for their downtowns:

embarrassment for the stumpy buildings with the faded paint advertisements for 1950s evening wear; outmoded, sun-gnarled, now vintage shoes in window storefronts; musty hat boutiques with web-draped blocks and shapers. And Negroes. Detachments would spill from the colored neighborhoods and swarm: there were no jobs. The corner of Kettel and Mayburn would be where the homeless men would gather at sunrise for day-labor detail; there they'd molder well into the evening's redness. "A class-A cluster fuck, that's what it is," was how one councilman described it. Property in this part of town could be had for near nothing. So the city bought the plot of land.

Now high-rise apartments and the jail commanded a view of the river. As it was situated, the jail basked in both sunrise and sunset. Thick plastic slits—pretend-pretty, Teo Toak called them—bridged the inside to the outside with a milky opalescent band that couldn't be distinguished from the wash of fluorescent lighting that flooded the cells and halls.

Teo didn't like the jail. The light was unnatural, the sound unnatural (always some minuscule inchoate whine pricking like a mosquito in the room)—and the smell unnatural because it was all so neutral. The waiting area and visitor cells were ash white with pressed-plastic bench seating. Give him the old tank: puce and hospital green, a mosaic of dried vomit over in the corner; nigger sweat, flatulence, and food remnants. Where the flesh abides.

Teo had parked his monstrous automobile a block from the shade of the jail. His office was eighteenth in a line extending from the courthouse down to Adams Street. By his location in the row it was known that he could post close to twenty, thirty thousand dollars' bail. Teo's was one of the first colored-owned; as a young buck he'd been one of the more successful bondsmen in the city.

"—So this gorilla-faced skillet comes up to me like he was the Sheik of Araby. Grinning. Got this old white feller behind him, Mr. Murray, shaking his head. 'Mr. Murray's gonna pay me to take down his stuff.'" Two cronies were already wasting space on the scratchy-napped sectional piece along the wall. Elder lowlifes were always roaching about the office.

"You could've given me a ride—you saw me," Feddy said, leaning from the doorsill. He then tossed a set of keys that clattered across the metal desk. "Anyway, you owe me big time. " As a favor, Feddy had cleared all the trash out of his father's two new townhouse rentals.

"Don't interrupt, boy—see, Murray paid some son of a bitch for a billboard. . . ."

Feddy gave a half wave to the old men boogered on the couch as he was about to leave but Teo shouted at him, pointing to a chair, "You look tuckered out. Sit down, man!" He then motioned for a codger to unprop and close the door.

"Come on, Pops. I've got to go!" Feddy cried.

"—Murray's nails. You could see it for miles. On the billboard is the Crucifixion and underneath it says, 'They used Murray's nails.' Murray can't believe it. 'Man! Are you crazy? You're gonna get me killed!' 'All right, all right. Just take it easy,' the guy says. Next day, he picks him up. They get there and Murray loses it. Instead of Jesus on the cross, they have a body all bloody and heaped up at the foot. What does it say? 'They should have used Murray's nails.'"

The old men grinned at one another, with the one nearly prone at the door returning to his woolgathering, kneading a scalp piebald with vitiligo.

"All right, Pops. Buzz me out," Feddy said. He had gotten up well before the end of the joke and was now pressing his butt against the glass door.

Feddy had thought of becoming a priest while still the vulnerable teen at St. Stanislaus, and Teo, not being Catholic or anything else for that matter, had found this hard to stomach. He enjoyed any occasion to goad his son with sacrilege. He openly blamed a Father Clemons ('That wall-eyed, dusty-napped bastard!') for his son's brief descent into piety, and, long after he left the parish, he broadcast his threats to beat the man to a pulp if he ever ran into him. "You can tell me," Teo had said, addressing Feddy in a stage whisper a few months back at Peebo's Piccadilly Cafeteria. "The old fuck had his way with you, didn't he? Come on, Peanut. There's money to be made!"

Teo wanted his son to stay, so he provoked him. It was his nature. "You know, I hate that fuckin' mustache of yours, Feddy. Makes your mouth look like some seventies porn-star snatch. Why does every nigger feel the need to wear a mustache?" Teo propped his cowboy boots on the desk and, while staring at Feddy, popped his jaw.

"You're on a roll today, aren't you, old man?" Feddy asked. "Fess up. You're jealous because you can't grow one."

"Just might be the case. But I can tell you that the ladies like that skin-to-pussy contact."

Teo was accommodating because Teo had no sense of shame.

Feddy wore fatigue, though. Teo could see it on him. And Teo knew that as he became more tiresome and needling over the next few minutes—wiping about Feddy's face the embarrassment of a grown man not owning a goddam thing, not a pot to piss in or a window to throw it out of—he'd find himself feeling vindicated.

"That's all right, Pop. Clown for these jokers all you want. But I've got to go. Some of us still try working for a living," Feddy exclaimed.

"Come on, boy. There's no denying your mouth looks like a pussy!" Teo shouted as he buzzed his son out.

Feddy stood in the lee of the bus shelter to catch his breath for a minute. He was already a good mile from Theodore Toak: Bail Bonds. The afternoon storm that inflicted itself daily upon the summer had passed, and he was now able to walk the blocks to the Golfair Shopping Center relatively dry, once you subtracted the day's general mugginess. This was becoming increasingly hard to do, however. His slip-ons (half a size too large, a gift from his son Jesmond, who, in turn, had been gifted the shoes by way of his girlfriend), for example, sang out in a sullen basso squelch with each step. With the last blat Feddy decided enough was enough. He decided at that point to take the bus.

He refused to sit in the shelter, though. The indignity of being without his car didn't need to be compounded by what Feddy perceived as an attitude of collapse: resting on one's haunches or sitting exaggeratedly forward like in a church pew because slats were missing from a bench. To do so when you had gray at the temples was one more concession. Recently, he'd been running into Ace Walker, a contemporary of his father's. Ace had been a numbers man and a pimp in his youth. He'd also been a sparring partner of Sonny Liston. Teo, for a time, had used him as a strong arm. With hands as thick and a complexion as dark as a side of country ham, he intimidated most of the neighborhood. "Hey, Milk Dud!" he'd yell after Feddy, playing in the streets. "Boy! Come here!" Feddy had no choice but to go over to where Ace held court with his hangers-on. His kingdom was the empty lot behind Mr. Steve's Grocery. Usually, there'd be around eight of them, asses pressed into some broken backless kitchen chairs, each trying to squeeze into the shade of a skinny pine tree. "Milk Dud, run inside Mr. Steve's here and get me a pack of Kools and a Yoo-hoo." He'd stick out his hand with a few dollar bills. Feddy wouldn't immediately reach for it. "Take it, boy! There's a couple of nickels left for you." Ace would then half stand up and draw back his foot as if to give him a good swift kick; this, of course, elicited howls from his cronies. Worse, however, was when a street would be empty except for the two of them: then—a mouth full of dice-size yellow teeth—he would loom over Feddy, grabbing the scruff of his coat and pulling him up to his face, braying, threatening; picking him up, it seemed, just to exhale on him.

Ace was now in his seventies. The large black rectangle of a man had been replaced by a gimp's frame with an air hose. He spent the day perched on the brick sill in front of Mr. Steve's (now K.J.'s) with his oxygen tank in tow. "Whatcha doing, old man?" Feddy asked him as he was entering K.J.'s. "Dying," Ace grimaced. "Well, speed it up," Feddy said, hopping into the blast of the store's air-conditioning. "You taking too goddam long!" As he left, though, Feddy placed a brown bottle of Yoo-hoo next to him.

The number 40 bus could be seen advancing in lurches to Feddy's stop. The windows were propped open, a bad sign. "You gonna make it?" Feddy asked the driver as he boarded. The driver shrugged. "Maybe. The Number 36 is right behind—" "That's all right," Feddy said and collapsed into a seat behind a homeless woman balled up under an avalanche of soiled grocery bags; a faded green slip peeked from one of them.

For the past eight, ten months, Feddy had been living in one of Teo's rentals. Now he was in a duplex just off Golfair. His credit was shit. Close to five years now, these floating residences . . . His doing, his predicament: he'd been profligate and heedless in his youth, glazed and neglectful as an adult. Uncles Darley and Verk had conned him into getting them Discover Cards under his name. And the IRS had a lien on Feddy for close to sixty thousand dollars. He was still paying the government back in part for student loans.

Feddy shrank into his seat, his head partially out the window, hoping to improve the cell phone reception. He was trying to reach Medgar. Medgar Coots was the psychiatrist assigned to him by State Employees Medical years ago when he was actively drinking and drugging. Toak and Coots had a relationship that spanned three decades. They had been in medical school together. Feddy, however, had dropped out second year, preferring to hustle on charm and liquor. Medgar was a light-skinned man whom Feddy distinctly remembered attending class one day in riding boots, though Medgar denied it to this day. His father was one of the first black professors Feddy had ever met. He taught reproductive physiology. And he was a bodybuilding enthusiast. "Every day's a great day for gravity!" Dr. Coots would berate students foolish enough to follow him into the gym (Feddy tried). It'd been his smirking conceit to discover the contributions of anabolic steroids long before the lifting cognoscente. Unfortunately, lymphoma foamed through his brain because of the drug and he died at the age of fifty-four.

Medgar was not without sin. Coots Senior thought Medgar sly, amoral, and heedless; for Medgar's part, he thought the old man specious and vindictive—a dialogue of two abandoned mirrors. "In the end, you've got to attend to your own needs, social and pecuniary," Medgar informed Feddy, drawing him aside one day in the common room. There were six blacks in the first-year medical school class at Tulane. By the last year only Medgar and a woman with an interest in pathology remained.

Though his own necessities weren't pecuniary, Medgar paid off his college tuition dealing drugs. He continued in medical school, more or less as a hobby. His last transaction, in fact, was the quarter ounce Feddy snorted the day before his permanent leave of absence from the school. Feddy's choice resulted not only in a collapse of his finances but a narrowing of life's bandwidth for him, too. People like Medgar had full run of the spectrum if they played things correctly—from rubbing shoulders with developers to sneaking a little trim from the cleaning woman. Feddy? For the most he could take a few steps left or right but his radius of ambition remained limited to the few square miles that encompassed north Johnsonville.

"Medgar! I've won a week's vacation in the Bahamas and I want to spend it with you, man!" Feddy shouted into his cell phone.

"Feddy, Feddy, Feddy . . . I knew the day would come you'd be turning sweet on the doc. Pretty soon you'll be doing tricks for me on MLK!" In addition to his role as addiction consultant, Medgar coordinated psychiatric services for the city's Gay-AIDS Alliance. He wasn't empathetic to such issues but he covered his disdain by ruthlessly orchestrating group sessions held at the Comfort Inn, the first Tuesday of every month.

"How's Jesmond doing?"

"Doing all right. Not using." One day, when Jesmond was about eight years old, he came upon Feddy getting high with his mother—

the woman drooling on her satin bra, splayed out on the couch. It was the second time he'd seen his father getting high—of the two times he'd seen his father that year. Feddy wondered: in witnessing such things what was brought forth in his son?

"Back with the bitch? She's married to a military cop, for chrissakes! You know she leads him by his pecker with some 'danger gets me wet' crap."

"That's between you two. You can talk to him. Confidentiality issues with me as his shrink—"

Feddy closed the phone. He'd blame the disconnect on passing power lines.

Medgar had little regard for what bodies experienced outside of his own. Feddy got off at the stop across from the stadium.

He didn't consider himself an overly moral man: Feddy had invited a number of married women into his life. He understood to the core of his heart that sleeping with another man's wife was a hazardous pleasure. This he could attest to by the relief map of scars crisscrossing his belly.

When he was younger—old enough, though, that desire didn't beat upon him as some fist of need—he let out on a woman. He was her live-in. Devils Lake Reservation, North Dakota. He worked long hours stocking vending machines at the military base and federal sites such as the post office. The reservation was ninety-two thousand acres.

They hit it off quickly, Feddy and the Santee woman, Joy. They met in the federal highway-administration office, where she sat behind a metal desk directly across from the candy machine. Her husband was habitually unemployed. Those were her exact words to Feddy their first day, meeting and flirting coinciding. Feddy made it a point to return every day for a week, addressing the machine's paucity of Clark Bars and Almond Joys. Soon she put her husband out—her husband and his girlfriend trading places for the motels Feddy and Joy had been frequenting—and Feddy moved in.

Having sex while her children were in the house—for there were always children in the house, she had five of them, ranging in ages from six to twelve—was a bizarre, guilt-tinged undertaking. Domination, though: some other man's kids scratching at the locked bedroom door while Feddy was pounding the man's wife left him in awe of himself.

The novelty of each for the other faded in less than three months but neither had the energy nor the desire to end it. What they had was comfortable and made the gray and ugly winter pleasantly remote.

One day, a Friday in April—it was Lent; he remembered this because to abstain from meat, in North Dakota, he had to settle on fish sticks—Feddy pulled up the gravel road to Joy's cinder-block house and witnessed a rank-looking, jaundiced little white man trying to sprint to his pickup truck on the other side of the brown lawn. The yard was sloped and the man tripped over his feet but caught himself before falling. He saw Feddy, too—as soon as he stooped to adjust his boots he fixed his sights on Feddy's approaching car and hurriedly popped his arms through suspenders. He was shirtless; his chest and belly were sparse haired and yellow. It was cold enough that steam rose from him.

In the house, Feddy tried to pummel Joy. It was only for a minute or two because he suddenly became winded. For a short burst he flailed at her again. He then retreated to his powder-blue GTO, where he brooded, staring at her living-room window. He'd been there close to a half an hour, without the heat, when she strode up to the car as if coming to meet him. There was an old and contracted beet-colored scar on her chin, severe enough that when she smiled she seemed to wince. "Now how did you get that, again?" he wanted to ask her, have her tell him again, then and there, the story of the horse bite—anything to displace his puniness.

She was talking but he could not hear what she was saying so he rolled down the window. "—Not my husband. Not even my father ever beat me," she said and then emptied five rounds into the interior of his car.

So he sat in the driveway. She turned around and went back into the house. Everything immediately after that was gone from him. Except for a few things. He remembered the blue glow of a television as Joy entered the house. He remembered how his congealing blood served as a sort of grease to help him slide over to the passenger's side. He also remembered how the package of fish sticks on the seat had come to hold, oddly enough, two of the bullets.

II

Tilted over the freeway entrance to 95S from Williams Road was a billboard. The platform was constructed with oily creosote railroad ties for a poster displaying a young black man in cornrows and a cartoon balloon blistering from his lips. RACHEL GOT MY CASE THROWN OUT! read the caption. This billboard was new. An older version clung to the Arlington Expressway overpass—ACQUITTED!—with the same young man, though now with an Afro.

Rachel "Mule" Ennis would be here even for something as insignificant as a billboard unveiling. "Detail oriented," she called it. "That's what separates the big guns from the peashooters," she would say. Teo studied her for a few seconds more before shouting from his car window. At that precise moment, Rachel was pointing to a small split in the photograph seam and began berating one of the workmen. "Mule!" Teo yelled. "How's my favorite dyke?"

"Theodore Toak!" she responded, not taking her eyes from the spot in question, "How's my favorite ass-wipe?"

An only child, Rachel grew up underfoot of nearly everyone in the neighborhood. She was Feddy's contemporary, jostling her way into every pickup basket- and football game the boys played. She hustled, took hits, bled; wiping her nose, she got back onto the asphalt without complaint: hence, the nickname, Mule. Her mother, light skinned, too, was a social worker from New Jersey. Her father was the city's first black postal supervisor. Almost as a given she went to state on a basketball scholarship; then to law school. After passing the bar she returned to the city to practice, but as a lesbian with kinky, cropped hair, a tattoo of a fist on one shoulder and a feminist symbol on the other—there weren't too many firms interested in her hire. "So I rolled up next to a barbershop," she said. Most of her clients were the kind who paid in cash. It wasn't unusual for a man to pop open the trunk of his Mercedes and extract a black garbage bag full of loose bills. She did well, though she eventually tired and grew wary of large sums of money coming into her office, " . . . I told him just to put a couple of thousand on A & R Liquors"— she had a running tab of an account there and other places. Longish in torso with squat legs, a softly hairy upper lip, tobacco-breathed, coquettishly feline eyes: Teo would not have sought her out, but the woman was integral to what he wanted to accomplish.

"Say, isn't that Skullhead's boy?" Teo pointed to the billboard face.

"Still can tell?" Mule asked, leaning back from her spot on the sidewalk. "I had them change some stuff on the computer, make him more generic."

"Well . . . Naw, it's pretty good. Looks like any gang-banger."

Mule smirked. "So, cap'n. What's up?"

"Jus' want to see what's goin' on with the little fella. It's been a couple of months since we last spoke."

"A few weeks ago, Teo."

"Yeah? Forgot. Seems longer, though."

She was a good, mean attorney. Just as mulish in the docket . . . In addition to a few class-action suits that she steadily pressed forward, she took to cases with children. Teo was particularly interested in Bobby Jackson—he'd put up the bail for the boy.

Bobby Jackson, fourteen, had been riding his trail bike in the San Pedro area when he came upon a pair of legs jutting out from a hedge, the panty hose bunched at the ankles. He was appropriately wary; curiosity, though, led him to rut his bike a little farther into the packed clay on the north side of an apartment building. They were delicious legs, those of a thirty-two-year-old white police-woman, her handgun resting on her exposed breasts. Several detectives sleuthing traced the tread marks to his bike. His fingerprints were on her gun and thigh (curiosity, again). The boy was placed in adult detention for eight months. There he lost all his teeth and reluctantly acquired a heart, tattooed to his right cheek. The policewoman had been married to another officer. It would be Mule's doggedness that would lead to the revelation that it was the officer's husband who had murdered her—to frame yet another officer, one who'd been having an affair with his wife. "Mista Toak, could you hep us out, please?" the boy's West Indian aunt snuffled. This was the third case that year of a cop allegedly being killed by a Negro. The bail was almost undoable; other bondsmen had no doubt that the boy would be on the next plane back to Haiti, Aruba, wherever.

"Some punk's been pissing around, marking territory. Film student saying he's doing Jackson's story. 'Doing an independent thing,' he says." Teo jiggled a little finger into his ear and checked the results.

"Don't worry, Teo. But I'm glad you've Bobby's interest so much to heart," Rachel said, stooping to his window.

"Points, Mule! Points! In any movie deal these days you've gotta ask for distribution points. That's where the money is. Don't let them snow you with some flat fee for—"

"Gotta go, chief. Listen to me, though: the boy's welfare is the primary thing. We're going to make sure that, in the end, what he gets is all good." Rachel straightened back, slapping her hand on the hood. "When you gonna get rid of this monstrosity?" she asked.

"Love to you, sweetheart. And kiss mammy for me," Teo shouted and pulled off, fishtailing.

"Bitch," Teo muttered to her reflection as she returned to arguing with the billboard worker. He knew a little bit about the business; after all, he'd made a few commercials. And for the past several months, he'd studied how money was to be made in the movies. Internet, the library, trade magazines (he even had a subscription to *Variety*): if he learned anything it was that you don't let anyone else ride your history.

"Mista Toak, could you hep us out, please?" was how the first big-brimmed jig came scuffling up to his door. In the 1960s, Toak's first schemes, monkey money: five-dollar-a-week insurance policies, titties, and trifectas—running a few women, numbers; he even had, for a while, an off-track-betting room with races from Miami. Then: the Civil Rights Movement. Nobody white in these parts was putting up bail for Negroes.

"Mista Toak, Happy Inn put lye in the swimming pool down in St. Sebastian," the man panted.

"Happy Inn don't need me for a pool cleaner," said Toak.

"Happy Inn ain't the ones in jail, neither." The manager at the motel was prissy about Negroes checking in. A black father, angry that his little girl was swimming when the lye was dumped, had attacked the manager. The father was held for an eight-hundred-dollar bond.

The intermediary finally took off his hat and Teo could see the sweat compressed into his Afro, clear globules clinging to the black ringlets. People had come to him previously about loans; loan-sharking involved too much shoulder-checking.

"You from here?" Teo asked, though he already knew the answer. Teo Toak eyed people. He'd seen this one mouth-breathing up and down Lane Avenue, a barber down from Atlanta, some chicken-shack preacher. "Yassuh, near Baptist Hospital."

"Tell you what. Of that eight hundred dollars, I'll take care of the whole thing. But you, or whoever, has got to pay me."

"Huh?"

"Don't go stupid on me, Jasper. It's going to cost you twenty percent. Yeah-yeah, you tell me that the average cracker there charges fifteen but I'll tell you he ain't going to do it. I put up the eight hundred so your man can be out on bail. You tell me that you don't have the money to meet my requirements. I tell you, 'So, you have the eight hundred instead.' I then keep the one hundred and sixty you put up front." That was how the Civil Rights Movement gave birth to Toak's Bail Bonds. Though, by the 1970s, the mood shifted from pulpit to pissed. The city had its little fart response to Detroit's riots and Toak's Bail Bonds did well. There were wild bucks getting soused and firing guns, somebody accused of theft and deceit. But by the eighties, even Dixie-flagged Bubba was cautiously sticking his head in his door: "Mista Toak, could you hep us?"

Teo huffed his gold Cadillac into the space in front of his office. The twelve-by-four-foot patch was his by stature and in earlier years was never questioned. Now, some shit-stain would park in his spot. Back in the day, he would've had Ace address a windshield with a tire iron.

Bondsman Row. Teo looked up at the lighted, canary-yellow sign. . . . The only Negro for years. TEO SAUL TOAK, LICENSED BAIL BONDS BROKER—with just the sign and the telephone book, people assumed he was Jewish. That was fine, got them in. Then he'd play colored, black, Afro-American, mixed-blood Armenian, Cuban— whatever racial truss, as long as it worked.

"Mr. Toak, some woman keeps calling for you. Won't leave her name," Ernie said, rubbing his eyes as if he were wearing footed pajamas and waiting to be tucked in. Gargantuan Ernest, of the bald pate and ponytail! Ernie . . . From Ace to Ernie—God, how times have changed! At least he *looked* intimidating: commode head, heaped-up scalp that was waxy about the eyebrows, catcher's mitt hands. There was a picture of him on the desk with some bikers and a pro-wrestling star.

"Mr. Toak, I think she's back again. Line one." Ernest watched the blinking light.

"What's that, Jasper?"

"I think it's that woman again."

"Well, don't you think it would be a good idea to find out who it is before you interrupt me? I was getting ready to talk to my friends here." Teo winked at the crew on the couch.

Ernest—Ernie—doodled two intersecting circles, pig snout on one end. "Yes, ma'am, I understand, but Mr. Toaks don't take calls without first knowing who it is. Legal reasons. Jus' gimme your name and number and he'll be sure to get back with you." Ernie put the phone back in its cradle. "Said she was some Bayonne's mother and that you or Feddy would know the telephone number."

"Sadie Burnett? That burr-headed bitch? Dammit! Don't interrupt me with that shit!"

"She said it was important and if I didn't tell you *I'd* be in trouble," Ernie chuckled.

"Everything's earth-shaking to that cunt. What she want?"

"Dunno." The phone rang again. "One moment, lady," Ernie said and looked up knowingly at Teo.

Teo rolled his eyes. "Just let her sit. She'll get the message sooner or later. Why don't you just go back and get some more of that sleep I pay you for?" He let the back room to Ernie in lieu of what amounted to half of his salary.

Ernie was used to being around Negroes and was good with them, liked them, apparently, having grown up in a border neighborhood in Knoxville. He was an alcoholic—like Feddy—though he goose-stepped the twelve-step now like he was a preacher. No women—not that Teo ever saw, anyway. (The man stank too much. Smelled, when he got worked up, like grease trap from a McDonald's fry station.) But Ernie wasn't queer. A touch of the freak, though. Whenever the sister, mother, wife of a client came through the door and she was a looker, Ernie would steal glances while Teo was engaged with the woman—building her piecemeal in his head, Teo saw. Ernie would then steal off, a little conspiratorial grin aimed at Teo, and jerk off in the bathroom. When he was done he'd languidly loll back to his desk (Teo would listen intently for that faucet—Teo had told him not to take one fucking step out of the bathroom until he washed his hands), his trousers all hitched up to one side so that the seat rode over a buttock. Teo tried to embarrass him, initially. "How was it, Jasper?" he'd ask him. "With her? Fuckin' great!" Ernie would say. But how was he to respond? Secretly, he was a little intoxicated by the geek's transgression. And the geek was a solid six-five, good muscle.

"I saw Ace just this morning. Just a damn shame," one of the old men suddenly said, leaning forward on his cane, stretching his back. "You look at him now. You know, back in the day, he was the first to knock down both Sugar Ray *and* Liston. It was sparring, but still—"

"You're one naïve motherfucker! You'd have an eye up your ass and you still couldn't see shit," Teo snorted. "Some goddam insurance detective's got a tail on him. This is all some pretend-cancer crap. And you fell for it, too, just like the rest of the folks."

At least, that was what someone had told Teo. He wanted to believe it. "Ace looks like death eating crackers," an old parolee said to Teo last week as they watched him hump up the street, his oxygen bottle nestled next to a sweater in a shopping cart. Pushed, the best Ace could have been was a mediocre middleweight. But his pleasure was in hurting people and he delivered punches to that end. Teo could size them up pretty well, but occasionally there was an outlier—some Geechee or redneck who decided not to show for a hearing or somehow decided to skip town altogether. Ace would suddenly materialize and, with a few of his goon friends and a tire iron, convince the guilty that they were performing a bad act. He didn't need to resort to formal bounty hunters as long as Ace was in commission.

But Ace began to smell himself, making independence noises. Maybe Teo was a little too old for the business, he began to say. Teo let him go then and there. Initially Teo felt wounded but eventually the wounds became solid scars, anchoring flesh. Ace tried to make a go, first with a bar, then (briefly) a convenience store. He then became certifiably destitute. Teo told this matter-of-factly, but also with glee and all the proper embellishments.

His legacy, though, these clowns . . . They wouldn't leave now, not with all the gossip and cajoling.

Feddy always had the grace to humor without spite. Teo wanted to make them hurt. Sidesplitting: he relished the literalness of the word, enjoyed making them ache, either grabbing a rib or finally becoming arch in the face of their own stupidity. Feddy was too graceful.

Teo needed an airing. "Time to take a stroll!" he shouted to Ernie. "I'm out! Lock up. Leave the bitch hanging. Go whack yourself silly!"

Teo had wanted so badly for the business to be Toak and Son, but the boy wouldn't be open to any of it. When Feddy dragged back to town after his skedaddle ("Knocking up that bitch is enough to make me run to the other side of hell," Teo grunted in sympathy), Teo thought this was the opportunity. He had printed ink pens and refrigerator magnets with TOAK AND SON, BAIL BONDS. Watching Feddy skulk through the courthouse and jail, waggle through knots of prospective clients, left Teo with a brick in the pit of his stomach. "Trust me—some little fucker's grandmama's out there worried about her June Bug," he had whispered in his son's ear, pulling him aside. "She could be wearing a belly ring and a Bob Marley tattoo but—listen to me—she's out there and will do anything to keep June Bug from a rump roasting." But Feddy didn't have it, didn't have the snarl to make it in the business. "You don't go mumbling up to those fucks like you're a sissy in a washroom asking to suck dick. Man, they're the ones scared!" Teo tried to yell into him. He ended up storing the boxes and boxes of pens and rubberized magnets and key chains in the back room. He couldn't let them go to waste, though. The telephone number and address were good, and eventually the boxes were emptied, the magnets finding their way onto pay phones and storefront windowsills, the pens and key chains crammed into the pockets of every Mutt and Jeff floating through the neighborhood. No one even asked him about the AND SON part of the advertisement.

The real secret, he'd come to figure, was real estate. A tree bumped through the sidewalk in front of him, heaping and crumbling slabs; Teo determinedly walked atop the root and concrete pieces. He then stopped to survey the street in front of him: 1223 Krishnan Way was his; 1248 Krishnan Way was his—as was the clapboard duplex on

1251/52. He owned the strip mall around the corner. His renters included a barbershop, a Chinese takeout, a Domino's Pizza, and a nail parlor. Teo had property all over the city.

"Cheap rental stuff, Pop," Feddy said. "Stuff that's like the purple crap on a Monopoly board. No getting rich off of poor folk, Pops." Don't or can't? Because you inevitably *do* get rich, as Teo figured it—it just took more poor people to get it from. You had to keep hammering the pieces into place: buy adjacent pieces of land, snap up commercial properties near residential areas, and buy the residences (hoping for eminent domain), swallowing fallow land within the purr of a freeway. He'd purchased the cemetery grounds *and* the old Negro hospital, just off of the refinery.

Can not, that was Feddy's big to-do. More, *should not* . . . The makings for a decency but not really—his son yelped whenever he found himself fucking up but went ahead anyway. Not like his grandson . . .

Miss Audrey's Consignment Shop benefited from the recent change in zoning. Teo owned it—rather, owned the property. Teo suddenly decided to bully her for a coat. The owner of the store was Elena Koslov, recently from the Ukraine, who'd chosen the name Audrey because she admired the actress in *Breakfast at Tiffany's.*

His window for intimidation was closing; friends were already introducing her to some Siberian huskies in rut. Soon they'd be barking and snapping at Teo as he set foot in the shop.

The store was poorly lit and musty, but Teo liked the smell . . . cloacal memory: post-coital sheets. He scooted the clothes around the circular rack, randomly holding up pieces for quick inspection. "Hullo, Miss Audrey!" Teo cackled. The woman grimly smiled. She was a peroxide blonde pushing past forty. He knew she barely tolerated him.

"Annó," he said in Russian. "That's all the Russian I know," he quipped in English. "No, wait. 'Kahk sah-law´-meen-koy, pehsh mah-you' doo'-shoo,'" he said. She smiled even more grimly. Anna Akhma—something.

They had first met when she came to him for her son who'd been arrested for possession with intent to distribute. Teo made it his mission over the following week to learn the exact phrase—"You are as fine as frog's hair," checking dictionaries at the library, but the Russian masseur at the Y advised him he'd get farther with the little snip of Russian poetry.

Elena walked with a roll despite the thinness of her hips. She disappeared into a room off the side. Teo decided to follow her, knowing she hated the sight of him—

He caught himself holding an expansive black coat with a black velvet collar. There was a gold monogram on the breast pocket.

This had been Ace's jacket. Teo gave a start.

He could remember to the moment the last time he and Ace had ripped through Deville Street. Ace and his dazzling coat. The Atlas Club. But that was decades ago! Sitting five, six to a circular booth—smooth-shouldered, rump-thighed women in satin dresses, crushing in on each side. Good sweat, good God! The promise of flung bras on the dresser and crisscrossed limbs about his body in the morning. Teo began scooting hangers about the rack. The huge blue gabardine suit—Ricky Hatch; dead now. The beige cross-hatched sport coat with the leather shoulders—John Caruthers (Shiloh Christian Nursing Home, was it? The old fuck . . .). The worsted yellow wool pants with the wide pleats, a flamingo-pink bowling shirt, a white Cuban *guayabera* with a little devil in diapers on the shirt pocket. Suddenly he felt he knew the former inhabitants of each piece of clothing . . . Here's wishing a private hell for each and every one of them . . .

It was as if they were Legion—dwarfish, immaterial but for their clothes, swaying in unison—cigarette-burned trousers, wash-transparent shirts, Bermuda shorts, ratty wife beaters; all of the clothes that made them, all in movement out of the shop and up the road until they disappeared into the horizon.

III

I'm going to give you the pimp's insight," Skooch Miller said. Skooch Miller had an associate arts degree in business administration from Sarasota Community College and was the owner of the Rent-to-Own near the base. Four men in plastic chairs hunched forward in unison as Skooch spoke. There followed a protracted keen from the near-desiccated marker as he drew a stick man and a stick woman on the dry-erase board in one continuous line. "These people"—he thumped the board with the marker tip for effect—"Mr. And Mrs. Jones, come here because they don't have credit. They don't have money. So they come here thinking they can snake under the finance radar.

"Fine! You want them to think that. You want them to think that they're clever. Cleverer than shit. Feed in to them! But then I want you to be the torque wrench." He drew a hexagon on the board. "By the time they leave and have signed on the dotted line you should be able to tell how much twisting and turning you can do. They will want what you tell them to want. Yes, they will get another DVD player, this time for Junior's room. Yes, they can fit the jumbo-screen television with surround sound into their single-wide, no problem! And they will be obedient about their payments. They will not want to disappoint you. To have us come and repossess the fleur-de-lis sofa will be an insurmountable disappointment to you. Remember! You are the wrench—you have them by the nut!" Skooch made a point of staring into each set of eyes for a second or two. He lowered his head and they studied the part in his dyed hair.

Twice a month, Skooch gave a talk to his sales force. Skooch was a high school athlete (left tackle) who still liked to surround himself with other large men. Jesmond had heft; Eric was soft, but so tall that he often had to stoop through a doorway. Cash and Atkins hoofed it in the fall from city to city along the southeastern seaboard, vying for a spot on arena teams. Jesmond, recently hired, was the smallest of the crew but he lied at his interview, claiming he had once played tight end for Bedford, the black high school buried deep in the west side. Skooch lifted his head and looked pointedly again at Jesmond. His face was heavy, as if the thick features were what pulled his head down (he did that, though—lowered his head while speaking—because his instructor at the community college said serious men talked that way), the thick, burnished copper hair looking fake but it was all his.

"You boxed?" Skooch asked.

"No, sir, played ball. Like I told you."

"Look, I'm not asking you just because you're black so don't get your shorts all in a knot. But you know, you're a big-ass son of a bitch. Folks, and I mean all of them—the black and white low-life crap—try to beat you out of what's coming to you. The job's straightforward: people sign, you drop the stuff at their homes, and they're supposed to make their payments. If they don't make their payments, you go get the stuff." Skooch stopped talking and crunched on a few breath mints. He then blew into his hands, which he cupped around his nose.

"—Never simple. They lie, kite checks, write checks on dead accounts, lay sick kids and dying grandmas all over the furniture. You like pussy?"

"Sir?"

"They'll throw that at you. But with those I think I'll send my little white girl with you. Together with Samurai Sarah—tough little chick, will even go to the Berkshire projects—you'll be perfect. You all do that 'good cop, bad cop' thing. What the hell."

Skooch wiped his forehead and then slid against the board the flat pancake of his fist. The plastic surface had been, at one time, white; over the course of a few months it had achieved a mottled gray through washings with cheap substitutes for the cleaner—vinegar, dish soap, sweat. During Skooch's ramblings most of the men slouched and sprawled, though Eric curled in upon himself, a scoliotic pepper, snuffling in the vee of his arm. Atkins openly slept, fly dotting his chin. And Cash, grinding pork rinds and staring into the shop through the two-way mirror, flickered a scarious tongue at his ghost reflection.

Skooch suddenly whacked the board with his hand. "You fuckers didn't hear a thing I had to say here! That's why you ain't going to amount to shit. No attention span. Hell, I'd probably do better with my three-year-old grandson. Get the fuck out of here. Go make me money!" Skooch liked to end his talks with, "Go make me money!" That was another thing an instructor in his business psychology class had emphasized—tag lines, just like on TV; these little pointers could be extrapolated to a workforce.

"Jesmond! Wait a minute here. I want you to go with Cash to do a little run. A woman with her brothers off Monument, Nancy Peters. Time to cut bait. You two can pick up everything—Magnavox, portable dishwasher, console, chest of drawers."

"Mr. Miller, I can handle it. Don't take two of us."

"Yeah yeah. But that Peters gal's threatened me before with her brothers and boyfriend—all of them seen the inside of a jail, she says—if I come for the stuff. She says she would like to beat my ass. So I'm sending you guys."

Jesmond Toak didn't say a word. After enduring several months of unsteady employment, it came simple to him to keep his mouth shut. Ovoid, bristled mug. He watched Cash two chairs over, feeding. They got into it at their first meeting. Cash had dragged him to a lopsided, rusted-out trailer between two knobby and diseased maples not far from the store. He tried to get Jesmond to rent it. "I know you just got out of some trouble. You can get in this cheap." Cash pressed him hard for $450 a month. Cash had purchased it, Jesmond later found out, following a property-investment seminar he'd attended with Skooch; in fact, he had bought four other rat-traps that nearly bankrupted him.

The two were headed to pick up the woman's rental furniture in the blue Rent-to-Own van when Cash suddenly took a hard left at a light and then another at the end of the block. They pulled up to the trailer Cash had tried to pawn off on Jesmond. They sat there for a while, not saying a word to each other as Cash bongo-thumped the steering wheel. Jesmond's attention caught the hairs spiking over Cash's T-shirt. A fucking porcupine, Jesmond thought.

Cash abruptly began bleating the horn. The door to the trailer suddenly banged open and a frizzled blond head stuck out, squall-ing into the phone, cursed until she recognized Cash. Then she beamed. Missing her left upper teeth.

"Listen," Cash turned to Jesmond—he was leaning against a frayed cushion where the yellow foam had popped through, dust-ing his shoulders, "it'll be a few minutes. You know how it goes, a little rent dance."

"Yeah, she's cute," Jesmond replied. Cash ignored him.

As Cash arranged himself, the woman darted into the house and herded out a puny little boy of about six. He was a yellow-com-plected chit, red nappy hair. The woman alternated pushing and chasing the boy around the yard while slapping mosquito repellent about his bare chest and back. She then handed him a garden hose. Jesmond watched the boy intermittently squirt an overturned bike while furtively regarding his mother.

"Whatch y'all doing?" Cash asked the mother. Her eyes danced; she seemed oblivious of Jesmond.

"Waiting for you. You want to get high?"

"Maybe. Let's go inside first." Cash slammed the trailer door behind them.

The boy flicked the nib of his ear where she'd missed a spot. The mosquitoes were thick, aggressive, pricking the air above the dead scrub weeds next to the bike. The boy repeatedly thrashed the aluminum siding of the trailer with spray, setting the green wash of kudzu quivering. Jesmond watched the boy move from malice to boredom before turning his attention to the van.

His eyes met Jesmond's. Before Jesmond could complete his thought, though, the boy sprayed the windshield.

Jesmond got out of the van. The boy didn't seem intimidated, staring up at Jesmond with his hand tense on the handle. "How old are you?" Jesmond asked, walking over to the boy.

"Seven," the boy said.

"No you're not."

"Why'd you ask me then?"

Mosquitoes lighted upon Jesmond's neck and arms and he swatted himself repeatedly. "For a little man your mouth's a little big, don't you think?" Jesmond asked. He took the hose from the boy's hand. "That your daddy in there?" Jesmond sprayed the window of the trailer.

"Naw," the boy replied. "Yours?"

Jesmond laughed. He suddenly felt the urge to call Peaches Richmond but he was out of minutes on his cell phone. He recalled passing a Lil' Champ with a pay phone a block or so from where they were.

"Hey!" Jesmond yelled. "I'm gonna go over to the store up here. I'll be back in a few." There was no response. Jesmond looked at the boy. "You want to come?" The boy nodded. "And I'm taking the boy with me! We'll be back in a little bit."

At the store Jesmond sent the boy in with two dollars and began punching numbers into the pay phone. Next to him a stood a thick woman in a near-transparent cotton shift talking on an adjacent phone. Her breasts were the size of udders and hung loosely under the garment. Her gray-brown hair was unwashed and in two braids thick as baby arms, and while she spoke she would coil and uncoil a braid atop her head, grimacing into the phone. Jesmond found himself looking into a mass of damp armpit hair; he turned toward the street. "Hey, baby," he chirped into the receiver.

"Jesmond? Honey, I'm so glad you've called. I've been thinking about you. And you know what I've been thinking about when I'm thinking about you, right?" Jesmond grinned. "And what am I thinking?" she continued.

"What you up to?" Jesmond caught himself smiling like a Cheshire cat at his reflection from the window of a parked car.

"Eddie's not home, baby. He and some officers went to Pensacola for a drill. You should come over." Eddie Richmond was Peaches's husband. He was a military policeman stationed at the base now for close to twenty years. Eddie Richmond enjoyed the perks of his job: he was a first lieutenant, the highest-ranking military police officer on base, and he loved to bully people. He was considerably older than his wife, fifty-three to her thirty-four-years. And, according to Peaches, wasn't all that lovable. Photographs of Ed dominated most rooms. From the moment he'd set foot in the house, Jesmond had felt scrutinized by the wizened, brown man in the black horn-rimmed glasses smirking in every room from either a wall or a desk. His hobby was crime-scene paraphernalia. For example, an old brown Leica camera from an off-base pawnshop sat on the buffet. The previous owner had been convicted through unrelated evidence and was now serving a life sentence at Leavenworth. It contained the vacation pictures of a woman murdered back in the 1980s—at least that's what Eddie believed. And over their bed billowed a red and white canopy from a jumper whose chute had failed to deploy. "Special Ed's a freak," Jesmond would whisper to Peaches' temple as they huddled naked under the sheets, watching the parachute flutter with the breath of the air conditioner. Peaches liked the nickname Jesmond had for her husband—Special Ed; she thought it hilarious and often told Jesmond as much.

"I'll try coming by this evening."

"I'll be waiting." She paused. "Lover. And Special Ed'll be gone for almost the whole week."

The boy was quite talkative on the walk back. He told Jesmond that people called him Kobe though his name was Caleb; that he liked to ride his bike (but a big kid broke the chain); that he and his mother had two cats but one was run over by a car. Jesmond simply nodded, answering with an occasional, "Oh, really."

Inside the van, Cash nodded at the trailer. "You want some of that? She's so fuckin' ripped she don't care. Like I told Skooch, I can handle those dicks at the pickup."

"That's okay, man. I'll pass."

Cash turned the ignition. "Don't like seconds?"

"I don't like stoned chicks."

The woman at the pickup, the woman whose threats as channeled through Skooch portended mayhem, was surprisingly docile. There were no men at the apartment. When Jesmond and Cash arrived she sullenly stepped aside, pointing to the rental items. She had collected the portable dishwasher as well as the emptied chest of drawers into the living room alongside the television and console. It seemed odd to Jesmond to see an open dishwasher in the middle of the living room; briefly, he felt sad.

As they carried the items down the stairs to the van, the woman remained standing at the door, holding it open, though it wasn't necessary. It had begun to rain, and the concrete, staining in gray splotches, began to steam. Just as they returned to pick up the last piece, the television, a little girl materialized from the back of the apartment and wrapped her arms about her mother's leg. Cash squatted eye-level with the girl. "Don't worry, sweetheart. All mama's got to do is pay up her account and you'll be watching Barney next week." The little girl suddenly struck out and scratched Cash across the face. "Goddammit!" Cash yelled. He fell back onto his haunches, collected himself. "Your mama ain't got nothing to worry about with you around, does she?" he finally said.

The ride back met light rain that evaporated as soon as the spatter hit the ground. Jesmond speculated that somewhere west, through this gray mist, probably at the end of Golfair Avenue, they could find a semblance of the sun.

They passed a lawn-service truck with a white wraith leaning forward in the cab as if facing a headwind. Negro laborers were packed into the back of the pickup. One of the men waved at Jesmond and Cash as they drove by and Jesmond found himself wondering if he knew the man.

After they unloaded, Jesmond had Cash drop him off at a Laundromat near the place he was staying. He had left underwear, socks, and towels in a washing machine. An aubergine-hued woman turned her chair partly to Jesmond so as to watch what he removed from the medium-load corner machine.

"You couldn't let me have one of them big towels, could ye?" the woman asked. Shaped like the vegetable, too. Two little girls in plaits were playing beside the woman, one with her arm in a fluorescent cast. "You know, I could've taken those things and you never know'd who done it."

Jesmond motioned for one of the little girls to come over to him. The taller girl, the one with her arm in the cast, coyly shrank into the woman's excess with her eyes fixed on Jesmond. The smaller of the two, however, ran up to him. He judged her to be close to five. "Give this to your mama," he said, holding out a damp towel.

"That ain't my mama. That my auntie!" she shyly grinned. Glued to her top teeth were silver caps.

"You put caps in that little girl's mouth?" Jesmond asked.

"It her mama's boyfriend got 'em, not me." The woman shrugged. "—Now go put that in that dryer!" the woman shouted.

Just behind the woman, through the plate glass, a gummy crone doddered behind a wheelchair. Above the edge of the sill were a gray plaited scalp and a pair of rheumy eyes. The wheelchair stopped, and alongside the head a hand began pebbling the glass, trying to attract the attention of the girls.

Jesmond threw his items into a Winn-Dixie bag and headed north. Though it was muggy and threatening rain again, people lounged on porches, and cars squatted mid-street, torsos half-swallowed by windows. A basketball game being played at an asphalt park with yelps and harangues heralded Jesmond's approach. He bumped a man leaning into a passenger window. The man jerked around to confront him; dangling from his eyetooth was a long thread of dental floss.

Decrepit men, derelict cars: both cluttered driveways, the wan men nodding suspiciously to Jesmond as he passed. And he walked toward a young woman with a heart-shaped tumor on her face; she turned away from him as she tried to purse her lips about a straw.

The sodium lamps erupted and Jesmond and the basketball players were thrown into sordid yellow relief. All exposed. Jesmond broke into a trot down the street to his current abode.

It was one of several ranch-style bungalows belonging to Dr. Medgar Coots, though Jesmond understood that the doctor occasionally used the garage as an office.

Presently, the house was in disrepair. Doors were off-hinged. Tacky, glue-exposed concrete. Bowling-ball-size craters marred the den. Still, Jesmond, enlisted as caretaker, was allowed to live there for free, and his friend Bayonne had begun to squat part-time.

Medgar had two Dobermans patrolling the premises. Jesmond got along well with the dogs. Bayonne, though, was not well liked by Ashley and Sarah (the names Medgar insisted that the dogs be called, though the collars spoke Spinster and Baal), nor was *his* pet, a Capuchin monkey.

Entering the house through the bedroom window (he'd left Bayonne the key), Jesmond stumbled over his friend, who whimpered. He was high and gathered into a ball on a corner of the mattress. The room was fetid. "Goddam, you act the bitch!" Jesmond shouted at Bayonne as he tripped. The dogs were in a squabble outside the bedroom door—which was odd, for Jesmond had locked the dogs in the garage office in anticipation of Bayonne.

Jesmond found he had to climb back out through the window and come in through the front door. The dogs were so riled, he didn't want to chance being cornered in a small room with them.

Lil' Monkey! Jesmond discovered the poor thing shivering inside a wall sconce. As he lifted it the creature bit him, skittering up his neck and leaping from the fireplace mantel onto the thermostat, then back to the mantel. Ashley, launching against Jesmond, snapped at Lil' Monkey but missed. Sarah, after her own third or so futile hurl into space, doubled back and bookended the mantel opposite her sister. The monkey, in desperation, made another seemingly hopeless leap onto the thermostat before a split-second ricochet back into the sconce.

"I didn't see them when I came in," Bayonne remarked to Jesmond as he entered—through the bedroom door. Jesmond suffered a few welts and gouges—challenges to his dominance—getting them back into the garage. "I think the motherfuckers were waiting."

"I had them in the garage when I left this morning," Jesmond said. The two of them watched Lil' Monkey pant atop Bayonne's multicolored Afro wig: the creature applied itself securely to the top shelf of the closet. "Serious, Bayonne. I don't think that pet of yours is going to make it in this environment. And quit watching your gay shit in my room!" Jesmond snapped. At the foot of the mattress on the floor, Jesmond's DVD player displayed silent crepuscular images of nude men.

"Get this, man. I trained Lil' Monkey to jack me off."

"Bullshit!"

"Sike!" Bayonne made some exaggerated gangster signs and fell back onto the mattress. As Jesmond sensed it would be, Bayonne would forever be in tow—his homunculus, his child-creature lacking the facility to translate the world. Recently, Jesmond had seen *The Miracle Worker*. The caretaker of the deaf and blind girl was the only person who could convey "sense" to the child. It rang too uncomfortably familiar.

"Come on and help me clean up. There's dog shit all over the place," Jesmond said, standing from a squat. "There's some detergent and stuff under the kitchen sink."

"Hurly Burly Hurly Burly Hurly Burly! I went back to Hurly Burly last night!" Bayonne sang in falsetto. Hurly Burly was a gay white club that restricted its number of black patrons by sudden, outrageous stipulations. One night it was six pieces of photo identification; another—passports. It was there that Bayonne, in his thug phase, had met Smullian. "He stinks good. Dirty enough, too," was what Smullian had said, lingering—then choosing Bayonne over another hoodlum manqué.

"I'm happy for you. Now get your butt up and—"

Upon opening the door, Jesmond nearly stumbled over Sarah. No bark or growl. Seemed to wink at him.

"Jesmond, Jesmond, Jesmond. Come on out here. Take a load off. Set a spell," a voice yelled from the center of the house.

"Wonderful social constructs—dogs. Parasites, really," Medgar began as Jesmond approached. Sarah, jogging past Jesmond, scuttled up to huddle with Ashley at Medgar's feet. "We're so greedy as humans. We want to see every fawning look, every tongue-hanging pant as an affirmation of love. 'The world may treat me horribly but Sophie' and he or she snuggles up to the little Lhasa apso aquiver in his or her lap—'my Sophié loves me, without question.' And they'll go on to swear their little lapdog is smiling up at them.

"But the trick is they mold to you. Conning little fuckers." While Medgar spoke Ashley raised her pointy head and began licking Medgar's palm. "Evolution has taught them how to freeload. Trick us into thinking they care for us. They are little Prousts. Sophie, the whole domesticated species, unknowingly guileful, traffic in human intent and play upon the nuances of our expectations.

"I read somewhere that the ancient Hebrew word for dog is *kelev*, also slang back then for male temple prostitutes. Speaking of which, how's your friend Bayonne?"

Medgar was perched on a high stool, legs crossed at the ankles. Such mass—the kind of bulk associated with odor. Hooded eyes, fish lips; brick shoulders but womanish hips—"embarrassment of bitches"—oddly, he had said this to Jesmond about himself at their first session, invading Jesmond's space with his face barely six inches away. But no intertriginous stench, big as he was: always, instead, the lingering scent of Mark Jacobs when he left the room.

"Sit. Sit down." Medgar pointed to a solitary kitchen chair in the otherwise empty den. "Our friend Dr. Finchem is out there pouting on the lanai. He'll be joining us soon."

"Bayonne's all right," Jesmond responded.

"Wonderful. And it's good you're here. We've a few housekeeping issues to address regarding our little business."

"What's wrong with Dr. Finchem?"

"Work issues, I suppose." Medgar leaned back and sprawled against the counter. Drummed a hand atop the Formica.

It was Adam Finchem's bad luck to have undergone two divorces in his fifty-eight years (seven children between the exes), as well as the loss of his plastic surgery partner (stroke), and a financial thrashing following a malpractice case—a case in which the company that purportedly carried his policy was, in fact, a dummy holding. ("The Brothers McKendree, up there in Georgia," as Medgar had explained to Jesmond. "Whole passel of 'em. Scam artists and crooked businessmen. However, so very rich.")

"Adam! So you've finally decided to grace us with your presence. Come on here where I can see you." He was a man who men hated to watch talk. Stout and barrel-chested, with waxy lips that collapsed and expanded a strand of paste, sparse eyebrows, pewter tongue . . . Adding to his misfortune was an extensive reprimand from the medical board.

His viatical investments.

For Dr. Finchem served as Medgar's medical screener. Medgar couldn't do it himself—it would be viewed as a conflict of interest. So Finchem was paid to place a stethoscope to the chests of young men with terminal diseases—AIDS, cancer—and declare them suitable for enrollment.

And he was paid very well, both in money and in shares.

"The board is looking into the new things now. That I lied on the evaluations of candidates, cheated for policies." Finchem, agitated, paced about the remnants of the kitchen, touching everything repeatedly: tapping the sink (faucetless), tapping the stove (burner-less and without its oven door), tapping the counter before finally coming to rest in the spot where a refrigerator had once stood. Finchem, draped in a blue work shirt, sweated moons under each arm. Panting like a fledgling.

As Jesmond understood the viatical process, it was for the AIDS patient who was very sick and couldn't afford day-to-day living, much less medications. There were investors willing to lay out cash for the gentleman's life insurance policy and take over the premium payments. Those who desperately needed it got the money; in turn, they hadn't long to go—hypothetically—and the investors would get a nice policy payout.

"Adam, you are the seismograph. Your manifestation of the healing arts discerns who is the appropriate candidate. No, better yet— the vintner! You have to pick those patients that are right at the cusp and harvest the grape. Too soon and we have the predicament of—ghoulish as it sounds—losing money."

"Some goddam investors want to sue me!" Dr. Finchem shouted, startling the dogs. Medgar waved them calm, though. "This on top of all the other shit I've got to deal with. I can't take it now! Can't! They paid out half of this man's five-hundred-thousand-dollar policy, this man who'd lost his health insurance, was at death's door, I'm telling you—but then started the phone calls, sending me certified letters. 'Why is he still alive?' they keep asking me.

"Because, with the money now, you dumb fucks, the man's able to buy his anti-virals! He is living. He's *alive!* They wanted to sue *him* for breach of contract, my attorney tells me, they wanted to sue the dying man with AIDS, but that would look too bad. No, no. So they go after me." Finchem, worked up, began jabbing his finger at Medgar. "You—you must think I'm a fucking idiot! I am not going to be the man left holding this shit, Medgar. Find another dumb-ass. And I'll be the first to let them know who's got the deep pockets here if they keep coming after me." His breath had become rubbed spit, string between the lips. Spirit so carnal as to be obscene.

Medgar smiled naïvely at Finchem. "But you do a good thing, Adam. Don't forget that the people that—" he nodded in the direction of Jesmond, "our friends help solicit would be brushed over like flyspecks. Those are the people you've turned a blind eye to. But I'm a little confused: which hat is it you're complaining about wearing? The screener or the insurance-house doctor?" Medgar's eyes hardened but the naïve smile remained. "Let me let you in on a little secret. There're other corporations out of state—West Virginia and Kentucky, I believe—that know some policies were obtained fraudulently, due to your misrepresentation of the client's health status. Now, don't get upset. See, you help poor folks . . ."

It was by stacking. Jesmond, Bayonne, and others let it be known that Dr. Coots had ways to get them money. At the county hospital, at the nursing homes, at the public clinics, solicitation brought the elderly and HIV-positive to Dr. Medgar Coots. They were mostly black men. Those with terminal diagnoses purchased multiple policies from different companies—were stacked—and their medical conditions were hidden by the reviewing doctor. The insurance policies were generally piddling—twenty-five thousand, fifty thousand—but their low value kept them from any severe scrutiny.

"Our friends don't want to be placed on the radar. Even individually, they're much, much larger than your nemesis, Adam. It wouldn't pay to piss them off. Please, I know what of I speak. As I've told you, settle down and it'll be taken care of it."

Nothing could sway Dr. Finchem, though he made a show, in leaving, of some semblance of reconciliation. Still—ending anxious, rigidly righteous.

"Fuck it. Let the bastard screw himself," Medgar mumbled. The serpentine Dobermans mirrored each other at the foot of Medgar's chair. Sejant, the dogs: as on some heraldic banner, in some ruinous castle of a miscreant Hungarian count somewhere in the Carpathians.

"So you're gainfully employed now," Medgar said, the naïve smile returning, giving the full bore of his attention to Jesmond. "Marvelous. How about Bayonne?"

"He's asleep," Jesmond said.

"That limits industrious activity," Medgar said, "But as a functioning employee—I take it he's still on his old man's payroll?"

"Last he said. Though he's been messed up the past few days, weeks. I don't think he can even do what I'm doing, this Rent-to-Own crap. I was thinking about bringing him along but the guy who runs it considers himself a hard-ass."

So he told Medgar about all the large men, of the classroom antics, of the sidelong flattering, the cajoling. The burgeoning enmity.

"The pimp's insight? Young Mr. Toak, let me give you the pimp's insight—" Medgar offered. They were cocooned within the shaded interior of Medgar's Mercedes sedan. Jesmond watched as Medgar's eyes jigged between the rearview mirror and the road. He had agreed to drop Jesmond off at Peaches Richmond's home; he just had a few quick stops to make. "It's not being a grifter or a con artist, contrary to what you'd think. The grifter, son, exploits the basic human weakness of perceived gain. That's why I find it hard to muster up much anger or resentment at a good scam. There's an almost ethical balance to it. Ask your papa about *his* business venture sometime. Feddy Toak had one for the ages. Used pacemakers. Better than his current status, Port Authority factotum—

"But a true pimp has figured out something. (I couldn't be one— I'm too lazy to be that aggressive.) A true pimp understands what the majority of the population does not. He makes the map of the world huge. Take rape. Rape is about them begging you to stop and you don't have to: truly, the loss of privacy. A pimp makes a weapon of this basic want, too. He makes sure of this: no longer is anything private for his intended.

"I had a friend, an endocrinologist, who was fascinated by this hustler he'd met. They hung out together. He said the man was 'schooling' him. 'The psychology, man, the psychology!' He had my friend sit at the kitchen table with him while he rode into this woman. He shouted at the woman to open her mouth, open it wider—at which point he stuck his hand down her throat. 'Now bite me, bitch! I dare you!' They sat like that for almost an hour. Her jaw was dislocated. My friend got himself all lathered up and excited telling me this.

"After a few months I lost touch with him. The next thing I hear, though, is that he'd moved in with the man and had begun turning over his university paycheck to him. And the last I've heard since is that he now has my gland expert in hoop earrings, peddling hole in Tallahassee."

They parked behind a block-stumped pickup truck on a road where most of the streetlights were either burned out or broken. A yellow eye-slit of lamp glowed in front of C. P. Frapple Mortuary. Even with the windows rolled up the discharge from the coffee-processing plant—initially pleasant; then acrid, near-bituminous—diffused through the car. Medgar leaped out and, leading with his hips, swagged up to the entrance and knocked lightly on a glass door. He waited awhile before finally slipping an envelope into the mail slot. "I guess you can't expect these places to be on the Waffle House clock," he chuckled as he settled into the driver's seat.

Their final stop was off Phillips Highway, an adult-stay motel. Three or four Gator City taxies were parked near the check-in. Wind-pressed newspaper shivered against the Cyclone half-fence corralling the parking lot. One of the motel-room doors was open, the wall suffused with orange glow, playful shadows. A woman of indeterminate age sat staring at the car from a dark window. Jesmond wanted to see more of everything.

"Recognize the place?" Medgar said, "Your grandpappy's. Country Hearth Inn. He bought this firetrap in 1986 for a little less than ninety thousand dollars. The lot itself now is easily worth two-ten, two-fifty. And if I'm not mistaken he also owns the defunct little diner down the street there." He pointed somewhere vaguely into the night horizon.

Medgar got out but stood beside the car, continued to talk. Jesmond could see only his waist. "Why don't you come in with me?" Medgar finally said. His voice came from above the vehicle. The woman in the dark room had grown very still.

The tiny lobby rushed upon and seized them. Two beryl green bristly sofas that, once Jesmond sat down, made him reflexively scratch his thigh. The soundless vintage television. He could hear Medgar talking at the counter but couldn't make out what was said. The other voice had some Eastern European accent.

The television had been bled of most of its color and light; there were only the ghostly remnants of a talk show. A man—rasping, wheezing, damp, shirtless, with an amateurish portraiture in blue ink on his chest—glowered at Jesmond. The tattoo (more an outline) was of a round, bald head with a pointed beard. Tangerine-size knobs collapsed the ears; the navel made for a harelip depression. The old man's square hand relentlessly stroked a Boston Chicken take-out bag where the golden rump of a roaster winked from the end.

The man was explained to Jesmond when they left. "That is the supervisor's father," Medgar recounted as they rode across town to the off-base housing where Peaches Richmond lived. "Ukrainian. A Gulag survivor. Ninety years old." He had been sent to a Siberian forest in the 1940s, survived the camp as a movie projectionist. Revenge killings occurred in the darkened rooms, bodies borne out on stretchers under the light of Tom Mix cowboy serials. "But he was a common criminal. A crook. More specifically, a thief. What you saw on that paunch was Lenin's face."

Among thieves imprisoned in the Gulag—so it was told, at least—there was a firm belief that no execution squad would ever fire upon a portrait of Lenin or Stalin.

IV

"Mule!" Teo yelled, pounding the wooden door with the flat of his hand. He was standing outside Rachel Ennis's East Arlington law office on a bright Saturday afternoon. "Mule! I've got to talk to you, this is important!" The ring on his hand provided a resolute *clack,* a shot that repeatedly discharged the blue-black starlings—nits of fresh tar—abrading the phone lines. When the door opened slightly, Teo pushed into the vestibule.

"I told you all this dicking around would bite us in the ass! I told you that you can't sit on a hot property, that when you have the opportunity you've got to move it! But—no! You just had me sitting there!" he shouted, waving a furled, thumb-thick newspaper like a tomahawk before collecting himself and handing it over to Rachel.

The *Tanner Gazette* was the African-American alternative weekly. Deals between the city and black-owned businesses were reported, and local ministers provided advice and insight. Touring celebrities would sometimes consent to interviews. A recipe always took up the bottom left corner of the back page.

"Look on page four—Entertainment," Teo mumbled. Beneath a three-color photo print was the caption, "Bernard Irwin excited about film prospect in The First City."

Many an aspiring star and starlet will want to listen closely to the advice Mr. Irwin might give. Bernard Irwin, 38, the talented actor/singer who won an Emmy for the hit comedy series *Perch and Seizure* (1986), is committed to expanding his career and to now include serious, socially meaningful roles. "When I was a child I did child things," the thoughtful actor said. "'Jeeta, Messqueta!' was a great run and served its purpose in its day. But the Bobby Jackson tragedy needs to be told and it needs to be told right." The Reverend Dante Phillips, pastor of Greater Abyssinian Baptist, a close personal friend and spiritual counsel of Mr. Irwin, spoke. "There's a new fire and commitment to him that I haven't seen in years. That part of Bobby Jackson was made for him. He will do the boy's story justice."

"So?" Rachel asked.

"Kind of a coincidence, ain't it, that we get that movie student, director, producer—whatever the hell he is—sniffing around here and all the sudden this little fucker pops up."

"What's your point, Teo?"

"Deals are being made, Mule! Things are going on and we're out of the loop! Though for the life of me I don't see how he got picked. Smaller than me. Size of an elf— What did he play on TV?"

"A kid, Toak. He played a kid back then."

"Yeah, dwarf, midget—whatever he is, back then is back then. He's too old now. See the gut on him? I don't care how small he is. It'd be like having some *Oz* munchkin play Opie on Andy Griffith."

Rachel shook her head. "How'd you find me?"

"I know where you live, darlin', just that it's gated. You've got three law offices. I figured you'd be at the one closest to the criminal activity since Monday's docket day."

"You know what? You need to go now," Rachel said. "You need to peddle that tired movie crap somewhere else. In case you didn't understand then, please understand now: Teo Toak, I will be forever thankful to you in providing Mr. Robert Jackson's bail. But the gratitude is now at its end. You had your reasons to cover him—I don't have an issue with that. What I have an issue with is this sense of obligation, that we should submit to some scheme of yours as you try to turn this boy's misery into some bank.

"Between you and me: you putting all that time and energy into this movie-impresario bit is fucking stupid. You think *I'm* going to turn over the management of the boy to *you*? Think again, tiger. I've got your game, Toak."

Teo's eyes narrowed. "What's that? What do you mean?"

"Just that you aren't the picture of compassion. Look, the boy's aunt is telling me that she has to lead him by the wrist just to get him to the bathroom on time. He's near catatonic—a seventeen-year-old in Depends."

Bobbing his head while she spoke, agreeing. "But—listen to me. Irwin is second cousin or some such to that bullet-head preacher—what's his name?"

Rachel Ennis looked incredulous. "You really don't know when you need to stop, do you?"

"Come on. What's it say there? What's the guy's name?"

"Reverend Phillips, Teo."

"Now you watch. Just as sure as I'm fucking standing here that jackleg's probably got it hooked up so that black Opie's on the dance card. The man can operate—screwed me out of a piece of property, there on Leland, overlooking 95 North. Blackmailed the city council with some cock-and-bull that that old factory should be given to him. 'As a man of God and the Afro-American community!' Said he was going to turn it into a nursing home or some such. Now he's sitting on it so I can't, the shit!"

"Let me make you privy to a little inside dope, Teo: Bernard Irwin is actually going to emcee the heritage festival down at States Beach in a few weeks. A tribute to the first black female aviator, Bessie Coleman. I know this for a fact because I'm on the committee with Phillips that invited him. So think about that, Toak, and leave me the hell alone."

He left unhappy. Not surprised. Betrayed? But what should he have expected, that she'd be his buddy and share his interests? That was the problem, he did expect these things! And a few years earlier he would've been sharp enough not to. Old age was making him emotionally loose. What static electricity did to cheap rayon: somebody would walk by and he'd silently swoop and wrap him or her up.

He drove his ancient gold Cadillac across the Horton Bridge, tires whirring over the iron grating. Then: splash of bloodred bougainvilleas from the sides of houses. He was on his way to a meeting regarding his condemned hospital property, a discussion with "Medgar Coots and his associate."

Medgar's associates were always some sort of shill. Teo wouldn't be up to it, wouldn't have the energy to deal with one while keeping an eye on the other. He wondered if his younger self would've had any respect at all for the old coot he was now. He could not have cared less about the other way around: what the hell did young bucks care what old men thought of them anyway? No—he was like wet felt now, sodden stuff—young Teo Toak would've sucked his teeth and sized him up as good dick for the buzzards.

Teo parked the Caddy, straddling a huge split on the heat-split asphalt. Weeds sprouted through smaller seams: flowers of spent condoms, their wrappers. He opened the broad door onto the cavernous parking lot and heat engulfed him, whipping about like a sirocco. His feet looked tiny. Teo placed his small, boot-shod feet simultaneously onto the soft tar and both heels sank just a fraction.

A drunk lay sprawled in the shade of a frayed and clattering hospital awning, watching him.

"Say, Jasper, can I help you?" Teo yelled. "Maybe get you a pillow, some chocolates? Get off my goddam property!" The man scurried off, his coat scrolled tight about him as if shrink-wrapped.

There was a padlock and chain on the glass double door. Teo fumbled with the keys, finally opening onto the foyer. A metallic smell but also feral: sun-baked, relinquished automobiles. The flooring was linoleum and dark, the color, the smell of iodine. Warped, too—he nearly tripped over a ridge in front of the information desk.

The hospital was founded in 1922. Before? Colored patients were tended to in the basement of the public county hospital, beneath dripping pipes and sweating plaster. A discerning white business-man, wanting to create a Negro hospital, brought to the state legisla-ture the following observation: young white women were handling the bedpans of Negro men.

In its heyday the hospital had five Negro physicians and a full nursing school. A children's ward in back gazed upon a green cem-etery. And at its pinnacle the hospital boasted a bay for its robin's-egg-blue ambulance. (Before then, funeral homes would have to be called, and black-curtained hearses delivered the sick and injured to emergency-room doors—a business card tucked discreetly in a pocket or corset.)

Teo had arrived in Johnsonville, though, after the hospital had developed the reputation as an institution to be avoided. When Feddy broke his arm, for example, Teo had Ace drive due west, and they positioned Feddy under a client's tree just outside of Gaines-ville so that the ambulance would take him to University Hospi-tal. By the late 1970s the Negro hospital no longer took care of in-patients and ran, instead, walk-in clinics. There was an attempt at a medical park. By the mideighties the hospital was closed altogether. (Though, for a brief spell in the early nineties, Medgar had leased the building from the city as an in-patient drug and alcohol treat-ment unit. However, the well soon dried up: no insurance company was willing to pay such outrageous fees.)

Teo stood in the sun-drenched lobby, dust motes in a storm. Pigeons gurgled in the eaves beyond the large glass walls, and a brown, elephant-eared plant rasped minutely, delicately across the linoleum. There was a soft draft, some cross-circulation, though Teo couldn't figure out from where. "Old man seeks ghost," that's what he should advertise in the *Gazette*. Wasn't afraid of them anymore. When he was younger—that would be the stick he'd rib young buck Teo with—he had a country nigger's fear of the spirit world. Now . . .

Upstairs, the wards were empty except for a raft of rusted bed frames piled one atop another in an enormous room. There was no sound save for the remote chirring of insects deep in the lawn. Ceiling had given way in leaping patches, white-shrouded pipes and the white flock of the fireproofing. Winter in July.

But it still ate at Teo that Rachel was able to make him to feel that way—*I've got your game.* What did she mean? The fur-lipped bitch! She was talking to Jesmond's mother, Yvette, now that *that* bitch was sober. And she was probably eating at him, too, lying about him—God! Where was the end? Why can't the world just love him and him alone? And Yvette and Feddy? What a pair! But he loved Feddy; he loved him enough to look after the two of them—though both of them were always high. *Do it, Teo. I want you to come in me. Come on, baby, come in me,* that cunt—

Too quiet. But there was the noise in quiet things. The ground floor in the back had been the children's ward. The yellowed enameled cribs were still there; a stack of little teacups and saucers; a child's wooden wheelchair with Vulcan-rubber tires—freakishly small; an adult's, one-quarter scale—with a time-darkened, orange-faced doll in the seat. Teo hated toys, didn't understand them. They pulled energy, made time useless. . . . But the doll demanded to be picked up. Looking through the clouded glass doors, he caught himself absently stroking the painted head.

The cemetery could have been a fallow field, with its tall, broke-neck weeds, hazy spiderwebs. And the barnlike door to the ambulance bay was ajar—Teo thought he saw a cat enter.

He wanted to walk quickly through the basement. The basement opened onto the top of a hillock, sloping down to a small gravel lot where he was to meet Medgar and his associate. And the lot narrowed to an overgrown footpath leading to the cemetery. . . .

Though he'd had them remove the abominations—surgical scraps in the thick, green Pyrex jars—the stench remained. Fucking formaldehyde! Feddy used to work in the slop when he was at the county hospital, he smelled of it when he would come visit. Didn't seem to bother Feddy, though. Still a drunk, then. Teo had to get after him to shower when he was through work: no real man, that is, any man with any self-respect, would go around smelling like that.

In the corner: shrouded furniture and a room composed of chicken wire. It held medical records, mostly those from the late 1940s to about 1960. Teo knew the dates because *he'd* been nosy— poked through them himself. Somebody else had beat him to it, though. A cheap aluminum padlock had already been twisted and split by the time he arrived, and a pull-tab faded Fresca can was spill-glued to a wooden desk, right next to a pair of cheap drugstore reading glasses. The glasses rested on . . . whose record? Syphilis and shakes of somebody he should have known . . . It was probably Medgar who had beat him to the punch. Typical of the bastard— trying for the leg up and tabs on folks.

Teo crabbed sideways down the small hill. His knees had begun to bother him lately, and he found he had to use the sedge, covered with talcum-like dust, as grapplings to help steady the accelerating descent.

Medgar was at the bottom of the gray hill. He was leaning against his car and waving intermittently. Teo managed a brusque wave back. "Hey, young'un," Medgar sprightly greeted Teo as he skidded to a stop right in front of him.

"Hey, yourself," Teo said, brushing his hands on his trousers.

"So, how's it cooking?" Medgar asked.

"Not bad, not bad. So you've decided to see if you can play me for a chump today, eh? Sweet man, Coots." Stuck through the rear side window of the car was a veiny, pumpkin-headed geezer in sun-glasses, listening word for word to what was said. "That your asso-ciate?" Teo asked.

"Yep," Medgar replied.

The man tilted his head up. Teo got a direct view up a pair of por-cine, large-bore nostrils. The man immediately spat a gout of brown fluid.

"Cute," Teo said.

Medgar pointed to the hospital. "You've been doing the upkeep yourself?"

"Naw. Got people I pay to come by and do the lawns, take care of any broken windows, stuff like that."

"The place still renting out piecemeal?"

"Naw, baby. That's you and your cronies back in the day. Only thing I've got now is some Lebanese chick who hauls cross-country and pays to park her rig in the lot up there." The codger shot out another stream of tobacco juice. "He don't say much. The man a mute, Medgar?"

"Better. Two out of three: 'see none, speak none'—dumb and blind."

"And this is your business partner?"

"Best kind."

The man spat again. "Don't hold his chaw much, either," Teo said.

"Regular Vesuvius. For some reason, brings to mind a story I'd heard about Old Slave Erasmus in Virginia. There was a bet between two wealthy southern gentlemen that his slave, Erasmus, could carry a mouthful of his piss all the way from Richmond to Fredericksburg without swallowing or spilling a drop. He, in fact, succeeded."

"And what the fuck you telling me this for? You want me to piss down *your* throat?" Teo snorted. "Well, I'm glad we're all caught up. Now, let me take you through the place. I'd just walked through the main hospital building—"

"Slow down, old man. I'm not interested in the hospital."

"Then what you bring me down here for?"

"The cemetery, old man, the cemetery!"

V

I want to see what sort of agreement we can come to about that dilapidated old cemetery!" Medgar smiled. "Now I know that you got a little heads-up about an airport extension coming through. You and I know that that's not fair. Actually, by law that counts as insider trading. And there's all that mess regarding exhumation and reburial. I've already put our congressman on notice that just because it is a colored cemetery the African-American community won't tolerate its dead being disrespected."

"Coots Coots Coots. Kiss-My-Ass Coots. I should've known better. You win. I'm just stupid. Let me just sign this over to you." Teo began patting himself. "Wait a minute. I've got a pen somewhere—"

"Now, Toak. All I'm suggesting is that you sell me the cemetery at fifteen percent above fair market price. You can keep the hospital. Turn it into a mall."

"Fuck you, Coots." Teo, for the briefest moment, glared despairingly at the hill in front of him. He then sighed, hunched over, and began lurching up the trace. "Call me when you've got sense again," he said without looking back at Medgar. Halfway up, Teo did turn around. "And what in the hell do you want a graveyard for, man?"

"To bury people, of course," Medgar replied.

As Teo disappeared over the lip of the little hill, the man in the car again spat. This time a ribbon of brown rime adhered to the door. "That's him," the globe-head grunted.

"You got tobacco spit on my car. Clean it up."

"I tole you I never forget a voice. Knew it was him when I heard the television. First heard that commercial. And that crap—"

Medgar opened the rear passenger door. "Get out. Now," he said. Medgar didn't raise his voice. The pig-snouted man in the dark glasses tried to make himself small, retracting into the shade of the car's interior like a collapsing spider. Medgar reached inside and jerked him onto the gravel.

For he was truly blind. A papier-mâché head, oyster gums. Knees scuffed and splayed in a squat, leaking shame and fear. Anxiousness to please.

"Sure as I'm standing I'll leave you here, Toby. As I told you: you spat tobacco juice down the side of my car. Now I want you to clean it up." The man nodded, bewildered.

Medgar popped the trunk remotely, a button from his keys. An oddity, his trunk: it was all black space with deep recesses and crannies like a canyon. In the center was the expected tire well along with cleaning materials; but above it was a black, carpeted box. To the left and right of it were crevices containing accordion folders and papers; there were several trays with Velcro bindings holding strange tools.

A blazing Saturday in July. And there, just a hundred yards or so from a small, verdant cemetery, a hive-headed codger wearing large tinted spectacles minced about, haphazardly spraying and patting the side of a parked car, while a black man nonchalantly read a newspaper at the wheel.

"Bees?"

"Bees."

Feddy sat back from Seth. They were in the downtown Peebo's. Peebo's Cafeterias served his favorite meal and this was his favorite of the chain. Cheap fare: three chicken wings (extra-spicy; oil-splotched paper plate), dirty rice (here the restaurant used pulled pork), and four of their signature Golden Biscuits. What made the downtown eatery one of his favorite haunts were the faces: over years he recognized the people as they came in—who worked in the area or lived nearby. It helped assure him of his place in the world.

"You want me to take my work van—what I use to make a living—drive down to your loading section—"

"Section thirty-three. It's quiet out there, near the back parking lot. Look, you don't even have to come in. There's a gap in the fence—"

"And then you want to, want me to, load my van with bees."

"Stingless bees, man. Besides, they'll be knocked out or something. Smoke. And put in transport hives."

"And these things, you tell me, eat roadkill?"

Carrion bees. *Trigona necrophaga.*

One day, the past bountiful spring, Feddy sat in his little chicken-wire office, tucked up some plywood steps inside the warehouse. On the radio (FM, the only frequency that would come into the building) was a program regarding the plight of the American beekeeper. The American bee had become exceedingly susceptible to tracheal mites and the population was dwindling. The only way to curb the decline was to infuse the anemic American bee with a hardier, tropical strain. The African bee was too violent and aggressive. The Costa Rican carrion bee had a hardy constitution, too—and was stingerless as well. Though it was against the law to bring bees into the United States, by grace of the Internet Feddy found the name of a Belgian apiary concern. Then tracked down beekeepers in Arkansas who'd be interested in the indirect imports.

"Seth, check this out." Feddy pointed his butter knife at the buffet station: a squalid, gap-toothed man with two ginger braids and layers of clothes over a hospital gown stared defiantly at Feddy as he hurriedly scraped food from his plate into his mouth, his back to the register. For the cashier's attention was on the joyless woman in the too-large smock behind the steam table, Agnes. Mole-ridden Agnes, sculpted hair, gold teeth.

A dapper gentleman was holding up the line in a request for more string beans. "Come now—what it to you if you give me a little more string bean?" the man asked with a West Indian lilt.

"That all you get."

"What it to you?" the man insisted.

"No."

"It not your food. Not coming from your plate or pocketbook!"

Agnes stared at him, arms crossed, the ladle bouncing like a conductor's baton.

"Ignorant." The West Indian shook a finger in her face. "You see? Jus' plain ignorant."

Agnes sucked her teeth and looked away. "I ain't studying you."

"You acting de boss, doing minimum wage. Prob-be not a penny to yer name. Jus' look at you! Miss High-and-Mighty, standing der wit yer whole net wort up in yer mout!" Guffaws and whistles.

"God-dam!" Feddy barked.

"That's not right. Just not right," Seth said. In trying to suppress a laugh, he started snuffling, fell into a coughing fit.

Walking out to Seth's van, it occurred to Feddy that a service establishment might not relish having a broad-paneled truck advertising waste removal parked out in front. "Anyone ever ask you to set someplace else?" Feddy wondered, moving aside a yellow Sponge-Bob doll in the passenger's seat.

"Naw, not yet. Though I'm sure those sons of bitches at the bakery get pissed when I drive her to work," Seth chuckled. "Now, this ain't going to take too long, right? I've gotta pick up Bethena's little girl from her mama's house."

"Sadie seems to enjoy playing grandma," Feddy grinned. "You ready for the next one?"

"Yeah, I suppose. Anyways, I still got some stuff I've got to go over with my deacon for tomorrow. I can't spend all afternoon hanging with the likes of you."

"Shouldn't take us too long. Just want to get an idea of how we're going to move things from point A to point B." Fortunate that Melan was generous in his blindness: gave a blind eye to Feddy's sometimes cramped, nascent ventures. For example, on the up-and-up (nearly), Feddy had previously worked out the selling and sending of used clothes to a Namibian distributor at two West African ports. Melan bypassed the paperwork. The bees, of course, required another level of finesse. The importation of live insects brought the certitude of Fish and Wildlife wrath—though Feddy was ready with the excuse of Darwinian stowaways.

"Look at that!" Seth pointed from his side window. They were climbing an overpass. "Now that's something you don't see too often. Black limo driver sitting while Colonel Sanders polishes the Mercedes." But by the time Feddy turned to see, they were well onto the freeway.

They rode for several miles, listening to staticky and whistling gospel stations crammed at the end of the dial. "Bayonne's in some serious mess," Seth suddenly said. "Sadie tried to call on your pops. She wanted to see if he'd put up bail if this Smullian shit is pushed through."

"Probably nothing to worry about. Cops are just pissed off. I don't think Bayonne did anything."

"Look, Feddy, I know that he was sitting there right next to the man when he offed himself. Of course Bayonne wasn't there all the way from start to finish, you know, till the man was dead, but the fact of the matter is you just don't sit there and watch—let—someone gas themselves to death. They said the insurance is close to a half a million."

Even though they were deep into the west side they passed one of Rachel Ennis's billboards. "Don't see who she'd hope to get out here. Nothing but rednecks," Seth observed.

Slowed down. A known speed trap. Sure enough, behind a hairpin and smut grass was a teal sheriff's car. Feddy stretched across Seth and peeped a goodbye as they passed.

"Thought maybe your daddy might be able to work something out if we needed to. Giving him the heads-up. That bail business can be out of sight and I can't afford it when it gets too crazy. I was thinking he might let me, since I'm giving him the heads-up and all, pay a little each month when the time's needed."

"Nope. And I can tell you what he'll say, just as if he was sitting right here between us. 'Sethy—bail on the installment plan? Give me a fuckin' break.'"

It was an ugly sea, ugly little beach. Rose-gray mud sand and the susurrus of the under-dock lap and retreat. Tannic, the color of oversteeped tea: a power plant and pulp mill rilled the brown water into the adjacent estuary, then the Atlantic Ocean.

Johnsonville Port Authority was partially closed Saturday evenings. With his pass card Feddy clacked the electric gate, and Seth's van pulled into one of the herringbone spaces.

"I think it's over there." Feddy pulled a manifest from his shirt pocket, unfolded and studied it, crumpled it back into his pants pocket. "Caulder Line Shipping. They're on the east port dock. *Caribe Cabello* from Puerto Limon, Costa Rica. There it is!"

They'd been wandering through a maze of shipping containers, ending before a break-bulk trailer. It was a blue and white twenty-footer that had been shunted to the far edge of loading area, just off the lip of the macadam as it petered to a retention pond. "I shipped through Caulder," Feddy said, checking the numbers along the side. "They're a half-assed line with broke-down equipment." The bill of lading read, "Perishables: Meat"—this was supposed to mean a refrigerated container, but Feddy let them know off the record that he wanted the spoilage. "Supposed to be a box with a Freon leak. Goat carcasses, I think."

Otherworldly darkness and babel. Nothing makes the stomach lurch as when the hand is on the portal and the thrum of what's beyond the door seizes stank, pulls breath.

"Geeyawd in heaven, Frederick! What the hell did you let loose upon this earth?" Seth yelled, jerking a forearm to cover his nose.

Murmurous velum—the slant of white sun revealed them covering the offal. The bees, hundreds upon hundreds. Thousands, maybe. Obsidian drones draping carcass and remnant. Feddy swung the metal door wide, stepped back. Good God, stepped back again. "My name is Legion" flitted through his head—the multiplicities of Feddy in their vision, holding the singularity of their attention.

He turned and steadied his gaze about the cargo. Had done the work, the research. *Trigona necrophaga* was a species of bee that replaced pollen with flesh. Instead of honey, a pastelike muck. The bees sometimes made a little sweet glue from overripe fruit but were predatory enough to chew through wasp larvae and pupae.

"Look more like flies on a garbage heap to me," Seth said. A gape-mouthed wicker trunk served as a hive. "Sure smells like it. Smells like shit. No way I'm gonna let that hell-spawn in my van." Of the naked, exposed flanks of goat—the bones were leaping white.

"Okay. Let me get a hold of these guys that help me set this up. They've got all the smokers and the transport-hive stuff. They can load all this shit in *their* truck."

"Wonder if you've got to bring them something else to eat. Looks like they're about done," Seth asked Feddy as they clanged the door closed.

On the way back, the lumbering shadow of an egret darkened the windshield of the van. And though the weeds were crushed and the backs of the tall hurl flowers broken, the police cruiser was gone. "Father Clemons called me the other day. Somehow got a hold of me at work," Feddy suddenly said. Father Clemons had been the principal of the colored parochial school they had attended. Feddy at one time needed Father Clemons. Long ago he would habitually call the old priest—when he was drunk or high, depressed, needed a handholding.

"Hadn't thought of that man in years," Seth said.

"I talk to him every now and then. Said he was coming back to Johnsonville for a visit."

Seth shrugged. A tour bus and station wagon passed them in the opposite direction, a long gap in between. A mare's tail of cirrus cloud bled greenish pink across the sky with the hint of constellations emerging. Seth began to vigorously crowd the dashboard with gestures regarding the bakery's biannual site inspection, implicating Cygnus and Vega through the windshield.

VI

In town they stopped by the home of Feddy's girlfriend of five weeks, Sharon Davis. A thick-calved pony of a woman, she was the only white woman in her neighborhood and had dated only black men all her life. Her house was a spottily mildewed clapboard two-story with a parabolic roofline and tar shingles inclined toward and sliding into the rain gutter. Since she ran an unlicensed day care, the home roiled with children from six in the morning till six in the evening, weekdays.

The house smoldered disorder. Newspapers would yellow and furl in the corners along with stacked issues of her glossies, *Ebony, Redbook, Jet,* which accommodated three-legged divans. Plastic garbage bags contained children's clothes, doubled as beanbag seating for the tots. And what to make of a disemboweled Franklin stove with a television in its belly? It would pick up only NBC, only her stories—*The Guiding Light, The Young and the Restless.* Sacrosanct that no children were allowed upstairs. The kiddies were fond of her, though. And the downstairs was wholly their realm—a urinous reek tinged with Lysol, orange Creamsicles, and Dollar Store fruit drink.

Feddy and Seth were parked and talking a couple of houses down from Sharon's when she knocked on the passenger's window.

"You just gonna sit there? Hi, Seth." Stood and nibbled the dangling strip of crisp meat from a fried bologna sandwich. A cluster of ancien régime acne scars dotted the center of each cheek. She gestured for Seth to roll down the window. "What's this? Gonna burn a tank of gas so you two can snooze in air-conditioning?" she reprimanded. Stuck her frizzy head into the car interior. Inquisitorial green-gray eyes.

"Both of us were dreaming about you. Mine had his beat by a landslide, though," Feddy said.

"Y'all could of done your dreaming inside."

"You know how it is, sexy," Seth whispered, loud enough for Feddy to smirk. "I don't want to make that old guy jealous. Me? And *him*? And you'd have to choose?"

"Hmm," she replied, her mouth full. She swallowed, then pointed at Seth with the heel of her sandwich. "See, I know your kind." Her voice was all husk and smoke-stain. "One of those sweet, innocent-acting, quiet types. Got to keep my eye on you." She paused. "Feddy, better get your ass in the house."

The afternoon's experience had Feddy showering as soon as he set foot upstairs. They then fucked. Afterward, Feddy traced the whorl of soft puberulent hair at the base of her spine—a tight Fibonacci spiral. Sharon propped herself up on her elbows and looked over her shoulder. "Stop, Spot. That tickles."

"You're not moving."

"'Cause I'm paralyzed, Romeo."

He lightly drew his hands across the crease of her buttocks. With his middle finger, he playfully dabbed at her anus. "R-r-r-ose bud," he rasped—his best imitation *Citizen Kane*.

She reached back and slapped his hand. "Don't even think about it!" She then snuggled to the crook of his arm, read the Braille of his belly scars and crannies.

Contrary to expectation, Sharon rarely ran her window-unit air, not with the leaf shade of an enormous oak swiping through the room. Windows throughout the house opened to a moist breeze playing through the space, flapping fronds of the unglued seams of the flocked wallpaper.

On his back, the constant purr of air across Feddy's belly led to an erection. Sharon, still on her side, looked down and made exaggerated, Kewpie-doll eyes. "Eeeow—" she mouthed.

Feddy pulled up against the headboard. He then reached onto the night table for her reading glasses, propping them atop his penis. Sharon took some time glancing between Feddy's face and member—"I'm sorry, baby. But I'm choosing the guy with the bushy eyebrows."

"Now you've done it, precious. You've done gone and broke my heart," Feddy said. He then stood up and went to the bathroom, the glasses still precariously perched. When he returned he was flaccid, glasses askew. "Uh-huh," Sharon sighed. "As I figured. A pee-woody."

Spring of their new lust. Each, playing intimate, wanting to regale the other with stories of romantic misadventure and lost love.

She loved black men. She recounted the progression of her companions through the decades. She'd been an attractive, exuberant high school cherub in South Carolina per her photo album: shimmering in a spangled vermillion dress, octopus-groped by a tuxedoed, sepia-skinned singer ("Member of The Systoles—what the heart does, baby"), followed by a trio of photographs. Three brown, brawny U.S.N. sailors. Like a boardwalk cutout with a head insert—only the faces differed with each picture. Then: tan baby on Mum's knee; tan child with long braids next to now-broadening Mum; Mum in coffee klatch with like mums—light-brown babies, porcelain women. The tan baby evolved into a tan, scowling teenager freckled in pimples. Then there was an old, foxed photo of Mum, baby, and a tall black man in Malcolm X spectacles. A glamour photograph: shiny stock, soft focused.

"That's my son's father," Sharon said. "I called him my Dark Angel. From Mississippi. Used to dress me up with my hair colored to match his fantasy."

"Goddam, that's a *huge* son of a bitch!" Feddy said.

"That there's in my Marilyn Monroe period," Sharon said, ignoring the comment. "Loved having me hanging off his arm then."

"He looks like a preacher."

"*Simon*? Hell no. He grew up in all these foster homes, beaten up and stuff. He wore glasses—just glass in the frames, he didn't need them—'cause he wanted to look intelligent. Died, though. Kidneys and blood pressure. He never really had a fair shot."

As she sat up and pressed herself against the headboard, Feddy let himself fall face-first into her nest of hair. He loved the unwashed smell of her, nuzzled her nape, slid a tongue into the hollow formed by the neck and clavicle. Their teeth clicked when they kissed.

"Before you get yourself all worked up, baby, finish looking at these with me," Sharon chastised. A photograph of the angry young man now in an army corporal's uniform. "That's my boy," she sighed, proudly. "He's stationed at Fort Bragg."

There were photographs of her best friend, a fat, shifty-eyed, sun-blotched woman with no discernible waist and thin banana breasts: friend at a picnic dangling a beer can; friend sitting in a nightclub, trying to look seductive; friend with *her* son of about twelve (white) standing beside her and a toddler on her knee—while behind them, smirking at the camera, was a Snoop Dogg lookalike.

"—She was a fool to have a baby by him. Found out he had two other children coming at the same time!"

Feddy stared at the shirtless man with the washboard stomach. He reminded him of a customer he knew during his North Dakota vending-machine days, a gas-station attendant who prided himself on having nine kids by five different white women. "I give them all little niggas, man!" What was this, Feddy wondered, what's left when you see your seed as contagion?

"How many kids do you have, Feddy?" Sharon asked. "I know you've got the one boy here. But I know your kind. You just step off a bus anywhere in the U.S. and you hear 'daddy.'"

"Nope. Just the boy. Jesmond."

"You never wanted more?"

"You trying to tell me something?"

"Baby, I took care of those issues a long time ago." She made a scissoring motion through the air. "Does he live with you?"

"Jesmond? No. No, no." Feddy stretched across and dented her waist for the opposing night table, fingertips reaching a cup.

It was the quiet of late afternoon, just before the sun sets. A Tarzan yodel from a television somewhere broke the silence.

Feddy settled into the center sag of the mattress with the coils pressing into his tailbone. He rested his hand and cup on her naked thigh before finally taking a sip of cold coffee. "Who does he take after?" Sharon asked. His turn.

"Dunno. His mom, I guess."

"You two hang out much?"

"I'm going to tell you something you won't mind hearing, darling. His mother was shit. That's explaining some of the boy's bad habits. Still—the boy and I don't see each other much."

"I know it's not my place but I can tell you, from my son. Young men need a father's presence."

Young men need only pussy, he wanted to say.

But he fed in to her urgent sincerity, gave her the story about Jesmond's abysmal cross-country trek to see him when he was twelve. "—About thirty-six hours on a Trailways from here to Milwaukee. March. He'd never seen snow before. His mother was still a drunk and smoking everything. I'd stopped drinking for the time, though I was still trifling. I sent Jesmond a ticket and a fifty-dollar money order. His ma then put him on the bus with just ten bucks, a couple of Jack in the Box burgers, and her expired American Express card. It was an old account that'd been closed for years. 'You can use it but only in a really bad emergency,' she told him."

The bus had engine trouble in the Smoky Mountains, where the heater stopped working. Jesmond's mother had packed only a pullover and her windbreaker for the cold. One passenger was kind enough to give him a blanket; another groped him. And the boy was ravenous when he arrived. "I didn't do much better. I was staying in an old house that they'd converted into apartments, just outside downtown Milwaukee. When we get back to my place there are all these flashing lights and an ambulance. Somebody had a heart attack downstairs and died. They couldn't bring him down the stairs so they had to jerry-rig a pulley through a window." One pitiful thing follows another, Feddy thought.

"Anyway. I called up some Chinese food, put money on the table, and left. I told Jesmond I had an important appointment that I couldn't cancel. It was really only a girlfriend. Sometimes you deliberately choose to be shit. I got back at two, three in the morning and he was still up. Scared, all that stuff with the ambulance."

Sharon had gotten up, put on a mint-green satin robe, and gone over to her dressing table while Feddy was talking. She sat on her foot, perched on a hard velour cushion with tuffs around the padding, bouncing lightly when she shifted. Sharon made a point of catching Feddy's eye in the mirror while he spoke and did her best to look thoughtful.

"That sort of thing leaves deep scars," Sharon said. "Excuse me, but you were such a jerk, Feddy. Who *was* the male in his life while you were away? Your father? He lives here, right? At least he might've played catch or baseball or something."

Feddy sprawled again across the bed, reaching under the night table for a telephone book peeking out from some dusty tabloids. "Here!" He sped through the phone book before throwing it open on the foot of the bed. "Take a look at that."

"My stars!" she exclaimed after a moment or two, reading. "That's some pitch!"

Toak and Son Bail Bonds. Professional. Discreet. *"Let us get to you before your cellmate can!"* Teo Toak smiling.

"Yeah. A classic. He actually went on and made a TV commercial with that. Fuck baseball. No, for fun, my old man's idea of father-and-son bonding was to take me to the courthouse and watch trials. For a while I used to think it was some kind of spur to get me to become a lawyer. Or moral instruction. But really it was all for him. All study and homework. 'Look at the hands, first, boy, *then* look at the face. And when you look at the face, don't pay any attention to what they're saying but watch what they do *with* the face while they're saying it!' He loved looking at criminals."

75

"So, no—my pops didn't hook up with my son. He had a hard enough time trying to figure me out. I think he gave up on kids after me."

He watched her: Sharon pushed up from her butt-engulfed foot and extended toward Feddy. Eyelids glittered cerulean, fluttered; their breaths mingled. They fell back into the shallow dent of the mattress, Feddy vigorously kneading the mound of rump.

She persuaded Feddy to call his son. She'd taken his cell phone and snuggled it between her breasts. "You're not getting it back until you promise to speak to him. Today." Feddy had seen it coming: soulmates-to-be—the crash of hurried truths, lorded concern. At one point, during the throes of passion, she croaked that they'd fucked in ancient Egypt. Lovers now, she leaped at the responsibilities of his familial intimacies—so long they weren't competition.

When Feddy got a hold of Jesmond, his son was cruising about town in a car he'd just purchased: a used 1983 Toyota Corolla. Such a cascade of embarrassing memories! First—he had to use Jesmond's credit report a few years back. The boy was only twenty-three and Feddy forged his name in order to get his utilities. In the end he screwed him. And he used his son's loan, his onetime student loan, to buy a car. And prior to that—when Feddy and the boy's mother were both drinking (but not together, Feddy couldn't stand even to look at her at that point)—there was the awkwardness and shame of watching Yvette approach the boy at his valet job for money (and she'd limp away . . . She was taller than Feddy. . . . A big-boned woman, reluctant to occupy space; a woman who gathered a limp when tired—vestige from a bout with polio), Feddy watching from a remove in his parked GTO, just a hair's breadth from doing the same. . . .

Through Sharon's prodding Feddy invited his son to her house. Jesmond was receptive to the idea. Almost giddy that Feddy called.

There were things he wanted to discuss, things about his friend Bay-onne—issues in his life.

"See? Aren't you glad you listened to me?" Sharon gloated. "I should run to the store to make sure you all have something to eat. Let me just check the refrigerator." He decided to push into her sense of accomplishment. "You're smart. Got a lot of insight into the workings of people," he said.

"It's the children. Children are little people, too," she shouted, bumping down the stairs. He could hear her tidying up: the squeak of squeeze toys, the clang of skillets, the rhythmic blatting of the push-toy rushed across the den. Might as well get out of bed and tidy up, too.

He nosed through her toiletries, picking up her lipstick (Passion Flower), sprayed into the air a puff of perfume (Youth Dew). Hair Mayonnaise ("Treatment for Damaged Hair"), astringent, Vaseline, cotton cosmetic squares, eye pencils (she drew in such broad lines, like Japanese cartoons), eye shadow, an angled dental mirror (curious), Eucerin Dry Skin Therapy. He worked a large dab of the Eucerin cream between his palms (stiff, like melted wax) and rubbed it into his elbows and forearms. A pair of translucent panties draped one of his tripartite reflections like a caul.

"Feddy, honey, I think he's here!" Sharon bellowed from the stairwell. "What kind of car is he driving?"

"A Toyota Corolla, blue! Midnight blue!" Feddy shouted. His shirt was still lipstick smudged, snail tracked, and damp. But not just sex sweat: he'd put it on, initially, right after their shower, just before the two of them fell into each other and began gnawing. He did not want his son to see him this way—some moist, ruinous satyr, sponging off near-menopausal women. But what was he to do? Maybe Sharon had a man's shirt—

"I think it's him! I keep seeing this little blue car going up and down the street here. Hey—!"

So, dressed in a chocolate-brown UNEF T-shirt and his jeans, Feddy descended the stairs to embrace his son. Sharon and Jesmond had met; she'd seated him on the couch. Jesmond was nibbling from a bowl of potato chips set upon the coffee table. "I'll leave you two. Don't need me to referee, do you?" she giggled, leaping up the stairs.

Hugging, Feddy actually kissed Jesmond on the cheek. Stubble, and the fleeting thought: Bayonne? Is this what Bayonne appreciates? Jesmond looked at him quizzically.

"New job, if I remember correctly," Feddy said.

"It's a paycheck."

"One thing they'll always be able to say about you is that you could hustle. 'Always gainfully employed.'"

"Yeah. I guess. Sharon seems pretty nice."

Feddy studied a potato chip, meticulously, a potato chip inspector. "You were telling me you were worried about Bayonne. His old man's worried. Seth informed me of what's going on."

And Jesmond went on to break down, point by point, his view of Bayonne's life presently, their part in Medgar's enterprise. "He is, in his way, serene about the whole business."

"Seth told me about Bayonne being named in that Smullian guy's insurance. What do you know? Is the boy gonna be rich?"

"Depends on how the legal stuff plays out. All these relatives sued but the lawyer tried to get them to settle out of court. Then somebody came up with this suicide-murder crap."

"You telling me that the Bayonne boy had sense enough to get an attorney?" Feddy asked. Jesmond looked away, shrugged. "You tied up in this mess?

It had never been the nature of Jesmond to confront his father. When Jesmond made the cross-country trek to see him, a day or so after the horrible first night he quietly came up to Feddy in the kitchen, holding in front of him a letter from his mother. "She says there's stuff you need to know." Jesmond hesitantly offered the letter. It was a thick, bulging airmail envelope. Feddy saw a shrieking missive. He took the letter from the boy and, in the manner of an old late-night comedy routine, held it to his temple. "What do you think, son? Death in the family, family tree, letter of amends for her fourth step, papal secrets?" He then raked the envelope's edge over the cluster of flat brown moles on his cheek. "Your mother's sick, boy. A mean drunk. She even enjoyed watching the animals suffer. Getting the pets high. She'd put vodka in the dog's bowl and howl as it staggered, knocking into the wall. So I doubt she has anything nice for me. For you, either. But come on. We'll answer it." He led Jesmond to the sink, took a cigarette lighter to both ends. They watched it blacken, rise, curl in on itself. The boy said nothing.

"Anyway, son. Got a woman in your life?" Change approach, Feddy figured.

Jesmond smirked. He knew that Feddy knew. Described her as chocolate, delicious. Slight, with a slim, small jaw. Shiny black hair that was hot combed, not permed. And a nice rolling walk—butt shifting in slow metronome ticks. "When Peaches passes, every man in the sight line suffers a whiplash." They had met at his one and only temp job at the hospital, during the construction of the emergency-room wing.

"Her husband's crazy," Feddy said. For he'd heard about Richmond—one of the evergreen topics of the ex-navy loaders working with him.

Jesmond went on to detail how much so. "He brought her home some things he took from a dead woman's dresser." The woman had been shot in the mouth by her husband, a chief petty officer. And Special Ed made Peaches parade around naked in sequined heels— shoes from a transvestite bludgeoned to death in an off-base motel by two Marines. He told Feddy about the Leica camera; about tying her to the bedposts with yellow Police: No Trespassing tape; about christening each new car with a lovemaking session in the backseat (Ed prided himself on collecting and repairing Volvos). But the final straw for Peaches, was the day Special Ed came home with the grocery bag. "'The shit's mine now!' Those were his words. The bag marked EXHIBIT A. Because the case was thrown out." He tore open the bag and flung out the contents, blossomed a crimson and white parachute. The chute had belonged to one of two jumpers—a murder and suicide between Navy SEALS.

"—One decides to off the other in a practice jump. So when Peaches refused to do it in the chute, Special Ed thought maybe if he fixed it into something nice hanging over the bed—"

I think I can understand this, thought Feddy. This emotional diarrhea. Because he doesn't know what to do with all this . . . "stuff." He's supposed to be grown. How's he supposed to respond? He feels he's responsible for her and for so much of this—living—that this woman's thrown at the feet of this twenty-six-year-old man.

"—Then he really got goofy. Went about ranting and raving and begging. Special Ed started threatening her. It was only after she'd locked herself in the bathroom and had his C.O. talk to him on the phone did he give up." For a while Ed went around sulking. Then, all of a sudden, his mood changed. "Peaches said she knew what it was when he began carrying around an extra cell phone. 'He's got himself another woman,' she said."

"While he's taking a shower, the other phone rings and she answers it. Of course a woman's on the other end. 'And guess who Special Ed is fucking? His flunky!' she says. 'He's messing with that mannish bitch who's his assistant. Those chicks are nothing but a bunch of dykes!' So now? Now she decides to let me know that Ed's suspicious."

"Goddammit, that's stupid! He's a cop! Boy, the easiest thing in the world for him to do is to have you knocked off. And he doesn't have to do it himself. I'm sure he knows enough lowlifes to do it for him. Take that car of yours. Cut the brake line, for example. Or have somebody come up and stick a knife in you to make it look like a mugging. And she's putting you through the hoops, son, one of the world's oldest hoops: Let's Get Back At My Husband."

In the last few weeks Special Ed had begun leaving on her nightstand cutouts from newspaper columns.

"There was an article from *Stars and Stripes* about an MP in Okinawa leaving the head of his wife's lover on the nightstand. Of course she's scared now. So she asks him what's his problem. 'You,' he says. 'And what about that female partner of yours?' 'That's just a woman I fuck,' he tells her. Then it hits me. I ask her, 'Why, all the sudden, *is* he so suspicious?' Understand, she's telling me all this over the phone. She tells me to hold on for a minute—and I hear this loud noise, banging. 'Sorry,' she says, she dropped the phone. Then this hissing noise like she's opening a soda. You understand, right?—I've just got this death threat, possibly about somebody cutting off my head, and there she is laid-back and sipping a Bud Lite. 'Why's he so suspicious, Peaches?' I ask her again. 'He found a piece of paper with your number on it in my purse,' she finally says. 'But I told him it was from some doctor at the hospital.'"

If I were in my twenties—his age—maybe even fifteen years or so ago, Feddy thought, I would've found this exchange all hot-breathed and exciting, too. A young woman, egging on her hus-band, hitting the switches in order to make him jealous. There and then, the flush of testosterone. Feddy could see himself caught up playing cat and mouse with the cuckold. Now, though, his graying hair brought a harsh light to the subject. "Special Ed's like all cops. Loves to intimidate. Through Peaches—Intimidation-by-proxy. That's not your home phone, is it?"

"My cell."

"Well, I doubt he'll be able to trace the number to you. And he's military. Doesn't have any say over civilians off—base. Still, with him being an MP, he probably has connections with Johnsonville sheriff or other assholes in the police department. Now's the time to cut bait, son."

"So why did she write my number down anyway? And put it where he could find it? She then calls me back after she hangs up. She called me from her house. I checked. Something told me I shouldn't answer but I did anyway. Somebody was breathing on the other end. Didn't say a word. Finally—'Feddy?'—It turned out to be Peaches. 'Something else the bastard said,' she says. Dad—she's quiet. At first I thought she might be crying but I don't think so. 'He says you don't care about me. All you really want is something under you. 'Pump and dump,' Ed calls it. Then—nothing. Both of us said nothing. Just there on the phone. "

His son finally stopped, spent. He took a drink of a bottled water Sharon had centered tastefully in a fan spread of Easter bunny napkins.

"She's pregnant, Pop."

"And?" Feddy asked.

"Ed doesn't know."

"You believe that? In the first place, that she's pregnant. And in the second—even if she is—that her husband doesn't know. Come on, Jesmond! He's married to the bitch, I'm pretty sure he's not so stupid that he can't count."

Jesmond took another swig of water.

"Well? What do you want me to say? I'm sorry, son, but for some reason I don't think congratulations are in order. What's the plan? You two gonna run off together? You might want to get a paternity test first. Or maybe the three of you'll just cozy up, Eddy and you taking turns playing daddy. This is a bunch of bullshit." Feddy stood up. "God, you're one stupid son of a bitch." Looked out the window. "Bastards making bastards."

"Motherfucker."

Feddy backhanded his son.

Jesmond seized his father's hand and began kissing it, fawning over it as if Feddy were a pope or liberator. Startling Feddy, before rising in a punch that doubled over his father. Pulling Feddy into his fist. Like his mother before him—the boy towered over his father.

Feddy flailed about and was able to grab a handful of Jesmond's Afro, wrenching him between his body and forearm and pushing his face onto the coffee table. He held him to it with all of his weight before hitting him twice midface with his fist. "Settle down, now. You settling down?" Feddy repeated, and Jesmond, gurgling, tried to pull away. He spat blood fed from a gashed lip. The boy then reared back and threw Feddy and himself against a pole lamp, all to the floor.

Sharon arrived in full wail. "Oh my, oh my goodness— Stop! Please stop!" She Irish-jigged around the two. But they rolled into her, brought her down on top of them. Jesmond drove Feddy's cheek into the splintery hardwood with his shoulder, using Feddy's groin as a pivot for his heel. The two rolled about the floor, punctuating their exhaustion with sporadic, heaving blows.

"Son," Feddy repeatedly pleaded.

Gathering his hulk, coming to his feet, Jesmond threw a final elbow into Feddy's throat for good measure. Feddy wheezed while Jesmond panted. Jesmond finalized his argument by savaging Feddy's ribs with kicks. Then staggered to the door.

Humming concern. Feddy in limbo—halfway between some blather on the television and a needling awareness of his right flank. A blizzard of writhing yellow sea horses gusted through the bedroom.

"Sharon?"

"Yes, baby." Humming again. She was sitting next to him on top of the bed, clad only in her panties, painting her toenails, toes splayed in a foam separator.

"What the hell did you give me?"

"Valium, Ambien, a couple Lortabs, and some NyQuil."

"Yes. That's okay." He tried turning onto his back, which led to a searing pain. "What time is it?"

"About two in the morning."

"I keep you up?"

"Naw, sweetie. Watching this old movie. Feeling any better?" she said, falling gingerly against him, her soft breasts against his back. Why, then, did he feel so alone?

"Nearly beat the shit out of me."

"I know. But we can talk about it in the morning. Best now to get some sleep." She reached behind her and turned off the lamp. He felt he barely knew this woman enough.

She fell asleep frozen to him, her hand cupping his chin. He lay half asleep or half awake, but fully regretful, stroking her naked thigh draped over his battered torso.

Book Two

VII

As Slocum Consolidated Enterprises began to accelerate its purchases of funeral homes, florists, and cemeteries in the late twentieth century, stock analyst Isabel Caldwell in her annual report for Beecham and Sully summed up SCE's market niche as follows: "It looks to remain perpetually profitable. . . . The demographic trends are favorable and they are insulated from competition. They have been able to maintain a startling growth rate alongside a yearly profit margin approaching 90 percent." The company, begun in the early 1940s on the plains of Kansas, was the brainchild of an Albert Darymple, a failed inventor (he had tried introducing an egg-candling device, patent pending) who had married Henrietta Slocum, widow of the late Lester Slocum. Slocum Funeral Home had been a family establishment for two generations; however, with Lester Slocum's death, the town of Kettle, Kansas was in danger of losing its only mortuary. The closest funeral home to the Slocums' was in a town more than thirty miles away. The genius of Arthur Darymple lay in his foresight, first to reach across and purchase the mortuary in the town over, then to buy outright two of the town's three cemeteries. He became very close to his stepson, Lester Slocum, Jr. After the boy's graduation from a mortuary college in Missouri, Lester Junior returned and, with Arthur, began the slow acquisition of several other funeral homes and cemeteries across the county.

Through successive generations the family bought cemeteries and crematoria and mortuaries covering a three-state area, bought casket businesses and floral businesses, bought a stone masonry—flirted briefly with a bereavement travel agency and a mortgage company for those who wanted pre-need trusts. Over the decades, Slocum Enterprises continued to grow. As to be expected, such growth led to the inevitable geographic migration—from Kansas City, Kansas to Kansas City, Missouri; from Kansas City, Missouri to Tulsa—before its final site in Dallas.

The behemoth paid well. On the average, with two million deaths a year in the United States, Slocum Consolidated Enterprises had buried four hundred thousand of the country's dead.

Why, then, were there not more funereal enterprises in the United States? Funeral homes have had the lowest failure rates as well as the lowest start-up costs of any business in America. Funerals are big-ticket items: the third-largest purchase in the United States after a house and a car. And the customer base—rarely do buyers comparison shop.

Maybe because the hours were long and the overhead is high and the profit margin narrows with each passing year. But Arthur Darymple demonstrated that more money could be made in sharing directors, gravediggers, hearses, and equipment among several funeral homes, all under the aegis of one entity. SCE had gross revenues of close to one billion dollars annually. It employed thirty thousand workers, owned 2,086 mortuaries, seven hundred cemeteries, two hundred floral businesses (in addition to a flower-growing concern in Honduras), and casket factories in Mexico, Belize, and (recently) China. The company operated in nearly a thousand cities in the United States, Canada, and Australia—with the metropolitan areas demonstrating even further cost reductions by way of embalming centers and SCE-owned limo-hearse services.

Still, the vast majority of funeral homes in the United States were still mom-and-pop run—with owners pushing into their later years and their children showing little, if any, interest in following in their parents' footsteps. All of which translated into more potential acquisitions for the monolith of Slocum Consolidated Enterprises.

Medgar Coots had purchased four mortuaries and three cemeteries and was on the verge of losing them all. Deliberately. The first three mortuaries—Tewell, Page, and Hall—were on the north side, funeral homes that were family owned and operated, with Page, the oldest of the three, going back as far as 1934. Tewell's Eternity Creations was also black owned and had developed a clearly defined marketing strategy of affordable funerals, ranging from simple cremations (six hundred dollars) to a chapel service with the use of an oak casket and cremation to follow (twenty-four hundred dollars). Hall's Green Ridge Mortuary and Monument Company provided a relatively new twist for Johnsonville, stone masonry specializing in Hebrew and Cyrillic lettering. Johnson Heights Cemetery and Well Spring Cemetery were small, neglected graveyards whose byzantine ownership needed to be traced through reams of courthouse documents; Chapel View was felt to be too near the airport. And C. L. Frapple Mortuary, the most recent purchase, was isolated and downtown and in receivership.

Tobias McKendree and his nephew, Henry, were in line with Medgar: they, too, purchased failure. Broken-down white mortuaries—family names that had been affixed to the scalloped-glass doors for generations, now demonstrating only ghostly tracings of "Frapple" or "Tate"—still felt they could sell only to white buyers. Medgar Coots dismissively agreed with affixing MCKENDREE MORTUARY CORP. to the window and bus benches.

"What do I care? I've got the controlling interest! But God, I hate to hear those yokels yawp!" Medgar was recounting to Jesmond the renaming of his funeral home in Clay County.

Mid May, and the spent grass patched in front of the downtown clinic was springy and crisp—bouncing atop steel wool. Medgar rocked back and forth on his heels in the middle of the playpen square of lawn, pointing out the misalignment of the cinder-block addition that was being installed. He'd hired day laborers from his patient lists and the men looked guilty and confused, fumbling with the strings and mortar. A banner had been strung between rutted and gouged stucco balustrades—Medgar relented after a community leader's incessant begging, BESSIE COLEMAN'S DAY AT STATES BEACH: pictured was a goggle-eyed Bernard Irwin pointing at a dainty little plane putt-putting into the horizon. The banner sagged quite a bit, wilted in the heat. "Your grandfather's been paying people to tear them down," Medgar remarked. Teo, yipping loudly and stomping about, had embarked upon a one-man campaign to oust Irwin as master of ceremonies in celebration of the African-American aviatrix. "For grins I double what he pays to keep them up. Old Granddad has a knack for endearing himself with the gen pop." They jogged from the midday heat into the cold slosh of the air-conditioning. Medgar was about to gush *his* gossipy tidbit: old man Toak possibly looking at aggravated assault charges from years before Jesmond was born. But discretion . . . Sometimes he ran ahead of himself.

"You hear anything from Finchem?" Jesmond asked. Medgar's eyes went flat. (Maybe it would have been appropriate to enlighten the boy as to his grandpappy's escapades. . . .) Dr. Finchem continued to be a sore spot with him and Medgar felt the boy knew as much. For Finchem had left him in a lurch—a Tallahassee politico friend had stepped in and extricated the man from his business heartbreak. Happy, he married again (his third now), and, to add insult, he was building a little mansion on the St. Johns River. "Oh, the son of a bitch is well connected. Probably promised thirty-eight double-Ds for the girlfriends. Found some folks to run interference for him and now loves rubbing it in my face!" Brow puckered, brown-streaked sclerae glistening, Medgar rocked sideways onto a buttock and perched on a calf, drummed his fingers on the table. Then—"Blam!" he shouted, slapping the window. Blam was a punctilious. Rastafarian. T-shirt sleeves rolled precisely and the neat, triangular red bandanna gathered his dreadlocks into a purgatory of black rope. Presented a man of meticulous gestures and studied gaze. But drops of sweat trailed erratically behind him onto the cool tile from the noon sun's beating: he played pretend-foreman to the pretend-builders. Medgar pulled out a brass money clip with a Susan B. Anthony emblem. He handed the man a fifty. "I need you to take the truck and go down to Muckets in Bayport and buy about thirty pounds of bait fish. You know, some of that gar, goo, shrimp, whatever. Frozen. And I need you to tell them you want it in those vacuum-sealed plastic bags. Then I want you to go over to this address—" Medgar wetted a pencil to his tongue and scribbled on a Post-it, cupping the money clip in the same hand. "Ask for this Ukrainian fellow named Lerni. He'll handle it from there." The man, for the briefest moment, looked soulfully at Medgar: *I can be of the best assistance,* he wanted to say. He then turned on his heels, not without looking over his shoulder and delivering a knowing smirk of understanding. The sweat was like blood splatter. Marking dime-size spots in drip from his dreads.

"Time-delay. That's the secret to our friend. I know the foreman to his builder. And I know his *real* boss. They're supposed to move in next week. Between the Sheetrock in the master bathroom if they haven't papered it yet. By the time he's pulled the pipes, dredged the septic tank, accused·Mrs. Finchem the Third of some god-awful STD, the rot will have leached on through the wall into the dining-room ceiling. Probably be sitting at some fund-raiser for refugees or manatees when a plop of swill lands in a glass of champagne."

Jesmond stared at the violet soda in the wax Taco Bell cup. Atop the meniscus bobbed a peanut hull. One of the laborers, a near-manic, could be heard outside screeching that there was no sin, only economic disparities.

"Darlin'. It's beautiful." Ce-Ce grinned at Melan as she twirled upright from her chair before heading to the restroom.

"Feddy," Melan whispered, nudging Feddy as Ce-Ce stopped to chastise Leon for not participating more in the States Beach Heritage Festival (though Leon pointed out the fluorescent pink mimeographed advertisements staccatoed across the bar front and back wall). "Ce-Ce's a wonderful chick. Jet-black skin, beautiful teeth—I still wonder how in the hell she and her family ended up in Wyoming—but come on, man! A tattoo? 'My name,' she said. All these bright reds and greens and yellows, she says. Why? I can't really see it. Really: I can't see it—might as well be skywriting at night."

A rhomboid of light fell from the door across the red vinyl bar front, and two men entered. Melan glanced at his watch. "On time, for a change. Listen, Feddy. I've got to talk to those two union representatives there. When Ce-Ce gets back, tell her I want your opinion about her tat." He stood up. "It's in a place that won't disappoint." Melan winked. "And sometime soon we've got to talk about this beekeeping business you're taking up. I heard it ain't pretty."

The after-work crowd at the He Ain't Here on a Thursday evening: lately Leon had tried to pull in more of the coat-and-tie crowd with a tuxedoed jazz pianist and happy-hour snacks. Tonight he had microwavable miniquiche and drumettes. The miniquiche sat untouched, except by a few cautious flies exploring the margins. Feddy thumbed one of the miniature piecrusts on his paper plate. Wet newspaper. And he was certain he'd seen a Norway rat slink along the stage's back wall.

"What say, Feddy." Standing over Feddy was a burly gentleman with a shaved head wearing a wife beater and a denim jacket. He precariously balanced a grease-warped paper plate on top of a mug of beer.

"Hey, Jakes. Why don't you sit?"

"Let me get Hammond—Hammond!"

"Say, boy! Toak!" Both men flopped into chairs across from Feddy. Sweating like a summer block of ice. "Looking for you, man. Looky here." Hammond extracted and unfolded a newspaper from his coat pocket, meticulously spreading it across the tabletop. It was the *Tanner Gazette*. "Guess who died?" he asked.

A meteor of uncompromising strength and grit has passed from us. Ace Walker, 78 years young, has died. World renown in the "gentleman's science," Ace was a world-class heavyweight boxer who had, at one time, defeated both Sonny Liston and Sugar Ray Louis. From 1964, Johnsonville had been his home. Following his retirement from boxing, Mr. Walker had been a fixture in the Johnsonville business community, working in law enforcement and as a small business owner.

Sweet Cherry Chicken
One 3-pound chicken, cut up for frying
Salt and pepper
¾ cup apple cider or juice
½ cup pineapple juice
1 cup canned Bing cherries
1 onion, chopped
½ cup olive oil
2 tablespoons honey
Salt and pepper chicken pieces, then marinate
* chicken in cherry juice mixture for an hour or so.*

"Yep. Last Tuesday. The bitch is dead," Feddy said.

Not just for Feddy: he was the bane of every child's existence from Lanesboro Boulevard to Church Street. After losing the store, shambling down MLK—drunk, towering, imposing, with his taped-tip metal walking rod. Made little Rachel Ennis fondle his purse on the deserted loading lot behind the Piggly Wiggly. Broke a tibia in a boy's leg—Ace's claim was that he was being robbed. Rumor had him soliciting—what he persisted in doing until tethered to his oxygen hose-umbilicus.

"Well, I've got his things: all the crap he prized most he kept hidden in a suitcase under his bed. My nephew rented a room in that piecy shotgun he had behind the post office. Boy felt he was *owed* the stuff for all the mess he'd to put up with. Then he got scared and left the shit with me. The suitcase's in the car."

"Then bring it in, man! Let's see what this son of a bitch felt he needed to hold on to," Feddy said. "Rachel!" he shouted, as she entered He Ain't Here. "—The esteemed Ace Walker has decided to take leave of us and we are now the sole heirs of his good fortune."

"Feddy, between you and me, I went and danced the boogaloo on the motherfucker's grave!" Rachel shouted as she straddled a chair.

At the table, Feddy could see face powder beaded in the down hovering above her lip. The fat folds bunched on Jake's shaved neck looked like a package of bristly frankfurters as he turned and grinned at Rachel.

Hammond returned with a wicker suitcase, flopped it on top of the table. Rachel laid her hands upon it.

"Quiet! Quiet! We will commence with the reading of Ace Walker's will." The shake and burr of a pedestal fan near the stage was distracting. "Leon, the fan!" Feddy hollered, and the contraption was silenced.

The contents of the suitcase: a pair of bubble sunglasses with orange lenses and an ivory frame; family photo (sepia tint: man, woman, two boys, girl); a Silver Creek High School diploma; certificates; a set of brass knuckles; letters; a yellowed cellophane casing holding a row of five gray coins ("Indian-head nickels, for all you coin collectors," Rachel announced); birthday cards; a mummified brown dinner roll the size and shape of a horse turd; staged boxing glossies; a photograph of Ace with Liston; a photograph of Ace with Rocky Marciano; a child's boxing glove; a 1952 IBF middleweight-championship belt buckle; menus from New York restaurants dating from the early 1960s; *Peterson's Field Guide to Eastern Trees*; a Braille Bible ("I think I heard oncet that his mother was blind," Hammond muttered to Feddy); a March 1967 *Ebony* magazine with Sammy Davis Junior on the cover; three 45-rpm vinyl records (Ink Spots, Ace Cannon, Ike and Tina Turner); an autographed album cover, Dinah Washington's *What a Difference a Day Made* ("If I

weren't already married, you thick hunk of man! Mmmm-mmm!"
Dinah); a clock with palpable hands that Rachel demonstrated also
announced the time; a straightedge razor with a blade brown from
use.

Two people mock fought over the pair of sunglasses; pictures
and magazines and placards were flung like playing cards, and
Rachel dramatically ground her heel into one of the posed boxing
glossies. The straightedge stood tentatively upright, jabbed into the
table, handle as a pedestal. Feddy held on to the album cover (a hazy
sense-memory from somewhere around age four—in the dark of his
room and getting caught up in Dinah Washington's voice while his
parents threw a party). Leon took the clock and the Bible and his
waitress was given the 45s ("And what the hell am I supposed to do
with these?").

Rachel then dramatically held the roll over her head. "Understand—that for the repose of Ace Walker's soul, whosoever con-
sumes this bread consummates his or her role as Sin Eater, releasing
the motherfucker from the yoke of his foul acts in this world and
freeing him from his divine and everlasting punishment in the life
hereafter. Any takers? Yes?" Rachel paused. "I thought not!" And
with an exaggerated windup, hurled the petrified bread into the
long kitchen corridor—whereupon, unseen by any human eye, the
furtive, greasy Norway leaped upon the roll and slicked it through a
broken-toothed floor drain.

Again Rachel raised her arms, now loudly clearing her throat.
"We will now close the reading of the will. Those that got, got. And
those that got nothin', don't got shit!"

As if on cue, Hammond's cellular phone chirped from his chest
pocket. He mumbled briefly. "What?" he then yelled, pulling the
phone from his mouth. "Wait a minute. Repeat that, boy." He then
pressed Speaker and handed the phone to Rachel, mouthing that it
was his nephew.

"Hey, I want the old man's sunglasses," his nephew said. "They's
Ray-Bans, right?"

"What?" Rachel asked.

"I want the old dude's sunglasses—"

"Nephew—we have already formally concluded the reading of the will," Rachel announced and abruptly closed the phone, which led to the pounding of tables and a cacophony of shrieks and laughter.

The suitcase, and whatever remained in it, was tossed to the fire exit in the back hallway.

("That damn blind man's clock"—Leon, a few months later, out of the blue came up with the complaint as Feddy and them sat at the bar, watching a football game. "The motherfuckin' thing's now broke. Every goddam hour at night, all night—'It is now two AM. It is now three AM. . . . ' ")

VIII

Father Ignatius Clemons was born in Alexandria, Louisiana, and brought up in and around Natchitoches, Louisiana, at a time of economic despair and cruelty of color—the Judas Boy was hanged the winter following the Great Depression. Father Clemons was nine; the Judas Boy, twelve: an apparently charismatic black gamin wily enough to entice others to theft or licentious behavior, whereupon the other youths would be arrested while he would stand at a remove, kicking at dead leaves in the gutter. That summer thirty-eight children had seen the inside of the parish jail. Some were shipped to boys' facilities in Shreveport and Lafayette; most were cowed and returned to their homes, remaining indoors throughout the sweltering summer; a few were imprisoned in adult facilities following trial by a circuit judge; one was castrated. The fortnight before the Judas Boy was hanged he had been caught a half a mile from the nude corpse of a white girl of six. A circuit judge was to return with the coming spring, in only five more weeks, but the pack of men seething through the small town square—rapacious, slavering wolves—removed the boy from the jail and hoisted him into the town center's grand sycamore. Father Clemons, as a child, saw the boy hanging from the thick bough while the crowd frolicked under the elongated corpse. A woman appeared and leered at a camera, holding up a bottle of Dixie Beer while a splayed-toed foot dangled over her head. He was about to disappear into a side street when, having dropped a parcel of moldy bacon (his mother had requested that he bring it home from her Baptist-minister employer), the woman gleefully pointed him out. The crowd suddenly surged over him, and with hands that throbbed about his body, neck, and legs, carried him to the tree. He was terrified and he was enraptured. He had been dragged to the trunk (he could remember the hemp bristles pricking his neck) when he heard, "Let that nigger go. He'd nothing to do with it." The crowd freed him. Later, he would articulate that it was an act of God that he was alive. He grew up to be a questioning but deeply contented man. He told Feddy he had learned to persistently forgive.

His first Mass was said in the choir loft of a church in Lafayette, Louisiana. He had trained for the priesthood not as part of an order but rather as part of a household of four snarling, parish-constrained priests. They had plucked him out of his seminary in St. Martin Parish, LA. He would later recount to Feddy evenings in which all five sat at the dining-room table for supper while the housekeeper served them. He had set upon this memory—forever fixed in him, a bubble in amber—because it was the early 1950s and the housekeeper was a white Cajun woman and he was a youthful black man. But he would also return to the sensation of himself at the train station in Lafayette. Here was Father Clemons leaving the rectory with the priests, all bunched together in the same shiny black sedan, arriving at the same train station, then moving to opposite ends of the platform with Father Clemons separating from the four—and they appearing not to know him nor he them. They each entered into their segregated cars on the same train, bound for New Orleans—him within the chrysalis of his cassock.

His first Mass had been said in the choir loft of a small cathedral in Lafayette because the congregation would not allow a Negro to say Mass upon the altar. So his first benediction was made looking across a space of pews empty of family and friends. There was a refectory table improvised as an altar. He did not remember that first sermon. What remained, though, was the briefest moment when, upon looking across directly into the light strained through the colored glass, he saw some bird outside—probably a sparrow or a pigeon, he reminisced to Feddy—fluttering about the hollow of a cornice. An irritating draft furled and unfurled the corporal. And through the doxology, Father Clemons gazed down upon the smattering of celebrants in veils looking up—what did they see, what did they think, him aping grace?

He had been the pastor of the church that Feddy attended, its school a small campus of mustard-colored brick buildings run by Oblate sisters. "'I enrich God, because before I existed He did not think of me as existing, because I am one more—one more even though among an infinity of others—who, having lived, suffered, and loved, abide in His bosom.' That was Unamuno's insight," Father Clemons explained to Feddy.

Father Clemons carried the community. Within a few months of his arrival he had obtained for them the discarded textbooks from the white Catholic school across town; they were to replace the foxed, coverless, outdated crap (for example, though it was 1967, there were still only forty-eight states in Feddy's fourth-grade geography book). In a year's time he had formed a band that would become a perennial award winner and established a speech and debate team whose alumni would include a New Mexico Supreme Court judge and a CNN correspondent. "Millions upon millions upon *millions* of departed souls inhabiting the ether, Feddy—I think that's why we have churches, so the living have some manner of amplifying their voice." For the elderly and the shut-in in the community, Father Clemons and the sisters began a visiting service with meals. And he engineered scholarships for the brightest black students, originally to northern Catholic universities (Notre Dame one year, Marquette the next), then to whatever school would be willing to provide full scholarships (Feddy—Loyola of New Orleans).

Feddy woke up at nine that morning, a Saturday. He now had a car: a beige Gremlin, two-door. Feddy had paid cash. A stump-legged hillbilly at a dealership on Phillips Highway, a few blocks up from his father's motel, had obliquely disparaged him for beating down the price—"That's the reason why you all don't do NASCAR"—and limply shook hands with Feddy over a sandbag ashtray gorged with gum wrappers and cigarette butts.

From his apartment in town he drove to the Mayport ferry. The late-morning sun smeared the horizon a peeled peach while wind pebbled the cars onboard with crumbly sand and shell pieces. He slowed down considerably atop the old cement ramp of highway that straddled the inlet sectioning the island. Zigzagged through the fishing poles crowding the span like comb teeth. He still crushed a Styrofoam cooler.

There was a brief stretch of red-clay farmland containing an off-angle roadside house with a collapsed porch. A rusted, spring-tooth harrow was precariously balanced against a shed alongside a hump of white marl midfield. To his surprise, the door flew open and an odd creature in a green turban and dark denim spurted to the shoulder, waggled a doll head at the car as it passed.

Now came the developments, the communities, the florid conceits. Mill Downs Plantation. Carrington Whispers. Monet Pines. Traffic circles crippled cars to a pause while golf carts trundled between the mustard lines. Feddy looked to the treetops. A *V* of birds dipped almond then chocolate with the glancing light.

He had wanted to stop at States Beach, almost missing the turn except for the hand-painted sign. A HISTORICAL LANDMARK, AN AFRI-CAN-AMERICAN COMMUNITY . . . ESTABLISHED 1945.

They were clustered at a remove from the sea. The houses. Simple cottages. Teo hadn't been exactly welcomed in the community in its heyday. Summer homes for doctors, insurance men, lawyers, all from up north—it was only when the community was in its slow decline that his father began frequenting States Beach. For Feddy this meant the sweat of thick summer evenings licked with breezes from the Atlantic Ocean, pretty brown little girls.

A For Sale By Owner sign tilting from a yard caught Feddy's attention. He pulled over immediately. For all his noise about what he would do with States Beach property, Teo never could bring himself to follow through on a purchase. The old man's one tic, when he got really anxious, was to bloody his cuticles. Back then he seemed always to get to the edge of a beach home but something always blocked him up. Chewed himself miserable.

Feddy approached the house. A young man and an old man (sockless, in black Florsheims) sat on a porch while watching a television propped in the doorway. " . . . And I'm a telling you—you listening? YOU WILL BE LIT UP WITH THE HOLY SPIRIT! ON FIRE! Come to Greater Abyssinian Baptist. Come on now. Don't just wave at salvation and walk on by. Greater Abyssinian Baptist. Come on and join us. Let's get kronked for Christ." Feddy recognized the man on the television. It was the Reverend Dante Phillips. "Go ahead and throw your money into those Wal-Mart, megamall churches!" Seth would harangue whenever he was in earshot of the man's voice.

"Hey. How you all doing?" Feddy asked.

"Hey." It was the young man who responded.

"You all thinking of selling this place?"

The young man nodded toward the old man. "My paw-paw is. Deddy back in Philly. He told him he don't want it. Rather get the money."

"How much you asking?"

The young man quoted him a price. "He trying to sell it to other black folks that are interested," the young man said.

"What you say?" the old man suddenly chimed in.

"THAT DEDDY TRYING TO SELL ONLY TO BLACK FOLKS!"

"Yeah. That's right." The old man mumbled his contribution.

Feddy thanked them for their time and then drove down to the miniature boardwalk. The gray weedy end of the street was cordoned off by a Cyclone fence. Feddy parked on top of a spalled sidewalk next to a cinder-block two-story painted brick red, its stenciled signs still present. As a boy he'd constructed fantasies as to what went on in the overhead rooms—imagined the transactions between the caravans of glandular sedans and pimpified convertibles that crept and halted in the parking lot and sandy streets and the languid women attendant to their windows.

Feddy left the car and stood outside the locked restaurant with its barred windows, missing glass. The booths were strewn with refuse and animal droppings. Feral cats fumed over specked counters and wried stoves—one basking tom stared at Feddy without interest.

This property was for sale, too. From the crumbly steps bleeding rust at the exposed rebar to the gaping rooms upstairs exposed to the sea. He saw now. On the stairs as he stepped into the room where the plate glass would have been. With the mattress end-split and rain-bloated. Inhabited. For there had been mice, now mice remnants; now there was even a nice dark-green mold, sandwiched between a layer of some black rot and tawny cotton stuffing, all heaped and twisted together like agate. The kitchenette floor propped by a rotted two-by-four crossbar. But there was the nice view of the sea. A half a million was the asking price. Realtor flyers—once or twice even in the *Tanner Gazette*. Teo had read them and was apoplectic. Balked now at the conceit of seaside property—"Great idea, Peanut! Why didn't I think of it? Let me buy smack-dab in the crotch of Hurricane Alley. And uninsurable to boot? God, you're priceless!"

Feddy wandered back to his car and drove due north then northeast for a minute or two before coming to a halt, for the resort where Father Clemons was staying bordered States Beach, was simply on the other side of the Cyclone fence.

Feddy asked the valet to point him in the direction of the swimming pool and Jacuzzi. Father Clemons had told him that's where he'd probably find him. The priest had prostate cancer that had now spread to his spine. With hydrotherapy, he said, he felt better.

It was Father Clemons who'd encouraged Feddy to pursue medicine. Feddy's summers as a diener—Father Clemons had sought out the job at the county hospital for him when he was a teenager so as to keep him out of trouble. Even after Feddy failed—by then he had begun to use cocaine regularly, and Father Clemons had returned to Louisiana for a ministry at Angola penitentiary—the priest would not disparage him. "When you see fit, you'll finish your studies," Father Clemons wrote to him. He wrote him and continued to write to him even after Feddy demonstrated that he had no real resolve. "You're still loved, Feddy, that's without question," he expressed in response to Feddy's query. "But as to whether God pities you—no. Pity is crap. A human failing—compassion looking through the wrong end of a telescope."

"Man, it's good soaking the bones!" Father Clemons shouted, climbing from the roil of the Jacuzzi, first to shake Feddy's hand, then, thinking twice, he pulled Feddy into a crabby, chlorinated embrace.

The wet spot clinging to Feddy's belly took a chill when they entered the air-conditioned corridor. Father Clemons, spindly legs and protuberant gut, wore only a pair of black swimming trunks. "All I can say is—thank God they're not Speedos. Come on, Padre," Feddy said, rubbing his cooled stomach underneath the newly wet shirt. "They keep it cold enough to hang meat in here."

The balcony of Father Clemons's eighth-floor room overlooked the twelfth hole. Beyond the greens, the sands were white and the sea was harsh. Feddy, across the patio table from Father Clemons, caught himself gawking at the priest's arms: sinewy and smoked and violet like beef jerky, but with those tense curlicues of white hair. And white eyelashes with a Sartrean eye—Teo always said he hated talking to the man, swore the walleye ogled body parts while the man's mouth moved.

The citronella candle guttered with dipping breezes from the shore. "The Civil Rights Movement had its peculiar tangents," Father Clemons began, reaching for the beer Feddy held out to him. "In Louisiana—I'm sure in Florida, too—there was the gravity of the implied threat that made you reflect on how you'd even ask for a newspaper at a stand, or how you'd walk on the sidewalk when someone white approached. I took this as the arc of my life. More an asymptote: approaching but not reaching some perceived, better state. And later, instead of grace, took to it as pure luck."

"By the midsixties, before I came to Johnsonville, I had my own little church—colored—in a little town called Opelousas. Cajun country. My church had a school just like the one here. I was the principal there, too, but that school only went up to the sixth grade.

"There was a cotton mill on the outskirts of the town where they employed blacks and whites, and by 'sixty-two, 'sixty-three—both were actually working in the same building, a Quonset hut. Men and women. And there was a young white woman, Madeline Gastineau, Maddy—somewhere in her early thirties, thirty-one, thirty-two—who had just married a black man. They didn't parade this about town—they weren't idiots. But for whatever reason, she was one of the few whites that came to my church. That's how I met her—at the church, at the end of the service. One of those busty, big-hipped women with dark hair that almost made you think she was a pale Italian. And chirpy. She'd peck at you while she talked, picking lint off your collar, smoothing a lapel—"

Feddy made the suggestion that she was coming on to him.

"Maybe. But she did the same with anyone, male or female. The first time I met her was after a service, she was standing there with her head cocked to one side like she was hard of hearing. 'You give a fine sermon, Father,' she said, 'but why do you always preach to the bleachers?' She was talking about the way I looked up into the rafters during my homily. I became flustered and stuttered some apology when she let go what sounded like a bark. That was the way she laughed—belly laugh leading to a coughing fit. I suddenly had to slap this new, strange woman on her back a few times. All the while she was laughing and coughing, though, she was sizing me up—one of those folks that could be talking with their mouths going a mile a minute but their eyes and mind are working hard, checking you out. I passed muster and she let her guard down.

"As I told you, her husband was a black man. Samuel. I'd seen him around town but never met him. One of those big Mandingo Negroes. At the mill some of the other white women were attracted to the black men, and vice versa. Till then, very few people in Opelousas acted upon these feelings. Suddenly, the earth seemed to be turning in a different direction. Friends of her husband, when they'd meet at their place to play cards, would approach her about some woman friend or another in the sorting line—'You think she'd be interested in talking to me?'—And she'd relay the inquiry. After a while she found herself playing go-between and setting up meetings. A girlfriend would stop by for a visit; a while later, her husband would come home with a 'friend.'

"Of course, she didn't tell me all this that afternoon after my service. This was all over the course of time. Usually in the rectory front parlor. And I made sure my housekeeper was present anytime she stopped by. I was still afraid in those days. . . .

"She had confided in me that things were becoming complicated. Maddy told me that she and her husband were being threatened directly. White men. Rednecks, I thought. On this one day she sat across from me in the chaise longue, twisting her hair about her finger. 'Just a little thing. Folks loving each other is all'—a cliché but she meant it, winding her finger into a lock of hair. When she transferred her tic to the window cord, the blinds came suddenly clattering down and she jumped up and ran out of the rectory.

"But the next day she called me. The police had beaten a buddy of her husband who'd been seeing a woman at the mill. Then some people took to calling her house in the middle of the night with these wild and graphic insults and threats. She was all flustered, agitated when she was telling me this. Afterwards I didn't hear from Maddy for a good two or three weeks.

"Then one day my phone rang and it was Maddy asking me to please come see her husband in the hospital. They had burned him up. Apparently those demons came through with their threats. They didn't harm her. But him—they dragged him off into a field, doused him with gasoline, prodded him with a torch till he caught fire; then they watched him burn. They stood in a circle, pushing him back into the center with sticks until the fire went out. They then tossed him like a sack of potatoes into the bed of a pickup and drove to Maddy's house, where they pitched him onto the porch. My first time meeting this man—my first time meeting him and you could almost still smell his flesh cooking. . . .

"He was wrapped in wet gauze except for the head. His hair had melted to his skull and his eyes shook. Jiggled. I'm introduced and all I can do is hold his finger wrapped in gauze. 'You know the men?' I finally asked him. But he didn't say anything. Even his eyes didn't speak—"

Feddy watched as Father Clemons excused himself to go to the bathroom. He heard a brief gush into the commode. Feddy noticed that the only light around came from the candle. When Father Clemons stepped back onto the terrace, though, he continued as if he hadn't left.

"—He'd begun to stink. I don't think we had burn units or centers then. Opelousas certainly didn't. The fact of the matter was that the hospital was still segregated, and black patients were put in that hot and humid basement. They did give him something for the pain. Morphine. I visited him daily. I remember once sitting next to him at the bedside and, inadvertently, grabbing his calf. It was squishy, as if I were grabbing hold of a wet cardboard box.

"Maddy had stopped coming. It was just me and this woman's husband and the dog days of summer." Father Clemons paused to smile at Feddy. He took an emptying swig. "Virgil wrote in the third book of the *Aeneid* on the appearance of Sirius, the Dog Star. According to the ancients it brought hell to earth, that withering part of summer. I remember I had a head cold, some summer bug, sweltering at his bedside. Minus the typical editorial screeds in the newspaper, no one tried to find the perpetrators. By the third week, in this swill of summer, he still hadn't died. At that time a man from the FBI came around.

"The agent was a good man. For all the things we hear about them now, the harassment and wiretappings, the bullying, the nastiness, Herbert Hoover—this man was compassionate. A good man. He bulldogged leads, patiently went over pictures with Samuel in those rare moments he was lucid. One day, the FBI agent was really agitated. We were standing over Samuel—he was to die a few days later—when he motioned for me to follow him into the hall. He reached into the briefcase that he always seemed to carry and extracted photographs. That was where I learned that among the murderers were a local doctor and banker. The agent said it was doubtful that they'd ever be formally brought to trial but he'd spend his last breath attempting to do it.

"What bothered him was that, in his dogging of the banker, shadowing him, taking apart his life up to that point—he saw that the banker was suffering. The banker suffered guilt. And that my FBI man felt pity for this demon while standing over the bed of the dying man . . .

"This is where we misinterpret—'Love the sinner, hate the sin.' No. This is more a spiritual laziness. I went through something like it watching Maddy retreat—as if understanding releases you from the burden of knowing. Human love doesn't heal; it doesn't even open doors and hearts. For all we know, it's a chemical imbalance. There's an old tale that recommends a spoonful of ant's eggs for those suffering from infatuation—the sacs supposedly contain antiendorphins, some chemicals that block the love state. Yet for the vast majority of human beings it's to be the sanctified glue that should hold our lives together.

"The service was simple. He was buried on the flat of a brand-new, sloping cemetery. Supposedly integrated! He was one of only three occupants of that ground. Samuel Woods was brought up in Chicago so he had only a few cousins in attendance; Maddy's family didn't show up. But the FBI agent was there with me graveside. We remained in touch over the years."

Father Clemons leaned across the table for his sport coat and pulled out his wallet. "The agent went on to get his law degree at American University in D.C. He encouraged me to proceed with my PhD at Georgetown." Father Clemons extracted a photograph and handed it over to Feddy. "I ran into him a few years ago. He still had this." It was an old photo of a balding blond man in a button-down shirt and tie.

"That's the banker—one of the handful of people convicted at that time for a civil-rights-related murder. Mainly because of his conscience: my FBI friend convinced him that that was the thing to do. That was it, though. He would only implicate himself. He was apparently murdered at Angola a few months after he arrived. When I was chaplain up there in the eighties I tried digging through records to find out what exactly happened but that was futile. Like so much else I didn't accomplish there—all an exercise in futility . . .

"You know, I became very fond of that man, my FBI agent. One of my favorite people. After you, of course, Feddy. He had a marvelous capacity for understanding. Understanding and humor.

"I've something now to ask of you. I am going to be cremated when I die. And I would like you to spread my ashes upon the convict's cemetery back at Angola. The prison is about a hundred and fifty miles from New Orleans, with the cemetery stuck in some swamp brush way beyond that. That is what I want to do, Feddy—I want to meet the Second Coming with my charges."

IX

Teo deliberately provided his clients with uncomfortable aluminum chairs: metal seat pans with edges that pinched and cut, back bars that poked. One chair listed toward the desk—Ernie had sat down hard in it one day, buckling a leg. Ernie was instructed to plant the brash, mouthy client in this listing seat, putting him or her in the predicament of having to look up, all the while straining to stay balanced so as not to fall into the desk.

"Whatever, Teo. Just do what you need to do. Let's get this shit over with," Seth Burnett said, pushing from the desk. Bayonne had been arrested the day before and was being held in detention. "You know, man, this could very well be you sitting here. Still might. Your grandson may be tied up in this, too." Seth's granddaughter, Bochelle, sat openmouthed asleep in the adjacent chair, her multicolored plaits crimped against the metal frame.

"Could be," Teo barked. "But let's play a little goddam Court TV, examine the evidence," he proceeded, heedless of the sleeping little girl. "Bayonne's boyfriend to the dead man, right? Two queers in love. Smullian had an insurance policy. Why? And no insurance policy on Bayonne, right?

"So you've got a pansy that all the sudden takes out insurance made out to his boyfriend." Teo paused and stared at Seth. "Me? I'm thinking the boy's got AIDS. Would be a good way to look out for the sweetheart when you're gone. Plus, if you think about it, it's kind of an insurance on the insurance policy, 'If I decide to off it, either he goes with me or the motherfucker ain't getting shit'—

because there's no company that pays out a suicide. So Two Tons of Fun gets the last laugh: Bayonne backs out, Bayonne goes broke."

"So why they arrest him?"

"Stupidity's no free pass, Rev. Trust me, I see it every day. To the cops he's just another stupid SOB with a fucked-up scheme."

Seth suddenly stood up, awakening Bochelle with a start. "You know, Jesmond was the one who got Smullian the insurance," Seth said. "You should look into the mess he's in with Medgar Coots."

"Yeah, I heard about it," Teo muttered. "Sit your ass down! We're not done yet! No need to get all righteous. Look, I ain't the one who wrote the script. Listen, Burnett, as Feddy told you I don't usually do this, but I'm willing to post bail at the standard rate blah-blah-blah—and you won't have to pay me back till the arraignment. Course, there's something you could do for me— Ernie!" Bochelle, scalp bedecked with yellow and red and green rubber bands, was wide awake now, playing peek-a-boo with Teo's assistant. "Jughead, do something useful! Go down to the detention center and see if any of the newcomers need posting!" Teo turned back to Seth. "Anyway, Burnett, Ace Walker died at home. I got word that the coroner's ruled it a natural death, with his cancer and all. The city's got your business to do the cleanup, right?"

"Heading to the jail, boss!" Ernie yelled and left.

"I lost touch with the bastard over time," Teo continued. "When you all go to do your work there I want to come with you. Want to take a peek as to see what the old goat'd been up to all these years."

Seth shrugged his shoulders. "Fine with me. But we're set now; set as far as Bayonne goes. Right?"

"Right as rain, Rev. Right as rain."

Teo stood in front of the house that had, at one time, belonged to Ace Walker. A brown house. Carob. With pink trim. "Good God, that's ugly," Teo said to no one in particular. Seth and sons, pillowed in white Tyvek suits, swarmed back and forth between the van and the door that opened onto the porch. To Teo's irritation, Rachel's BMW drove past (3DJD was the license plate) and slid to the gravel curb a few houses down. The passenger door discharged a spry, small, bowlegged man in a black windbreaker. Teo immediately recognized Bernard Irwin. It didn't hurt that DIRECTOR was stenciled on the back of his jacket. Rachel bustled to the back passenger door, extracted a frail wraith. The Jackson boy. The young man nearly collapsed as she escorted him to the sidewalk. Teo decided to make his presence known and took to shouting her and the boy's name as he then bounded toward them.

"Oh God, not you!" was Rachel's greeting.

"Mr. Irwin, it's a pleasure," Teo began, ignoring his reception. "Teo Toak, bail bondsman, developer, entrepreneur. Love your work. *Perches and Seizures*? Got the DVD box set. And how you doing, tiger?" Teo continued, starting a little jab toward the boy before dropping the punch. Teo turned to Rachel. "My lady—you hurt me so!" Teo clutched his chest, feigned grief. He then turned to Irwin. "Ennis here will tell you, I helped this kid out big-time and long-time." Teo took a moment to size up Irwin. "You not going to play the kid?" Teo asked, narrowing his eyes. The small man was cursed with the sin of cuteness: large black eyes, feathery lashes, lacrimoid frame, narrow pick-me-up-please shoulders—fine with kiddies but freakish in middle-aged men.

"Nah-nah-nah, man! Too old! Too old for that role! But my company will be producing and directing his biography. And the young man here wants to star in it." The three exchanged glances among themselves while the boy tepidly grinned. "Sees it as his passport to Hollywood. Whatever, though, he's my first assistant, my ace-boon!" The boy attempted a ferocious smile.

"Must be doing—what you call it—background work, eh?" Teo asked, watching Rachel. "Ideas for directing and such?"

"Yeah. Mining the terrain," Irwin said, "Mining the terrain."

Teo left, not without presenting Irwin with a business card. "Never know." Teo winked.

"Yeah, that's true," Irwin halfheartedly laughed in response.

Teo squeezed between the wind-bloated work crew, the hazmat suits fluttering. Sails skittering about the porch.

The walls in the kitchen were the covers of *Gourmet* magazine. Ace had glued them on top of every vertical surface: around the refrigerator, the stove, the little kitchenette set. Teo stood alongside one of Seth's teenage sons, speechless.

"The man was a little freaky," Teo finally said. The boy shrugged. *Chilled Caribbean Cerviche: Sole on Ice!* Met Teo at eye level.

"What choo here for? You his brother or somethin'?" the boy asked.

"Might buy it," Teo replied, picking at a glue bubble alongside a sun-pinked soufflé. "Buy the place and turn it into a skating rink or tattoo joint. Maybe both. Interested?" Teo said, turning to him, but the boy already had disappeared with a waste bag through the back door.

The other rooms were surprisingly dainty, but with a second-hand feel, as if Ace had purchased the house in toto following some spinster's death: chintz curtains, fringed lamps, red velvet Victorian furniture. A yellowish cast covered most things, however. A tinge of nicotine—with the drapes gummy to the touch and the once-white popcorn ceiling like miniature yellow stalactites.

There was a teak palanquin in Ace's bedroom. Teo picked up a like-framed picture on top of a mantel over a bricked-up fireplace. It was a photograph of a hyped and circusy prefight weigh-in with Ace seated in the palanquin. In the corner, "1957" was printed in blue ink. Teo, in fact, had been there. Ace had been borne on the shoulders of towel-wrapped coolies, his head and hands jutting from the open shutters, waving and grinning and gibbering like an idiot while glad-handing everyone within reach. Actually, if he remembered correctly, the litter-bearers were dancers from some touring chitlin-circuit revue. . . .

Decomposition had, in the end, glued Ace to the yellowed plastic slipcovers. So at least the evidence suggested. Teo stood between two looming boys and the trio stared at the caked depression in the corner of the sofa.

"Only the plastic," Teo mumbled.

"Pops said somethin' about saving the sofa," the taller of the two young men said to the other. "You clean out the fridge?" His face was peculiarly flat, the tallest—as if he'd been cartoonishly hit in the face with a frying pan. Was this the one who flew face-first from the school roof onto the asphalt? When Teo thought about it, it seemed that a number of Burnett's kids suffered skull abnormalities.

"This shit fuckin' stank! He sat here for how long?"

"What the hell you expect? Look, the zipper to the covers are right along the top edge there. You—"

"Nobody died and left you head Negro. You want those plastic covers off, you best do it."

"Just get your punk ass over to the end of the couch—naw, man, you get the funky end—and we'll dump it out back. I'll tell Pops that it was too corrupt or somethin' like that."

Teo rummaged through what made for the boxer's library: a voluminous shelf holding six puny CDs. And two shelves, on the opposite side of the console, filled with VHS tapes—all porn, by the look of the titles. The old fuck's surrender to attempted self-abuse. Already the collection was gapped, like missing teeth—probably the discretion of Seth's kiddies, pocketing select videos. Years and years ago Ace told him a secret: that he couldn't get a hard-on anymore. That was truly the curse—pitiful and sexually desperate in decrepitude. Teo could imagine Ace naked on the sofa, pulling his pud. Soft. Kneading putty. And, for all the movies to choose from, probably watching the same snatch and fuck over and over—to nothing. Nothing but frustration and impotence and back. Really, though, so what if you had trouble getting hard? Viagra took care of that nowadays.

"You can take your pick. Whatever you want," Seth said.

"I don't want any of that shit!"

The son with the flat nose, on the face devoid of cheekbones, came up to his father and began joshing with him.

Softening him up for half-assed work.

Seth, though, well versed in his children's tactics, easily saw through the feign, pointedly asking about the chemical washing and fumigation of the den while his foot dug at a cigarette burn in the carpet. The son began a long diatribe against his brothers, stating that they were lazy, they were always lazy and he had to carry his work and theirs, too, with no compensation. Teo was spared further details when somebody called the young man's name from the street and he, without missing a beat, excused himself.

Teo paced through the rooms of the house, calculating the estimated square footage. He entered the backyard through the ratty porch off the kitchen. A rusted auto seat spring dangled from the roof of a shed. And the sofa had been tossed onto a pash of soaked mattresses, damp and pasty Sheetrock, compost swill, and old clothes. The corner of the sofa, in fact, straddled a pair of denim coveralls, legs splayed.

Teo wiped his eyes. It could have been the sun baking the curdled sofa on top of whatever offal—like the spackling there on the plastic. He carefully stepped through the weed-choked lot of chalky turds and seething ant mounds to the narrow space between houses, where the air spawned insects. Teo pulled back the black plastic covering the broken window of the adjacent house and peeked inside. Darkness absorbed his vision.

As if it'd crept across the sidewalk on its own initiative, Teo's Cadillac sprawled atop the neighboring fibrous lawn like a sunning cat. He was approaching the car by the passenger side when he ran smack into his grandson, Jesmond.

Teo knew he had tried to avoid him. That Jesmond had recognized the car, leading Jesmond to holler for Seth's son from the street.

"Hey, boy!" Teo greeted Jesmond. He knew a little bit about

the scuffle between father and son, which would probably lead to another extended period of the two not speaking to each other. This was fine with Teo. He didn't like the boy. In fact, he raised the question to Feddy early on as to whether Jesmond was actually Feddy's. Yvette had been everyone's mattress. Being drunk, high—that was her business then. The two of them were sad sacks of shit.

"Hey, Teo," Jesmond responded. His alleged grandson didn't like him much either. Jesmond raised his chin in the direction of Seth's son reentering the house, shouting that he'd call him soon. "Ace Walker worked for you once, right?" he asked Teo.

"I'm thinking of buying the place," Teo said, ignoring the question. "Have the city designate it a historical landmark."

Jesmond shrugged. "Still driving the monster."

"Son, it's too hot to be standing out here for this over-the-fence chitchat." Teo wanly smiled, walking over to the driver's side of the Cadillac. Teo opened the door and rested his foot on the floor sill. "Why don't you just slide on in here and set a spell so we can catch up?"

"A car parked in the sun with its windows rolled up is gonna be cooler?"

"That's where you miss the boat, Jasper! In just thirty seconds there're be air cold enough to make a nun's nipples point." Jesmond again shrugged his shoulders, got in.

He studied the boy with side glances, prattling on about stupid things. Studied him. Smelled him—for Jesmond always seemed to have a feculent whiff that Teo detected, a half-wiped ass, partial hygiene, now magnified in the heat. Not particularly off-putting, though. Almost brought forth paternal feelings in Teo.

Teo caught himself lionizing attributes of everyone in the vicinity: Seth, Seth's sons, Jesmond. A case of nerves was what it was. Teo put the car in gear as a nonverbal prod for Jesmond to exit his car but he simply sat there looking out the window. Teo began to slowly back into the street, waiting for Jesmond to stop him so he could get out. He still didn't say anything.

It was now a contest of wills: the car crawling down the street, Jesmond wordless, studying scenery. At the corner, before pulling onto the main boulevard, Teo finally turned to Jesmond. "Anyplace I can take you?" he asked.

"Just waiting to see how long it took before you finally said something," Jesmond said, opening the car door and stepping out. "See you later, Teo." And he trundled down the street.

The boy made him react the way he did because the boy was an ugly constant. Teo had fucked the woman—his son's wife, woman, whatever. It haunted him that he might be Jesmond's daddy. Mule probably knew—*I've got your game.* Smoking dope cracked, yellowed, and cooked Yvette's teeth. The bitch's fang-toothed yap spewed history all over Mule's lap, and she—gingerly holding up the skirt ends, clopping about on those hooves—wanted Teo to know, *I've got your game.*

So why? Why did he do it? He loved his son without end; give up his own life for his in a heartbeat. Then as well as now—but pitied him more then. Feddy and Yvette scavenged only their neighborhood; their perimeter was so small. Teo let them live in a Section Eight clapboard that he owned just off Beaver Street. . . .

Porn.

Ace's collection stirred to memory a pallid middle-aged man Teo had seen in an upper-end mall a few months back. He had crinkly black hair and a damp round face that reflected the glow of a laptop. Teo sat at an adjacent table in the mall's food court. The man was blithely watching some heave-ho action right there, under all the community noise and agitation. He seemed restful and resigned, and at one point looked over to smile at Teo.

That was how he was able to fuck his son's woman—maybe not the why but how. Back then, he lived his life as if watching porno in public: a willful, greedy howdy to depravity. Life treated him well, then. Money, women—what was asked for was received. Then a boredom, a giddiness, a giving in. Finally—a sinking into a shit stream and riding it as far as it would carry him. Feddy, squeaking, scurrying about, surrendering to Teo. And Yvette, rutting about and lifting her rump but, unlike Feddy, still pretending to be in control—*Come on, Teo! Come in me*—

The car phone went off in the dashboard, beneath the radio. His one concession to the times was the car phone. No cell. Teo saw no advantage to being at some hayseed's beck and call while walking down a supermarket aisle.

"Yeah."

"Mr. Toak, this is Sergey. I am sorry not to call you on your work phone but we have need of you at the motel. It is almost urgent."

"And the problem?"

"There have been several complaints about infestations—"

"And the problem?"

"A woman has come to the office with bedbugs in a sandwich bag. She—"

"That's why we have 'infestations,' Boris. People eating their twelve courses and having buffets in their rooms. You know the exterminator we use. You don't need to call me with that shit."

"She says she will contact the television stations. There is, additionally, some personal matter where you are needed."

"Well? What is it?"

"They—he—did not say."

"Listen, Boris—"

"My name is Sergey, Mr. Toak. Sergey Belikov."

"I know what the fuck your name is. You'd do yourself better if you'd pay attention to how you're managing my motel rather than playing some goddam name game!" Christ! He rode through all of this before. First, the Cubans, then the Vietnamese, Pakistanis, Mexicans, Africans. Now the Russians—every new immigrant tried playing him for a chump.

"Hey, Mr. Toak. I make no rules. The man said it is very important that he see you."

"Hay is for cows, Boris. Tell him that I'll see him at my business office. Bail bonds."

"He said you need to come here now. That he will be here at two."

Teo felt his heart pumping against his palms pressed against the steering wheel. They had succeeded in riling him, made him run a red light, nearly sideswiped a Dumpster, punched a water-filled orange freeway barrier. Another sign of old age was the knowledge that certain buttons pushed would create stupid responses but you still responded as expected. He did not have the energy, now, to act to the contrary, but he had to fight against the tic of resignation.

And the world was getting too small. There, loitering at the desk, was Miss Audrey's—the renter of his little store space—son. He remembered him, the bail posted from a few years back. Four or five other pimpled and pasty adolescents cluttered the lobby while Sergey sat hunched over the computer, the boy chattering at him.

They all seemed Russian. At least they spoke what Teo took to be Russian. Trying to snarl, trying to menace, trying to look unrepentant for future violations about which Teo couldn't have cared less. A gangly, rufous boy with an Adam's apple the size of a goiter glared defiantly at Teo, his body sprawled across an overstuffed chair. Emblazoned across his T-shirt was I HAVE A NIGGER IN MY FAMILY TREE. He then stood up and deliberately crossed in front of Teo to the lobby window. The back of his shirt depicted a tree with a stick figure dangling from a noose. The boy stood at the large window as if studying the parking lot. The place already smelled of insecticide.

"Take a seat, Mr. Toak. The gentleman on phone said he will come at two."

"Who the hell are you to tell me to take a seat in my own goddam place, you borsch-eating communist son of a bitch!"

"Relax, Mr. Toak."

"Get the fuck out of here! Who the hell do you work for? Get your fat ass out of my chair!"

To Teo's surprise, his manager wanly smiled and looked not at Teo but at a point just above Teo's head, almost teasingly withholding eye contact or attention.

"He will be here momentarily Mr. Toak. Relax yourself."

"I said get your motherfuckin' fat ass out of my chair!"

Teo was suddenly aware of the redheaded boy standing at the plate glass behind him and the yellow sun pushing through the glass onto the two of them. He became aware, too, that he had chosen to be aware of something for distraction. He was suddenly aware that he was trying to avoid feeling shame.

"See! There he is. The man I told you about is here, Mr. Toak."

"Mr. Toak? I am hereby authorized by the state of Florida to serve you with these papers." The process server then turned on his heels and abruptly left.

He was being sued. Some man in Georgia was bringing a civil action against him for cumulative bodily injury sustained from an assault more than fifty years ago.

X

All oniony, a touch rancid—coital—was the air in the break room, the smell—after a search—emanating from Cash. A virid day, at least from the patch of green through the propped door. Jesmond got up every so often to catch a smack of clean air. It had rained earlier that morning and a constant breeze made for a clement afternoon, a breach in the summer's sprawling heat. Cinnamon. If he were to characterize the day by a taste or sensation, that was how Jesmond felt the day would best be described as he leaned through the fire door.

Cash wanted to tell his story. Their boss had gone to the Psychedelic Freak On—a black-light bowling party at the Cosmo Lanes for his granddaughter's birthday; he could be reached by his cell phone only in case of an emergency. "Jesmond! Sit your ass down! I want you to hear this!" Cash yelled, and motioned for Eric to hand Jesmond a can of Miller from the cooler. "When the cat's delay blah blah blah . . ." Eric grinned.

I was telling Eric about my buddy I grew up with, Tommy. "His mom was one of those straight-as-an-arrow Betty Crocker types. His old man was a trucker."

"BFD! My pops used to drive rigs," Jesmond challenged, raking a hand across his braids.

"Trust me, he probably didn't carry what this guy did and not do time. Anyway, I'm over at Tommy's house, playing with his toys and shit and his mama is getting ready to head out. PTA, Rotary Women's Auxiliary—that's the kind of woman she was. 'Now, Caleb,' she says, 'you keep an eye on those boys. Don't let them get into anything.' He's just flipping through a magazine and grunts as she leaves. Soon as he hears the car pull off, though, he looks up. 'Tommy, Cash—come on, let's go.' And he takes us to a bar.''

"They don't allow no kids in bars," Eric said.

"In Palatka they do. Anyway, it's one of those neighborhood strip-mall joints, everybody knows everybody and shit and as soon as we walk in they start hollering at the motherfucker, 'Hey! How y'all doing? What's up, Caleb?' and somebody is buying him a drink. He gives me and Tommy his pocketful of change and tells us to go play some pinball."

"You didn't play pinball. You played Pac-Man. Or Space Invaders. That's what they probably had back then. How old were you?" Eric asked.

"I was, I dunno, eleven or twelve. Yeah, I guess we played Pac-Man—what the fuck, asshole? Anyway, there's this dude with a pit. Claims this is the meanest pit bull this side of Georgia. Never lost a fight. Toughest thing on four legs, he says, maybe even two. Now Tommy's dad is listening to this joker talk all this crap about how bad a fighting dog this is. 'I don't think he can beat an orangutan,' he suddenly says. Tommy's daddy says this. It all of the sudden gets real quiet. 'I don't think that cocksucking dog of yours can beat an orangutan,' Tommy's daddy says again. This time he's smiling. The guy with the pit looks at Tommy's daddy like he's crazy. 'Well, I have no doubt that if there was an orangutan around here he'd tear the shit out of it, too,' the man says. He's laughing and grinning at everybody. 'I've got an orangutan,' Tommy's daddy says, 'and I bet you five hundred bucks he'll beat your dog'—"

"Give me a fuckin' break," Jesmond said.

"I'm serious. See, like I said, the old man used to haul more than just oranges from Orlando and one day some guy's short on a payment. So he gives Tommy's daddy the orangutan to make the difference.

"Anyway, everybody's all excited about this battle between the pit bull and the orangutan. Tommy's daddy bets the man that his orangutan will beat his pit bull. Everybody's now placing bets, calling up people. Before the guy leaves to get the pit, the old man tells him how to get to his place. See, when he got the ape, the first he does is build this huge concrete pen that takes up half their backyard."

"What's an orangutan look like?"

"Like Cameron Diaz, motherfucker. What do I look like, The Discovery Channel? So you got all these folks now over Tommy's house, the driveway and street all filled up with cars. Finally the guy shows up with his pit in a cage. Ferocious-looking little sucker. Can't fully recollect its name—Viper or Hellfire, something like that. Folks are now saying to Tommy's daddy that he's in shit now, that that little sucker is gonna tear his monkey up. And Tommy's daddy's just smiling. The orangutan—you've got to picture the saddest, most bored-, miserable-looking creature on God's earth in a diaper—is just sitting there on the concrete. These Stretch Armstrong arms out in front of him on the cement with the wrists touching. All this racket, everybody shouting—and the orangutan's just sitting there. The man goes to the door, takes off his pit bull's collar, and lets it loose in the pen. Understand that this is the guy's prize dog out of all his dogs and it's never lost a fight. The dog's now barking and snarling and snapping like crazy. And the orangutan is doing nothing but sitting there, looking bored, staring at nothing in front of him. The dog goes for the orangutan.

"—*Wham!* All the sudden that ape brought those two hands straight down on that poor dog's neck, quick as lightning. Broke it. Didn't know what hit him. And the orangutan goes back to just sitting there staring at those arms, looking bored out of its skull, as if nothing ever happened. Of course the guy is pissed but he can't say nothing. He was the one talking all this crap about his badass pit. Now he's got a dead dog—a dead prize dog—and he's got to pay up Tommy's daddy to boot.

"The funny thing is that the evening comes up and Tommy's mama turns the key in the door and there we are, in the den on the floor, playing with Tommy's army men. His daddy's in the recliner, watching TV. 'You boys must be bored silly,' she says. 'Caleb, why don't you give these young men a treat and take them down to Dairy Queen?'"

"Okay, so what then?" Eric was digging mud from the waffle sole of his shoe with a finger.

"So, Cool," Cash said to Jesmond, ignoring Eric, "you don't buy that my friend's daddy had an orangutan in their backyard?"

Jesmond had gotten up again, looked out the back door. "Hell," Jesmond said, turning around and heading back, "That's fuckin' Palatka. They're just as likely to be screwing an ape as do anything else. I think we've got a customer, though." Jesmond arranged himself in the two-way mirror before heading to the salesroom.

"Me?" Eric began, "I just as much sneak up on Skooch and show up there at bowl-a-rama. He should've invited us. Goddam! It's wild seeing those bright pink and blue bowling balls glowing down the lanes with that black light."

"See. Ying and yang," Cash said. "One time you needed a ride and I dropped you off. Now you do the same for me."

For the past several days, Cash had been without transportation since his wife left him, taking his beloved truck. Jesmond, unfortunately, had come to know every detail behind her departure since it was his number that Cash had entered into the speed-dial of his cell phone. And Cash felt it was only fair that he share and reconstruct the decline of his marriage for Jesmond in exchange for livery services.

"That was once. And it wasn't even your car. I ended up taking the bus the rest of the time. Let me see about getting you a schedule," Jesmond said.

"Don't be such a pussy. Just drop me off."

"Man, I'm not Driving Miss Daisy— You have me picking you up at the bitch's trailer and taking you back. Call a fuckin' cab!"

All four windows were rolled down and still Jesmond had to angle the air-conditioning vent toward his face. "Hell, man—don't you know anything about personal hygiene?"

Cash bobbed to the loping shadow of the telephone lines upon the sidewalk as they drove past. "Don't ever let them know how you truly feel about them. They will turn it against you, my friend," Cash said. According to Cash, his love for his ex-wife was so full, so violent, so larger-than-life that that was what had pushed her away. "Intense. That's the only way I can describe our relationship. I remember once—I was a stupid, thieving little fuck, I'll tell you that right now—me and my friends were out one night, stealing from this fisherman's net he had crossing a lead-in off the St. Johns. Now what the joker was doing was fucking illegal anyway—net-hook fishing. I'm out there in the water, cutting loose the ties, when all the sudden I slip and get caught up in all this net. Thing's covered in all these sharp little teeth, man. . . ." He was hooked all down his back and thigh, the net trailing behind him like a wedding train. His so-called friends doubled over, laughing at his stupidity and pain, put him belly-down in the back of a sedan and drove him home. But it was his old lady who came through for him, took him to County with him having to stand up in the bed of that beloved truck ("She didn't have to run off with that, goddammit!"), holding on to the roof for dear life. "She pulled right on up into emergency, right next to the ambulances. Got out and told those sons of bitches that this was her man and they better step to it because I was in need of some serious looking after."

His uxorial braying stopped at the kudzu-smothered trailer. "There's the jezebel that fuckin' destroyed my happy home," Cash said to Jesmond. The woman stood on a concrete stoop in a yellow halter and unbuttoned Daisy Dukes, lime-green panties. A purple shirt gaily bounced in the wind on an improvised clothesline. She brought up a hand to shield her eyes from the sun so as to look inside the car.

"She didn't twist your arm," Jesmond replied.

"I know. But I swear you'll never taste anything sweeter." The woman began gesturing for Cash to come out. Cash stared at her. "I ought not to be telling you this, but you won't believe how this chick used to make money. Take a fuckin' guess. On second thought, I've gotta tell you this one." Cash waved at the woman. She smirked, then stuck out her tongue at him. "In Gainesville, at the place where they keep the animals for the experiments for the medical school, this young lady breast-fed newborn monkeys," Cash said, nodding at her.

"Bullshit."

Cash shrugged. "She'd just given birth to that rug rat, the one you met. A buddy of hers who worked cleaning crap from the cages told her they were looking for a titty donor. Wet nurse's what they wanted. Wet nurse for a bunch of chimps whose mothers wouldn't feed. Felt from the chimp psychological perspective they needed human titty, not just milk in a bottle. Paid them real good, too."

Jesmond looked at him warily. "Sometimes I think you believe half the shit you say."

"All I can say is that she was bringing home two grand a month slinging tit. Now, the wild thing is they had to let her go. The little chimps were getting sick. Come to find out mama there had hepatitis and was spreading to the babes in her juice."

"But you still do her."

"Simple, chief. Just pull out before I unload." The woman began knocking on the window. "Besides, I've probably got the shit, too, all the women I've done. Don't kill humans. Give you, maybe—what did I hear some old crackhead call it?—'roaches of the liver.'"

"Cirrhosis."

"Yeah. Well, let me get out. Bitch'll be head-banging the window pretty soon. That fuckin' kid of hers—"

"Kobe?"

"Yeah. Little pervert. Since the wife left I sometimes spend the night here. We'll be getting to business and the little fucker will come right in on us. End up having to lock the kid outside till we're done."

A desiccated little land crab burped up from the snarl of shrubbery at the trailer's collapsed rubber wheel. Always made Jesmond's flesh crawl when he saw one of those brown things: seemed a hybrid of pregnant roach and lizard.

"Come on, Cash. It's a fucking little kid. You don't leave a kid standing alone outside here at night just so you can do the mom."

"If it ain't me it'd be somebody else. And who are you to talk, Saint Jesmond? Men dying for our country in Iraq and you're knocking boots with their wives—you're a real role model. Anyway, she's pissed. Let me get outta here. Talk to you later, boss."

Ashley and Sarah did little to betray their presence behind the house door to the garage but it didn't take much. A protracted whimper here, then a snuffle, a click of nails across the linoleum, sighs—these were the sounds Medgar's clients would try to piece together staring at the door.

With the abrupt departure of Adam Finchem, Medgar found himself wearing hats of both therapist and insurance examiner. Something he swore he wouldn't do but now he didn't appear to have a choice. Jesmond sat across the room in the half-dark.

"Who that?" It was a young man in a wheelchair, trying to point at Jesmond.

"My apprentice."

"What's that? What does an apprentice do?" the young man asked, now studying the door. Medgar's pinchers.

"It means he must work with me for years and years in order to master his craft. Even then he might not cut it. He might not have the necessary skill of empathy combined with constrained detachment, for example." Medgar removed his glasses and began polishing them on a Popeyes Chicken paper napkin. He then, reflexively, swiped his lips with the napkin. Liver-colored. For the first time Jesmond noticed how Medgar's lips were liver colored and cracked.

"But enough about me and what I do—how did you like my health lecture series at the public library?"

"Excuse me?"

"Nothing. Just a joke. Why did you end up in the wheelchair?"

The young man pulled up in his chair, wobbling in his oversized tracksuit like a wind-bounced flower. He then adjusted his legs.

He was one of two brothers, both in wheelchairs. Kevin was the young man across the desk from Medgar; Kelvin was the sib back home. The brothers lived in a stucco ranch-style house with their mother—a house similar to the Medgars', though their mother's home had black wrought-iron bars on the windows and doors of her house, and on the northwest corner of the roof a tin rooster would flicker and spin windward during a thunderstorm. With her two sons wheelchair bound, the city had provided her with a plywood ramp for the front steps and lift bars in one of the bathrooms. Kevin was the first to come to a wheelchair; his brother followed three years later.

They all had guns. At the end of nearly every Saturday night on the street in front of their mother's house, when most of the revelers from the He Ain't Here and other clubs and parties had disappeared into their respective homes, and the knots of young thugs eventually diminished in their floating from street to street to the five or so remaining—the five or so who were powerless in bringing the night to a close, standing there in front of *their* house (or if cold, in *their* garage); when everyone remaining at some point fell into the stupor of the evening, drifting (high or melancholic) in reveries of acts without consequence, or submerged in the dark hour of some radio's voice; when every proposed deed fell into a dispute or silence—then one of toughs would cuff another, provoking words and vengeance. Their streetlamps had wire mesh over them.

A relatively new man had fallen into the group. He shot Kevin one Saturday night after Kevin, high and belligerent, punched the newcomer.

The man deliberately shot Kevin in the neck—rather than the head or the chest—so as to paralyze him. "I've fucked up your life," he chortled, looming over Kevin. In three years his brother would come to his chair following an altercation over ownership of a video game at a party. Kevin's brother, to his disgust, still whimpered in his sleep.

"Is it true I'll never do it again, doc?" Kevin asked Medgar.

"Do what?"

"You know, fuck. Fuck a woman."

"I'm glad you've qualified it, 'fuck a woman.' Because you—as you know—can still 'be fucked.' But as the fucker rather than the fuckee—no, I'm afraid that time has passed. I bet with every new doc you see you ask the same question. A breakthrough in imagination is what you're hoping for. No, that gentleman robbed you of your manhood. Did you retaliate, Kevin?"

"What?"

"Did you go back for the gentleman, the new guy? An eye for an eye, tooth for a tooth. Revenge?"

"He not from around here. Split after he shot me."

"Weird. The antisuccubus. This demon, instead of damnation through intercourse, must nightly bring you right to the edge of lust and leave you stranded, horny without redemption, so to speak. And this leaves me sad. Now take off your shirt."

"What?"

"You want to be a millionaire, don't you? I need to examine you for the insurance company."

He was a reedy, concave man, complained of piles. A tulip of flesh blistered at the nape of his neck. Medgar had Jesmond help Kevin undress himself. Strapped to his sticklike brown thigh was a white plastic bulb. A tan rubber band held it in place and a rubber tube led from the bulb to his penis. Kevin said he had spells in which his heart would run and make him dizzy. Medgar probed Kevin's chest back and forth with a stethoscope, rubbed the wound nipple, had him cough twice. As if on cue, the three of them watched the white plastic bulb slowly fill with urine.

"Every group has its embarrassment, its rube or bumpkin. Every culture, every country," Medgar began. Though heat suffused the garage office, the unclothed young man had begun to shiver. Medgar seemed oblivious, however. "If I had time enough, another lifetime maybe, I'd get a Fulbright studying those facets of Americana—Redneck, Trailer Trash, Ghetto, Country, America's denizens of bad taste and Section Eight housing—as they manifest in every country. In England, they're chavs (which has replaced 'yobbo,' early twentieth century). Australia, bogans. Scangers in Ireland, *dres* in Poland, *ah beng* in Singapore. . . . I was in Denmark when I happened upon the tribe of 'Brians.' They'd been given the unique sobriquet by the home folk because of their quaint tic of naming their boys 'Brian.' They heard it as very American. *Bree-yan* was how they'd say it. And as an inversion of their trailer-park sisters here in the States, those lovely blond things would dye their hair black. So you'd see them and hear them, sandpaper-voiced and yelling at their children's hockey games (the pastime encouraged in their kiddies), lipped cigarettes, baby-blue track trousers girdling a flat ass. Though now midnight hair with white roots . . . Befuddling. No matter where in the world . . .

"Adaptation, Jesmond. These people survive, slide by, on the grease of anticipation. Fascists, each and every one: their eroticism simultaneously pure and effusive, guiltless. But they will become selfish and mean. Confronted with lives that persist beyond their ability to alter them, they become helpless in the end. Mores the pity! But none insincere; all, 'Keeping It Real!' . . . Someday, you might come across this story I am going to tell you about an eccentric Frenchman. He was a surrealist poet and actor who'd been forced to undergo more than sixty courses of electroshock treatment, and had been confined, for more than a decade, to a mental hospital in Rodez, France. His name was Antonin Artaud—get Kevin dressed now. He looks as if he's freezing." Jesmond reluctantly approached the young man, tugging his trousers back up from his ankles as Kevin scrunched, alternating buttocks in the wheelchair.

"On a night in 1947, billed as a 'Tête-à-tête with Antonin Artaud,' they sat the actor in a chair upon the stage. He read poems before an audience that included the likes of André Gide, Breton, Albert Camus. Though he was only fifty, he looked frail and gaunt. He clawed the air and sobbed, grunted. Nobody understood what he was saying—'O dedi, o dada orzoura, o dou zoura'—were his exact words. There would be these long pauses, minutes. Embarrassment. Then words shouted—'Syphilis.' 'Piss.' 'Electroshock.' At one point, he knocked over the lectern holding his manuscript, and in falling to his knees to retrieve his papers, his glasses fell from his nose and skittered across the stage. André Gide, an old man himself, crawled about the stage with him, handing him papers. He pathetically pulled himself back up into his seat. 'I put myself in your place,' he addressed the audience, 'and I can see that what I am telling you isn't at all interesting. It is still theater. What can I do to be truly sincere?'"

Medgar collapsed back into his chair, extended his legs, rubbed his shaved skull as if it were a crystal ball. His eyes then suddenly caught something on Kevin's ankle. "I missed that," he said. He reached over and pulled up the young man's pant leg. Revealed a house-arrest anklet. "And how did you come about this piece of jewelry?" Medgar asked.

Kevin shrugged. Nonchalant. "Weed," he finally said.

He told them how, for a time, he had been the most profitable dealer in his part of town. It took detectives several months to connect the paraplegic with the Care Bear-stickered wheelchair to marijuana distribution in the area. Out of pity the judge had sentenced him to a monitor that required he call an 800 number every time he left his mother's house. Even though the sentence had been completed months ago, he still wore the device as an emblem of his days as a man among men.

"Any-who," Medgar began, "the fact of the matter is that you now have AIDS. Your CD4 count is less than two hundred; you have a fever from a pneumonia (more than likely, pneumocystis); and you've got thrush. And yet you still find somebody that will cook and shoot for you—an (old school) man!" Medgar turned to Jesmond. "You know, your old man used to provide a similar public service. Back then he'd help a junkie out by providing him or her with a central line. All on the down low, of course. He even did an old doo-wop singer from the Platters. Whenever they needed access—veins had been disappearing or festering and they're teetering on withdrawal—your dad would be kind enough to bring them down into the morgue and pop in a large-bore IV. Free of charge. Right in the jugular or, if discretion was warranted, a subclavian vein. I swear if he'd finished he would've made a wonderful surgeon. As to you—" Medgar smiled grimly at the young man in the wheelchair.

The young man now suddenly appeared to have old, old hands. They were discernibly puffed and glossy. His fingernails were long and grotesquely curved. "You are a member of an unfortunate race, and, unfortunately, in a race against time. I'll get you approved for these policies, but it'll take at least a month before all the *i*s are dotted and the *t*s crossed, then another month or two before a check is cut. The best thing for you to do right now would be to get yourself admitted to County. Otherwise—to be blunt—it's a toss-up as to who'll get to you first: FedEx or Frapple Mortuary." Medgar stared at Kevin, who squirmed about his chair. Medgar then dug into his pants pocket, held his cell phone out in front of him. "This is what I'm about to do. I'm about to call a doctor at County, the one in charge of the TB and AIDS unit. I will discuss with him your plight, and I'm fairly certain you'll be admitted. I will take care of your transportation. Your only responsibility at this point, then, is to make sure your body is delivered to 655 West Eighth Street."

A short while later a Gator City taxi pulled up in front of the house. The gap-toothed driver cursed Jesmond and Kevin under his breath for having to help lift and fold Kevin into the backseat; at one point all of their limbs were crisscrossed and in a jumble as if playing Twister. The driver then had to collapse and disassemble the wheelchair and force-feed it into the trunk.

While the driver was struggling to fit the chair so that the trunk might close, Jesmond caught sight of a car two doors down and across the street with its parking lights on. There was someone at the wheel. Kevin had noticed the car, too, and stuck his head out the window. He lifted his arm through and scraped the dark but the figure did not respond. When the cab pulled away, Jesmond deliberately stayed in place. The car stayed, too. The day's heat roasted up through the soles of his flip-flops. It was only after Jesmond took steps toward the vehicle that the car pulled into the street and slowly rolled past. The windows were tinted but Jesmond could have sworn, from all the pictures he'd seen about the house, that it was Peaches's husband, Special Ed.

XI

Medgar was grinning at Jesmond when he returned. He was astride a chair, hugging the back. The grin suddenly disappeared and, to Jesmond's amazement, Medgar's face resembled Jesmond's. "You can always make your face register interest by mirroring the other person's expression," Medgar said after a time. "Long-married couples unconsciously do this to each other. In the 1960s, there was a psychologist called Sylvan Tompkins who had an uncanny ability to read and predict a person's or peoples' intentions—a murderous homosexual tribe in New Guinea, for example—by the set of the muscles in their face. What you learn to see is the moment-to-moment movement—like a swarm of insects—of sprawled emotions surging up through some facial torpor. From there you can learn how to elicit empathy.

"Usually, everyone regards other people with a vacuity, as if what it took to see into people was a different, overwrought sense other than sight. When in reality it's a very passive, receptive act. Your father, for example."

Jesmond made a face. "You ever work with my dad?"

"Many times. The best, though, was when he was a morgue assistant. From when he was in detention and treatment, Feddy read everything he could get a hold of regarding cardiac pacemakers. When he was released and working at County, he came to me with an idea of removing pacemakers from the dead and reusing them. We started at County, scratching out serial numbers and expiration dates. I pulled a few cardiologists into using the product. Your father, unfortunately, got cold feet. Pity, too. I went on to make quite a pocketful."

Medgar stiffly stood up and screaked the legs of the chair atop the concrete. He pointed to the chair for Jesmond to sit as he slowly let himself down onto the sofa. A near-mock medical station with a metal desk and chair and sphygmomanometer. And a living-room facsimile—well appointed, with Chippendale pairings and coffee table, a creaky Italian leather sofa, a Wainscot chair—all atop a bare concrete floor. Small lights leaked into the space, since Medgar turned off the overhead, from three diminished foci: the thin gap of the hall door, where the dogs' shadows turned and turned over the splintered light like shoveled earth; the moon, blistered and reflected through the top glass of the side door; a 40-watt desk lamp.

"I've seen my fair share of lunatics—the same with 'em, read 'em the same way. Actually, I have a theory that they suffer a gap between what they feel and what they want to feel. Constant state of tumult. At its worst it's like watching vintage television where the reception picks up two or three channels simultaneously."

Sprawled like an odalisque atop the sofa, Medgar studied a ribbon of tiny black ants making a trek from a crack in the outside wall to a desiccated rubber plant next to the chair. He extended his arm and crushed the column within reach into a smear with his thumb. Jesmond watched as Medgar then flicked the remnants into the shared darkness. "Lunatics. I had one that was convinced he needed electroshock therapy. I thought otherwise and told him as much. He ended up creating this device that he jerry-rigged off an electric cattle fence, a ways out on his parents' farm in Ocala. Each week Sparky would crouch in front of the fence, put a touch of Bengay to his forehead, and lean his head into this prod. Left him with a permanent brown spot, size of a quarter."

Medgar sat up, bouncing stiffly, lightly, upon the horsehair-stuffed sofa. Looking into the dark edges of the room, he hunched toward Jesmond, resembling a man on a john.

"—Your father had a life preserver all the while he was using and in treatment. A Father Clemons. Your old man would probably love to see the rake made a saint. 'The Beatification of Padre Clemons'—though something tells me there was a certain amount of brainwashing slap-and-tickle at play there." Medgar met the boy's angry gape.

"What? Short of some contrived, patient-doctor privilege nonsense, I'm not bound by any ecclesiastical writ. Misprision is the priest being damned in betraying the confessional, not me. I suspect the old boy was queer—but no, I never heard your father speak of any catamite as his particular Bone Daddy. But what follows, Jesmond, is the opportunity to squirt a little desire in the mix. As a young'un he was like, I suspect, most adolescents—fervor, lust, all one inchoate mess. With religiosity used as bait. Finally, in the end: 'I thank you from the bottom of my heart for the desperation you've caused me, and I detest the tranquility in which I lived before I knew you.' Not that it ever transpired with me, mind you.

"I finally came to the conclusion that after all the hue and cry is done, people stupidly equate being moral with being lovable. Love-worthy, more. I didn't see the need. It would be like everyone tacitly agreeing that there was this seventh sense that was essential to their movement about the world but that they couldn't describe. Had no vocabulary for it. And I still find myself getting about just fine. Oh, I've heard it described as what it'd be like if a sighted individual tried to describe vision to some congenitally blind bumpkin. But that emperor has no clothes, Jesmond. I saw those gentlemen and ladies stumbling about the world more so than me. Made me chuckle. In fact, something along those lines were my dear pap's last words, directed at me. To quote—'You laugh too goddam much. Wipe that smirk off your face.' He then kicked the bucket."

He had become toxically youthful. Even in the half-light Jesmond saw Medgar becoming animate, jouncing atop the sofa. The dogs, too, were becoming more agitated; Jesmond could hear them clatter behind the door. "You're becoming too simple. Too . . . uncomplicated. Boring. There's so much more to things if you fracture them, tumble them in a kaleidoscope," Medgar said.

"Are you gay?"

"Why you ask?"

"Dunno. Just that's the way that some guys hit on you, by making themselves seem real clever."

"Fuck you, boy—" but Medgar shrugged his shoulders. "That's where you're an idiot. Sex is play. Gay, straight. I accompanied my daddy, once, to an abortion, waiting in the car until he was finished. Afterwards, I came into the kitchen where the fetus sat in the garbage, pressed between waxed paper. What he called 'happiness's byproduct.'"

Medgar suddenly got up from the sofa and fell into the chair at the metal desk across from Jesmond. In the weak light his jowls appeared stippled, like the fresh burr at the bottom of a cake pan.

"You might not believe this, Jesmond, but sometimes I pray." Medgar greedily regarded Jesmond. "Our Father. Our Father, who art in heaven . . ." Jesmond sat across from him and watched Medgar repeat the prayer. His face became flat as he focused upon the dimming and quickening light coming from under the door connecting the garage and the house—the dogs scuffled. Beginning his fourth Our Father, Medgar rubbed his finger behind his ear, sniffed.

Medgar's face and voice were slack. The eyes, though, collapsed between mockery and confusion, demanded Jesmond's attention. Jesmond shouted over the recitation that he could not stay there the night, that Medgar was acting too fucking strange, and stood up to leave—Medgar never discontinued his drone, though his eyes, with a sort of dull hatred, seized upon the slap of the flip-flops hitting the dry fleshy heels of Jesmond's feet as he descended the driveway.

XII

The preparations for the inaugural celebration of Bessie Coleman's flight were a welcomed distraction. For the past several months the city, moving up the ranks, had embarrassingly acquired the title of Tenth Murder Capital in America. Since the first of the year there had been at least one murder a day. The deaths had devastated and debased the black community: contentious employees strangling bosses, handguns used to settle playground disputes, rejected suitors stabbing first loves. It was generally acknowledged that the citizenry were spiritually depleted. Embarrassment and scorn surfaced. And there was a call for soul searching, with the requisite prayer breakfast being held assembling the city's leading ministers.

Feddy sat in his chicken-wire-and-plywood office space listening to Seth on the phone. He was bemoaning his exclusion from the citywide spiritual meeting. Feddy stared at the screen saver of a raccoon. Melan had recently replaced all the screen savers of calendar girls with a menagerie from the Wildlife Fund. Melan swore he was in the dark on this one, blaming higher-ups in management and new policies regarding potential sexual harassment. Feddy argued that as far as shipping and loading went there were only men and dykes in the facility—both groups liked the pictures, he might add!—but Melan simply nodded in agreement, then winked and went about his business.

"—So I don't have my congregation turn in copies of their W2s. And I don't have a VIP entrance to my church. And I don't have an ATM in the lobby. But, what the hell, Feddy! Nobody has done more—and has a finger on the pulse of our community—than me! Hell, do you remember when some young banger came up behind me, right there in front of my church, *my* church, and pressed a gun into my ribs? He then stopped to ask me who I was—"

"Yep. Stickup men asking for identification about as often as they offer it."

"—But he then tells me that he once got a coat from the clothes bank we keep there, and he apologizes."

"What can I say, Seth? It's an unfair, crooked business, preaching. But the people that matter know the good you do."

Seth pressed on, venting, this time about Bayonne. The district attorney was now making appearances with a whole new slate of questions. He was suspicious. He floated inquires—had Bayonne been associated with this AIDS-for-money scheme? Was Smullian connected in any way? "Lucky for us, Rachel just shut him up. Told him he could do his, quote, 'fuckin' fishin' at some other fuckin' pond,' unquote."

"That's great, Sethy. Listen, though. I've got to go back to paying into your Social Security. The Greater Johnsonville Plan calls. I'll holler at you later." Feddy hung up.

Feddy contemplated his raccoon. Jiggling the mouse brought forth a spreadsheet. It was his intention to close his eyes just for a moment, just for a power nap, and the spreadsheet made him look busy.

There was a soothing, rhythmic pulse to the rain as it poppled against the corrugated warehouse roof. There would be a rush of wind, and then a silence would brush across the ceiling, and Feddy caught himself looking up as if he'd unconsciously bumped into someone and needed to apologize. He was able to tune out and sleep through the yelling and bustle of the storage personnel and lift operators and the lot traffic through the open bay doors. He closed his eyes.

The spreadsheet was still before him when he awoke.

He stood up hard and was, as usual, rejuvenated. He had decided earlier to drop in on Melan. It served him best to line up for his boss all his projects along with their projected obstacles, assessing their risks and benefits. For example, the bee group was eager to import again *Trigona necrophaga*. However, they now had several stipulations as to shipping arrangements and payment. Melan also had become something of a pain in the ass: Feddy couldn't use Caulder Shipping anymore ("Sorry, but I use those guys sometimes for my recreational imports and have to keep up a good rapport. That shit apparently stank to high heaven. Besides, it's too goddam weird, man"). Couldn't use the standard manifest. Melan also wanted a third of the *net* profit—meaning Feddy would have to eat all the expenses and any losses by himself.

The used-clothing exports, though . . . Those were becoming a gold mine. He'd learned from one of the Ugandan stevedores about selling the castoffs, *mitumba,* Swahili for "bale." In Togo the shipments were called "dead white men's clothing"—"Because nobody there could believe anybody living would throw away such clothes. They're a broke-ass country." Through union connections, Melan was able set up donation bins throughout Johnsonville. The metal containers were straightforward: PUT USED CLOTHES HERE. They were usually stationed strategically within the vicinity of a Goodwill or Salvation Army bin; after a week or so, when people became frustrated jamming their donations into the overstuffed Salvation Army or Goodwill containers, clothes were simply dumped into the accessible Put Used Clothes Here bins. The venture—however tenuous—was legitimate.

The new issue facing Feddy, though, was the request to presort the clothing before shipping. For one, his contact person called and offered to nearly double the purchase price if someone Stateside would, for example, separate out bras and panties from the rest of the clothes. "There's crisp money on the return, my friend, if you could get your workers to just make a pile of the woman's intimates. For my street and market vendors with their stalls, the—how you say? potluck!—the big bales is fine. They cut them open and jump in. But my high-end stores have a certain attitude about that sort of thing and I end up having to get people here to open and sort. Then they steal, so I have to get people to watch *them.* . . ." Feddy had already begun a project over in one of the closed-down, leaking warehouses. He just hadn't let Melan in on his little experiment yet.

There was a knock on the doorsill. It was one of the forklift operators, just discharged from the navy. He was a thickset, ruddy blond with a visibly repaired harelip who still believed that he operated within the military chain of command: for the past two weeks, every task he performed had to be rigorously reviewed by a superior. The young man had been passed from one floor boss to another before a secretary, in exasperation, finally pointed to Feddy's office. This was his third visit with Feddy of the day.

"Mr. Toak, sir?"

"Man . . . like I've told you, you're not in the navy anymore, you don't sir me."

"Okay. Okay . . . I don't know whether you want this billet 286 over there in dock forty-seven because, when you look at the actual papers here, it's not even supposed to be in that warehouse, much less—"

"You know what? I think the best person to handle these matters is Mike Brooks in warehouse three. I'll walk you down and point out his office to you." The raccoon popped on screen as soon as Feddy stepped from the office.

The automobiles and air gleamed post-tempest. Glistening windshields. And the sunset drew in tendrils of tangerine and lime, scarring the day with dying light through the clouds.

"You go to that double-wide situated right there next to the warehouse. Not in the warehouse—Brooks likes to remain at eye level," Feddy informed him. The young man bounced his head in agreement and lumbered forward, intent on his mission.

Feddy always felt reduced in Melan's office. As if the furniture, the windows, even paper and pencils, were all oversized. He knew he was cleverer than Melan, and older, and certainly had held the promise, at least, that came from a better education. And isolated, Feddy knew he carried his own weight and then some when with Melan. Here, though: he felt like a kid visiting Daddy's office. Not that Melan was a hard boss to work for, far from it. It was just that Feddy saw that he was at a point in his life that no amount of hard work or cleverness would remove him from the ranks of old men who had to kowtow to younger bosses.

What made the ritual easier to put up with, though, was Ce-Ce. It struck Feddy that Ce-Ce, having been hired close to a year ago, was still in the employ of Melan. Usually Melan hired pretty women during the summer—then he'd let them go by late spring.

"Hey, Fed-dy!" Her singsong greeting. She drew out the first syllable of his name, then clipped the second. Like a birdcall.

"Hey, sweetheart! Where's Skeletor?"

"He called me from downtown where he said some city councilman's got him tied up." She leaned in, motioned for Feddy to follow. "But, lover—between you and me, our favorite Negro is ready to haul you out right along with this mess you've pulled."

"What did I do, this time?"

"Using company folk on company time to play naughty with women's unmentionables is what! Feddy, Feddy, Feddy!"

"Sweetheart, I saved you a couple pair. Wait a minute—" Feddy looked down and feigned counting in his pocket. "I actually got you three—two Wednesdays and a smiley-face Sunday!"

"Used drawers? He-man, you certainly know the way to a woman's heart."

"I take it he ain't too keen on the idea."

"No."

Ce-Ce had a knack for dissolving even the most problematic moment into some *aqua regia* of lustful flirtation. Feddy found himself grinning—as would probably ninety-nine percent of men standing where he stood—and Ce-Ce warmly reciprocated. "Anyway, darlin', let me see that tattoo that's got your boss so hot and bothered. I'll show you mine if you'll show me yours," Feddy attempted.

"I'm sorry, baby, but it'll only frustrate and break your poor little heart. See, I've got one half of the tattoo and Melan's got the other. Only when we're together can the truth be known." Ce-Ce winked. "Just leave that to your imagination."

All the way to the ruinous Quonset warehouse, Feddy chuckled in stutters, bumped through a trio of orange caution cones. Maybe each thigh with half a heart? He scooted around to the minuscule side entrance. There Feddy confronted a puddle the size of a foot-ball field, barely a quarter of an inch deep, underneath a rent in an expansive metal roof. A small private plane had, not so long ago, missed the runway—hell, missed the airport!—and crashed into the roof.

Feddy, strolling up to two men sorting through a mountain of clothes, began exaggeratedly shaking his head and one of the men imitated his motion. The man wore a terry cloth bathrobe and a vest of grease-stained suede. A half-dozen bras were draped over each arm.

He had gone to a hamlet outside Atlanta for three days. Teo. Drove up in his lumbering Cadillac, the car wheezing down Interstate 95N. He cruised into a motel parking lot as the work day ended. Large reflecting windshields threw glary light on the wall behind him. The bed linens were damp, the carpet unpadded. A bird's nest rem-nant was stuck in a barred bathroom window. If Teo stood in the tub he could watch mudders spinning and spraying their monster tire trucks in an open field.

For the first day's reconnaissance he was up at 5:00 AM, having slept poorly. In the Huddle House, hunters in camouflage fatigues and loquacious men in gray windbreakers—up at dawn to fly remote-control planes—were the only other patrons. His own gasp-ing snore woke him up in the booth, accompanied by a head bob.

With his red-rimmed eyes he felt he was an object of easy derision and he left only a quarter tip.

A sullen morning, curdled ground mist: Teo pointed the behemoth west, onto State Road 3. The plaintiff, Tobias McKendree, lived with a passel of McKendrees in the speed trap of Euphonium, Georgia. A doe, nuzzling a Styrofoam cup at the edge of the road, stiffened as Teo sped past. One McKendree was an elected judge; another a tax collector—the family also owned several businesses in the town.

Teo rode past three antique barns, each with a clawfoot tub spewing purple phlox. It was Coots who had connected the dots. A series on cold cases involving law enforcement. Coots had been leafing through the *Atlanta Journal-Constitution* when he came across a news item about the blinding of a junior sheriff in western Georgia, back in the 1950s. The crime had been perpetrated by an African-American whose voice Tobias McKendree thought he recognized from television once, for he would "never forget that cold sinister voice." The irony was that the perpetrator was now apparently involved with the law, either as a bondsman or bailiff, McKendree couldn't remember.

Teo had cornered Mule, asked her to slap a libel suit or something like it against Medgar, hoped she'd give him legal representation. And Mule guffawed, saying that wasn't her shtick, told him to check the back of the phone book. Genghis Cunt, the bitch . . .

He found the usual two blocks of spindly structures perched near railroad tracks. Negro housing. Back in the day, all he'd have to do was tip some skillet to direct him to the proprietor of the main red-light establishment or juke joint to get the lay of the land. Now—integration had destroyed the colored kingpin. Essential folk were too spread out and the money too dilute.

The sun was a long time coming. It finally emerged, burning yellow-green through the maple, and Teo's window glided down to catch some of the morning coolness. He was backed up against the rotten wooden fence of a convenience store as a lanky mouse-colored man in a box shirt and shades loped gingerly toward him, his shadow leading atop the tarred road.

"Hey! Hey, brother!" Teo shouted from the window.

"Yeah?"

"Who does a fellow talk to around here to find shit out?"

"What?"

"To get information, who do I talk to?"

"You a cop?"

"Hell no! Just got some questions."

"Whatever!" the man yelled back and, without breaking his stride, continued on his way.

The convenience store, butted up against a house in the back, awakened from the rear to the front. When the shimmering roll of a beer sign's waterfall finally ignited in the store window, Teo decided to enter. Collared-greens stink hung in the air, and the galvanized metal shelves advertised a few dusty canned goods and nondescript bottled liquids. Teo was caught looking down a dingy corridor into a blue living room with plastic slipcovers. A glaring woman in housecoat and hairnet slammed the door from the end of the hall. "Can I help you?" came from the walk-in cooler in the back.

"Yeah, partner—six-pack of Miller Lite!"

Pneumatic lurching. A gravel-napped man huffed to the register clutching the six-pack and a half-open tin of Vienna sausages.

Teo pushed a twenty onto the Formica for the beer. "Might have one of those suckers myself," he said, pointing to the sausages. The old man held the tin out to him. Teo dug his fingers into the red, mealy juice and popped a frank between brown teeth. "Nice. Nice place. You own it?"

"Who you kiddin'? Naw. Cracker that owns it lets us stay with a cut."

Teo leaned in, wiped his fingers on a foul counter rag. "There's a McKendree making my life hell. Trying to cheat me out of some property."

"Nothing new, might as well pick you a number—which Mc-Kendree?"

"Heard he was some old cop. Blind joker."

"You talking, then, about Tobias. He ain't the richest of 'em. Thinks he knows everything and he don't know jack. They look after him, though. You see him sitting out in front of the courthouse. Something new to do with them digging up the street and all." On the way out, Teo ignored the man's wheezed protestations about change from his twenty.

Midafternoon the gold car came wending through the leafy, shadowed streets leading to the town's main square. Teo was unusually wary, gliding through on his initial approach. Old white men gathered at the wrought-iron bench encircling a large ironwood tree. Others sat facing the square in front of the courthouse. Doubling back, he parked on a side street a block or two from the courthouse. Adjusted his sunglasses and panama hat.

He was self-conscious in a way he hadn't been in a long time. An old black man among old white men.

Teo walked toward the steps of the courthouse. One of the men, a face crisscrossed with so many tiny wrinkles that it resembled a cutting block, nodded and smiled knowingly as Teo mounted the first step.

"Hey, buddy!"

"How you all doing today?"

"You here for the dig?" the man smirked, pointing to the trench with workers and shovels in the middle of the cobblestone street. His partner on the flower stoop steadily watched the activity. The man explained to Teo that a previously unknown gravesite had been discovered following a ruptured water main and was being excavated.

Across the street, a man, dappled piebald by the tree's shade, sat fidgeting with a battery-powered shaver he kept removing from a pocket of his overalls. He would worry it across one cheek, then the other. He'd then tilt his head sideways, rocking back and forth like an autistic. A few minutes later he repeated the little ritual.

"Local color?" Teo asked.

"Part of our permanent collection," the seated man snuffled. "He's all right, though. Just can't see nothing."

He was an hour back into his room when Teo decided to stop staring at the leak marks on the ceiling. He thought he might get some supper.

So what had Teo learned the first day? That the family had retained the counsel of Davenport, Sayles and Powers. Coots had probably put a bug in a McKendree lawyer's ear. Part of some grand vendetta against Toaks—Teo was sure of it.

He couldn't bring himself again to Huddle House. Teo settled for a Carolina-blue log cabin serving vaguely ethnic red sauce ladled into scabrous yellow tortilla shells with scorched hamburger meat. The next day was the same cardinal smear on top of a white wad billed as spaghetti.

As for the remaining Thursday and Friday, there was no new information. Teo found out that the family had made inquires into all his properties, his businesses, even his automobile.

But never spoke to him. To Tobias McKendree. Broad face, no neck, sidewall eyes. Pair of overalls, the same all three days in Teo's surveillance. Teo talked around him—found he was a piss-poor crooked cop before the blinding, rode sheriff's shotgun with his brother, nephews, then grandnephews till weakened generational responsibility had diminished obligation and they parked him comatose under a tree. Now: prospect of new money brought an awakening.

A white minister came to the excavation site, accompanied by a television crew. Tobias had been propped against the sandstone court building and Teo brought himself to stand next to him, observed his chafed jowls, his dried stalk of chaw adhering to the chin, his two-toned shoes, the sunglasses riding up his forehead as he repeatedly wiped the sweat from the bridge of his nose. In spite of himself, struck by how much the man's old dull bulbs reminded him of Pawpaw's—his father's—glaucous eyes. Then called himself an ass for not putting Tobias together with the mention of Coots' "silent partner" earlier.

The minister began what Teo took to be a sermon. His spectacles gleamed under the camera lighting overhead, two white disks, and he inclined his head much like a parrot contemplating a shiny object. "Before these, our dead, think on me, of John 11:33—"And Jesus lifted his eyes and said, "Father, I thank you for hearing me, and know that you always hear me; but because of the crowd that surrounds me I said it so that they should believe that you sent me." After saying this, he cried out in a great voice: Lazarus, come out here. And the man who had died came out, with his hands and feet wrapped in bandages, and his face tied up in cloth. Jesus said to them: untie him and let him go.'

"We have before us, some more of the dead arising—seventy-four, to be exact. But just as Jesus had admonished the townspeople, we too must—untie them. And let them go . . ."

"Preacher there can really preach, don't ye think?" the wrinkle-scarred curb-sitter whispered. He had made a beeline for Teo in the small crowd, sidling up beside him.

"He's all right," Teo nodded, noncommittal. For the intoned Bible verse and the blind joker beside him had pulled him into a past place, a nest he did not want to foul. Pawpaw used to have all nine of his boys line up. Sightless, held each in turn by the wrist in his claw. Had them reciting memorized scripture. Those that got it wrong got walloped.

On the ride back, the moon was a rat's yellow eye in a snout of raggedy cloud. Truth told, the Lazarus story frightened him. Always had. Teo's attention caught the fluorescent orange or bright green gauges of sports cars as they swooshed past. The man already died once. Ugly and painful, but it was done, finito. But then Lazarus was brought back and eventually had to do it all over again. And knew already what to expect.

XIII

Rachel's cat, for the past two weeks, had ruled her mother's house in the East Arlington neighborhood not far from Rachel's law office. Initially, the visit was to be for only a couple of weeks—following a breach in the roof by a falling tree, Rachel's home had become infested with small German roaches and needed to be tented and fumigated. The insecticide was said to be toxic for small animals days afterward; Rachel had planned to have the cat stay at her mother's place only as long as the vet deemed necessary. Rachel's mother, however, a ninety-two-year-old widow who lived by herself, was so completely taken with the creature (an obese but surprisingly spry yellow tabby) that she wheedled an extension with each visit.

The cat sprinted about the den floor between Rachel, Feddy, and Rachel's mother. For a second or two it would lie on its back, flipping a cracked beet-red rubber ring between both the hind- and forepaws; then it would suddenly fling the small rubber doughnut onto the carpet, leap into the air, and bounce after it. Feddy attempted to inject himself into the cat's play by grabbing at the toy but—as cats do, when you try to participate in their private games—the tabby immediately curled away and left in a huff.

Rachel's mother turned from the conversation with her daughter and addressed her attention to Feddy. "Hey, fatso! You're getting a little belly there. I bet there isn't a house between here and Gainesville where you couldn't find the kitchen." The skinny nonagenarian draped her arm over the back of her kitchen chair and grinned. Rachel simply shook her head.

Feddy, studying the old woman, couldn't recount the day when he'd seen Rachel's mother without her jogging suit and T-shirt. Today: ivy-green track pants and a T with a drawing of three little kittens approaching on the front, three little anuses under dancing tails on the back.

"You know—now no offense, Miss Ennis—but for someone who was once a social worker, a profession that requires an understanding of the human condition; knowledge and empathy regarding the pull of temptation—you've no heart. You are a sad stone of a woman," Feddy grinned back. The cat then sprinted back into the den, pouncing upon the rubber ring. "Isn't that a pessary?" Feddy asked.

"Hmm? You know, I think you're right. That little scamp's been into everything lately."

Moving through the house—he had excused himself to go to the old woman's bathroom since the downstairs commode was broken—Feddy was confounded with musk and memory. The blur—as if swimming in a warm sea and suddenly coming upon a cold current—led him to a spot at the foot of the stairs, a mote-speckled shaft of sunlight through a window looking out onto a backyard. Two bullet-headed black boys were missling rocks at bottles propped on cinder blocks. The sun-warmed mustiness seemed to rub in his face some memory of ancient perfume and first lust. Remote. Was it Rachel's mother? God forbid that skinny-assed harpy was the agent of his adolescent wet dreams . . . In the middle of the dark cool hallway, right in front of the bathroom, was a bottom-lit dusty painting of a dog, what looked to be a collie. A portrait. It was one of those 1950-style oils of muted aquamarine lines and beige and rose pastels. Found he was constipated before the visage staring through the bathroom door.

"Well, that's a first for me, Miss Ennis. A shrine to Lassie."

"The painting up there? That's Laiki, the Russian cosmonaut

dog. Picked it up in Cleveland, a few years after the collapse of the Soviet Union, all sorts of Russian art flooded the market. You know, up until Tipsy here, I've always been more of a dog person. And that dog's special: first living creature to die in outer space."

They supped by old-folk's clock: dinner at one in the afternoon. Rachel's mother had her carry from the kitchen a yellow oil and red syrup concoction with floating drumsticks. Followed that by a moist bloat of cabbage. She sat beaming.

Rachel and Feddy picked at their food, though Feddy, in trying to be polite, scooted his fork more vigorously about the plate.

Rachel calmly put her fork down.

"You win. In your day, you have come up with some winners. But this one belongs in your top fifty—no, top ten, Ma. What, for chrissakes, is this?"

"New recipe I found in the back of a *Tanner* that was lying about the house, with my own variations. Sweet and Sour Cherry Chicken."

The Bessie Coleman Tribute and Heritage Festival at States Beach was to begin that afternoon. For the second time in just as many months some shade-tree mechanic was working on Feddy's broke-down Gremlin, though he was easily able to cadge a ride to the island from Rachel. The work came in convincing Sharon that she shouldn't carry him. Feddy gave excuses of possible violence from the young hardheads and gangbangers (he was sure the idea of territorial shootings would grab her attention) and gas prices as deterrents. The truth of the matter was that he wanted to orchestrate running into Jesmond and he didn't need Sharon glued to his side. He hadn't spoken to his son since their battle royale. He found out from Seth's sons that Jesmond had been knocking back drinks in clubs and had to be escorted out on more than one occasion. And he checked up on Ed Richmond. Feddy had heard stories that Ed was also getting drunk at some bar off-base, and that he bragged about a prenuptial with his wife that included a sex schedule between them. When she came up pregnant he refused to allow her to leave the kitchen, interrogating her as to who was the baby's daddy until she peed on the kitchen floor. He then sat on her and rubbed her face in it. Swore that if she bore a child not of their union it was going to be an orphan.

It took Feddy and Rachel an hour and a half to get to States Beach with most of the tie-up occurring at the ferry. It was already oppressively hot. Dotted about a sandy hillock were three or four small fluorescent yellow yard posters advertising Adam Finchem for Fifth District councilman. A child in torn shorts removed one of the signs and ran up to its mother, flapping it before her like a fan.

The cars were packed eight deep in all six loading lanes. A food vendor panted from a webbed lawn chair beneath a beach umbrella, hiding from the sun. The shiny metal warmer was unfortunately positioned seemingly to maximize the number of people squinting—it was like a reflecting mirror. Auto visors were angled, as were heads, and some occupants took to standing outside their cars with their backs to the ferry gate, annoyed and brushing away midges. Finally somebody approached the vendor and, after a brief shouting match, he reluctantly wheeled the cart so that it was perpendicular to the sun.

The park adjacent to States Beach was already filled to capacity. Rachel glided her BMW from cluster to cluster of revelers, stopping and greeting each group with a toot of her horn and, leaning either through her window or across Feddy through his, exchanging pleasantries and gossip.

A quartet—three bald men, a stout busty woman—were playing bid whist on one of the few shaded picnic tables. They had arrived early that morning and by midday they were well into red-rimmed eyes. The woman wore a garishly sequined green and yellow blouse and camouflage Bermuda shorts along with a straw beach hat. Nesting in her spot, she looked smug and self-satisfied. Also had a watch on an ankle—Feddy caught her peering through her cards onto the crooked foot under the table.

Rachel was able to park near the stage, the VIP section. Red, white, and blue crepe ribbons crisscrossed the dais and white lilies bowed over the Plexiglas-vase centerpiece midtable. The Greater Timothy Gospel Singers were just leaving the platform as Bernard Irwin strode up to the microphone. He was somewhat deliberate in his approach to the podium because of a step his short legs needed to climb.

"The Greater Timothy Choir, ladies and gentlemen!" Bernard applauded. "Truly a blessing upon the community—"

"We have a CD!" one of the retreating singers shouted.

Bernard next introduced his right holiness, the Reverend Dante Phillips. The pastor strode up in what for all intents and purposes could only be called a Nehru jacket—a mustard-colored high-collared body coat over rust-colored pants, light brown shoes.

"How you all doing? Do we have the Lord's blessing today?"

The crowd roared back in the affirmative.

"We are gathered here, this special day, to honor a historical African-American woman, Bessie Coleman." The reverend wiped his forehead with a white handkerchief and waited for the crowd to settle. He took a sip of water from a plastic container beneath the microphone. "But wait a minute now— Who of you out there can tell me who this woman really was? Come on, somebody. You—" Reverend Phillips pointed at an old man leaning against a cane.

"First black woman flyer, airplanes, that is—from right here in Johnsonville," the old man shouted, beaming.

"That's right, sir— See what a repository of wisdom we have in our community? Yes, she was a strong black woman who climbed over many an obstacle to get a little closer to heaven. But I'm going to ask you all another question: How was she able to climb up there?" Reverend Phillips made a dog-paddling motion in the air. "She was not the angel Gabriel. God did not bless her with wings. No, man!" Phillips then gestured with both hands as if lifting a weight over his head. "See, an airplane is a mechanical thing, a *man*-made thing, God blessed her with a *community!* It was our *community* that was the wind beneath her wings . . ."

Feddy stirred through the crowd milling before the stage and headed toward the old miniature boardwalk. Since his last visit they had spruced up the place. The little diner had been cleaned and painted. And though the grill and kitchen were not formally being used, scantily clad brown bodies clamored and patted the counter for sandwiches and soft drinks. The stairs to the rooms had been closed off with a chicken-wire gate, and a security guard half dozed under an umbrella wedged above him.

Teo was pissed and confounded. Loyalties. Children.

The night before last he had been over at Feddy's apartment—no, *his* apartment! The boy pretending he's paying rent . . . And there was Feddy yammering about going to Louisiana sometime in the near future to spread Father Clemons's ashes.

"The man's not even dead yet."

"No, Pop."

"So you telling me this—what? Make me jealous? This a hint that you want me to hurry up? If I remember correctly, he's that walleyed motherfucker. Child molester."

"No, Pop. That was your buddy, Ace, that messed with kids."

"Hmm. But he was that walleyed son of a bitch though, right? No other relatives?"

"He has a brother and a sister. But his sister's got Alzheimer's and his brother, I think, is ten, twenty years older than him and in a nursing home."

"Hell. Suspect the whole passel of 'em's walleyed. Anyway, it's me you've got to worry about, son, here among the living. Not some dead—near dead—black-assed son of a bitch who I'm sure will be more than well buried by those idol worshipers in Rome. Should've never sent you to that school. Ruined you."

"So why'd you do it?"

"Only decent school for pickannies back then. You take what you can get."

It pissed Teo off that he might have needed to explain to Feddy the nuances of parental sensitivities. It pissed Teo off that he found himself getting almost teary-eyed and achy—jealous even—over his son's solicitousness over some old teacher's future as ash chunks and bone char. This was *his* son!

Feddy tried to make sure he understood.

The peace that surpasseth understanding.

"It's those priests and nuns that ran the little schools and churches that are in trouble. Taking a vow of poverty didn't leave them with much to fall back on. There's some colored priest-nun-whatever retirement home for them in Chicago but it's a shitty place, some warehouse or icehouse they converted."

"Sad to hear that the world's unfair. Just remember: I'm your deddy. Better be there for me, all I'm saying."

And to top it all off he had a pimple. Two. More than seventy years on the face of this planet and popping up with zits. Teo studied the red "sunny-side up" spots in his rearview mirror—maybe noseeum fly bites. Still, one didn't go begging favors from the grand pooh-bah looking like you've been eating Typhoid Mary's pussy. Teo pulled into a Circle K parking lot, came out with a box of Band-Aids. He situated the Disney-character tabs to cover the pimples the maximum distance from each other like a geometry problem.

The last time he had seen his moneyman, his Mr. Deep Pockets, his bank—a thin-as-a-whippet Irisher—was a decade ago, at least. And as to physically going down to his mansion on the river in Ortega? The early 1970s, when looking liberal looked good. Teo in his sculpted Afro, hunched over and signing papers with Mr. Deep Pockets and his muttonchops. What a photo op for the *Johnsonville Times Union*—a small-business loan and investment capital for a vigorous black entrepreneur. Teo never looked so good.

He stood on the aged pink brick steps of the house after his car had been buzzed in through the gate. Teo had to again buzz an intercom and was led through an obstacle course of low-lying tables with framed photographs, large books, and crap that, best he could describe, belied the title "knickknacks." An honest-to-God butler was his guide. The butler was much younger than Teo, looked to be in his midforties, slightly potbellied, in black jeans and a white polo shirt.

The two of them hopped up another short set of steps and stood before a closed pair of heavy wooden doors through which a loud thrum droned. "You can go on in," the butler said. He then left.

Inside, Teo found himself on a deck, standing above his Deep Pockets, his moneyman, his snarl of Irish muscle—the man churning furiously an Australian crawl in a stationary pool and some ear-splitting Wagner mayhem, "Ride of the Valkyries."

The soup of human events at the Bessie Coleman Festival bobbed forth groups of all kinds: pubescent glittery girls in thin plastic stiletto heels; boys in low-slung trousers over calico boxer shorts moving in Brownian motion; families with slack-jawed kiddies slung atop their fathers' necks. Jesmond was not yet visibly inebriated— though he did sway into the path of a boy running and twirling a sign like a helicopter propeller. The boy ricocheted from him and bounced into crowd aimed toward the beach.

Peaches walked beside him. Fearful and disgusted. She was afraid of Special Ed—but not so afraid as to avoid a chance to humiliate her husband, even if it meant being draped about some disgustingly high and drunk kid in public.

Jesmond finally allowed himself to be pulled in tow to the main stage, which held Bernard Irwin and the Reverend Dante Phillips. They were in the middle of an exchange of playful jibes between acts while the Four Blind Gospel Boys were being led off the stage, each with a hand upon the shoulder in front.

"You know, Bennie, I remember when before you became Mr. High and Mighty—Mr. Hollywood—that our little posse would be ripping through the neighborhood, right there on 133rd and Maxwell, and you'd be tagging behind, yelling, 'Wait for me! Wait for me!'"

"And, Rev, now that I'm in Hollywood, that's all I hear from you—'Wait for me! Wait for me!'"

A laugh rippled through the crowd.

"Well, unfortunately, you all will have to wait a little while longer—we still have a full plate of festivities before we get to the main event this evening. What is that again, Reverend Phillips?"

"A sister who is a direct spiritual descendant of Bessie Coleman, Leontyne Prunt, is gonna dazzle us with some aerial concoctions flying an old-fashioned airplane, along with fireworks—but till then let me introduce a group of young men and women very near and dear to my heart . . . Are you all ready?"

The crowd roared.

"I mean are you ready to get kronked? To get down and get kronked for Christ?" When the crowd only tepidly responded, Reverend Phillips pulled his lips closer to the microphone and yelled, "ARE YOU READY TO GET KRONKED FOR CHRIST?"

The crowd and Jesmond immediately shouted *"YES!"* And a bass, guitar, piano, and drums came in on the downbeat of a count.

From his vantage point Jesmond woozily thought he recognized Bayonne on the stage. If it was Bayonne, he was in costume. Jesmond was aware that in his altered state it all might be a trick of perception. Still, there among the line of performers in multicolored wigs and spangled costumes, Jesmond felt almost certain that it was Bayonne breakdancing with a partner behind a mimed reenactment of Jacob wrestling with the angel.

"I'm not going back to that rat hole!" Peaches seethed. For the past two nights they'd slept in Coots's house on the north side. Still with the mattress on the floor. Still with the growling Dobermans behind closed doors. Now with greasy take-out bags piled into greasy take-out bags like nesting dolls. Peaches and Jesmond weren't sure yet whether that was Special Ed's car at the bottom of the street. Cash had told Jesmond that pregnant women like to be thought of as sexy so Jesmond kept pawing at her cootie till she gave in the first night. The second night—the vault was shut. She slept bunched against the wall, her feet to him.

After the performance, Jesmond knew that it was Bayonne, for he strode up to the two of them, still in greasepaint and costume. "This is a powerful day," Bayonne said to them, breathless. "A powerful day! You hear me!"

Feddy was corralled into joining a game of pinochle under a portable canvas shade. Warm sea breezes carried the scent of pine and the smell of sausages and ribs from various grills. His stomach grumbled. Rachel had long disappeared, folding into the dignitaries tiered upon the stage and dais. Initially, Feddy was stuck meandering back and forth in the no-man's-land between parking lot A and the stage—stopping twice at a funnel-cake stand, making no purchase, however—when a sympathetic voice yelled his name. Melan was passing playing cards under a listlessly fluttering yellow and white easy-assemble canopy.

"All right. You hear me? We got it set now—this man here is my partner. Pete, why don't you get up a spell and let Feddy have your seat." A pallid green butterfly grazed Melan's hairy wrist as he held a card suspended, middeal.

The fourth at the table was Leontyne Prunt, the featured air performer. Melan winked at Feddy as he sat back in his chair. The woman was petite and tawny. Almond-shaped eyes, soft curly hair, muscular calves. Ce-Ce was nowhere to be seen.

"Jeeta Mess-qui-ta!" Bernard Irwin brayed from the podium.

"She's not even from here," Leontyne the Aviatrix began. "Actually from Atlanta—Bessie Coleman— Texas. Not Georgia. Lived in Chicago. Did a lot of flying all over, California, New York. Exhibitions in big places. Died here, though. She was gonna do a stunt right over there when the co-pilot lost control. The plane flipped over and she wasn't buckled in so she fell, some three thousand feet.

Copilot burned up in the plane when it hit a tree. We playing cut-throat?"

Feddy started for a moment. So farsighted, thought he saw Jesmond at a T-shirt booth.

What he lacks in style he makes up for in determination, Teo thought. Thrashed the water like a Weed Whacker. Splashes ghosted the window like watermarks. The music began to hurt Teo's ears.

Teo found a corner in this tiny, cluttered lanai, sat atop stacked eighty-pound sacks of water-softener salt. First Teo folded his earlobes into his ear canals, then hunted desperately for a surmised remote, which he found under a black silk Chinese bathrobe. (Groping through the robe left Teo feeling as if he'd been digging through the man's soiled laundry.) Held the gizmo over his head and pushed buttons for dear life. Teo saw it as a compromise, lowering the volume to *light pain* from *heavy*.

The man still fought water.

Forty-five minutes. Teo sat on top of the salt pile for forty-five minutes watching the man flail nonstop. And at no time did his one-time-benefactor acknowledge Teo's presence. Teo took this behavior as a response to his request earlier by phone. Finally, Teo had enough. Sun won't shine on the same dog's ass twice. Called moneybags a cocksucker. Upped and left.

Irwin gestured for them to lift Bobby Jackson up onto the stage. Feddy saw that the boy was petrified. Bobby Jackson stood in rictus with the stubby remains of his teeth bared while Irwin bunched him in close and pulled him to the microphone. The boy then tried to mirror the actor's maniacal strut and delivery. One looked like a bantam rooster on acid; the other, its sad simulacrum. They talked between them on the stage about the forthcoming film biography of Jackson's life.

The aviatrix had left. Feddy leaned across the table as Melan motioned him forward. "She don't have to be back home until Monday," Melan grinned. "I can't wait to see fly-girl."

"You're one lucky motherfucker. How'd you hook her?" Feddy asked.

Melan held up his backstage pass. Feddy shook his head. He then pointed to Bobby Jackson up on the stage. "The boy's scared shitless."

"Deer in headlights," Melan agreed.

It didn't take any advanced psychology degree to see that the Jackson boy was emotionally rickety. For a flicker, paternal pang from Feddy. Outrage against the wicked destroyers of men.

Feddy plunged into the swirl, bumping through security, one of whom held a cup of yellow coffee that plashed down his pant leg. Feddy's goal was just beyond the spot he thought he saw Jesmond. He would decide where to follow from there.

A woman approached him as he approached his target. The bottom and top parts of her bathing suit didn't match and she wore ridiculously oversized pink sunglasses. It was like staring at the Sunday funnies. Feddy smiled but the woman didn't reciprocate. It was hard to tell if she even saw him or was looking elsewhere. And he lost track of Jesmond.

Bayonne saw Feddy, though, and rushed up. "Damn, I'm glad to see you, Mr. Toak. You listening to that up there? For years Deddy's been kissing that woman's ass to help repair the roof in his church and get a learning center in the neighborhood. Now Reverend Phillip is cool and all, but why in the hell does he need a million bucks for a gym? You see that white Bentley he's got parked out here?" Up on the stage, the Jackson boy was squeezed between Irwin, Phillips, and one of the district councilwomen, each maniacally leering and gripping a gigantic replica of a check. The amount was for $1.1 million.

"Them that gots, gets, I guess," Feddy said. In front of them passed a stooped little man walking frantically behind some sort of guinea fowl. It wore a tiny green jacket tethered to a box the man was carrying. "I tell you, you see some goddam freaky things," Bayonne said. Continued: "They turned him out in County. That Jackson kid. It was a crime to put that boy in there with those adult men." A passel of children bobbed behind the man as he disappeared into the crowd. "You know, when I was in there somebody actually gave me a little paper book—*Who's your Daddy?*—it was how to survive in prison as somebody's punk." Feddy stared at Bayonne. Didn't know what to say so chucked him in the arm, then patted the spot.

"You seen Jesmond?" Feddy asked.

"About fifteen, twenty minutes ago. He's somewhere around."

"Thanks, son."

He was like a one-armed boxer at a carnival side event: so much strength and leftover poise but pitiful and a geek still, spilt. His decline made him think of certain things, lately. Teo had decided upon a simple funeral. None of this drama of special requests and field trips. Good casket, though. Lead-lined, with zinc, then wood, was what he'd already purchased. He had paid cash in advance a couple of years ago. Not that he kept it bedside; he tried to enlist Feddy's participation—Feddy's response was a simpleton's "yeah, okay"—and give him copies of the agreement so that at the last minute they didn't try to substitute that pressed-wood crap. And he would be buried at St. Timothy's, the little graveyard next to the church. (Not that depressing, deserted cemetery property. No! No upkeep—the last time anyone was put there was more than a quarter century ago.) Gravestone would be white marble; THEODORE TOAK it would say, then, FATHER . . . But then there was his family to consider, his brothers—Pritchett, Sonny, Ray, Simon, Zeke, Darley, Verk, Enoch, Toon. And Pawpaw. Maybe he should be buried with the family. Teo hurriedly pressed Feddy's number into the car phone.

A thin woman in beige slacks was the first to call attention to

Feddy as he approached the little posse of elderly men and women in their golf carts. They were stationed at the gated entrance to Carrington Whispers. "May I help you?" the Mr. Smith said of the two—Feddy assumed it was Mr. and Mrs. Smith, given the name sprawled across their cart. "You all must be security," Feddy said. "In a manner of speaking," Mr. Smith responded, gliding his cart up to Feddy. He stopped a dime short of Feddy's shoes. "You don't know what might pop up." From the main stage came the muffled thumping of a bass. "Interested in the area?" the man asked. "Got me a place at States Beach," Feddy lied. Feddy's phone was on pocket trill but he felt nothing, for his attention was caught up with the butt of a rifle jutting from a golf bag, poorly camouflaged with a too-small five-iron head cover.

Jesmond stood blinking through the diminishing daylight, spastically danced a few steps with Peaches at the foot of the stage. A sinewy, eel-like woman sang, a klaxon of brass instruments answered, and parts of the crowd shuffled in unison to a backbeat. Being drunk or high made you stupid, he knew that; knew that Peaches would just as soon chuck him as Special Ed but they had the baby's future to consider. She read too much into her tabloids and Montel Williams.

Feddy stood at the far end of the dancing mass, a good distance away from the live band. Feddy had not seen him but could imagine how his son felt—somebody standing on the edge there, looking to do you harm. It was unlikely Special Ed would do anything in public. Still . . .

People had begun to turn and shout and point. Across a lurid orange sky was the barest speck, then the larger bead of a propeller plane. Searchlights ignited the horizon, and an errant lime-green firework popped. The soft putt-putt of the plane could be heard before gradually emerging atop the violet edge of the sea.

He had driven to his hospital. Sat in the car with the windows down, air conditioner ticking. Teo caught himself counting the ticks. Under an ironwood tree—branches thick and sinewed like a wrestler's thighs—someone had parked a corrugated metal trailer. Self-pity now sloshed into shame—back and forth. And it was becoming dark. The purple outline of the trees fused to the shape of the building. Teo swore he saw folk scurrying to the back in shadow. The city was inconsistent in dealing with its homeless. He left the car, removed the padlock, and entered his building, shouting. But in the hollow that followed, nothing but the susurrus of a scraping leaf.

The little plane blatted over the beachfront, performed loop-the-loops and barrel rolls, pulling paper and particulate debris in its wake. A dollar bill pressed against Feddy's forehead for a moment before fluttering off in a gust. A little boy in puffed-up swim shorts leaped after it through the crowd before giving up with a moue. Feddy pushed his way back to the parking lot, uneasy, a huge mouth in the pit of his stomach that seemed to chew through his shirt, moaning and yelling at him for losing something, someone.

"Hey."

Feddy looked up. He'd been leaning against Rachel's BMW.

"Feddy—over here, dumb-ass." Melan sat up, submerged in a lawn chair in knee-high weeds behind the VIP cars. His feet were propped up on an ice chest. "Wasn't she a honey?"

"Don't know what she'd want with a moldy oldie conk-haired motherfucker like you."

"It'd be nice if you answered your cell. Tried to call you—tell you that I'd seen your son."

Feddy quickly reached into his pocket and pulled out his phone. Saw that Melan had called. Teo, too.

"Ain't gonna do shit to pick up now. He looked all right, Feddy. Had his pregnant chick with him. Cock on the block." Raked his mustache with a finger as he spoke.

Dark, the hospital gave Teo the willies. Loony-looking—with the meek dusk pushing through the untended trees that pressed and creaked and cracked the lobby glass, everything loony—the chairs, the counter, the photographs on the wall, the dead plants, the wheelchair at the end of the corridor. Had that been there? He spooked himself. Hurriedly wrapped chain and lock about the handles, then skedaddled.

They scattered in pursuit, drawn out like beads on a wire. Jesmond was very swift but Peaches was only able to half-run half-waddle through the crowd, so Special Ed's four beefy steroid- and hemorrhoid-hobbled henchmen gradually caught up and gathered about the woman, one by one, wheezing. Special Ed showed great poise in his meandering approach, stopping at a closing booth here and there, bought chili cheese fries, a huge grin for his wife by the time he met up with her. Jesmond had not turned around once, and chose the long drive back rather than risk being held up for the ferry.

"You think about it, all those stars and planets." Feddy was ruminating. On their drive back Rachel had opened the hatch roof. Feddy had reclined his seat. "They're all moving away. Starting with the one explosion, the Big Bang. Now normally an explosion, by definition, is a flash. It's only when you've got a special camera that can slow things down do we see the flying particles and garbage. So it's a matter of perspective: what's infinity to us, in our comprehension, so infinitesimally slow and loaded with darkness—is, somewhere, just a firecracker pop with crap to sweep up."

The radio mumbled scores of basketball games.

"Did you know the chick wasn't even born here? Bessie Coleman?" Feddy continued. The low moon poured graying light into the car.

"Didn't really find out about it till last week. We were so busy looking for what to celebrate that it kind of snowballed. Kinda sad, being that her only real connection with all this is that she died in Johnsonville. Pass me some of those Red Hots."

They drove in silence. Rachel cleared her throat. Two or three times a minute. Twenty, more or less. Then: "You know, what you said got me thinking. Darkness being probably a relative thing. Dark to us is night. But elsewhere it could be somebody's flash, or a full day.

"And when did we become scared of the dark? Ever wonder that? The womb's dark but we don't know anything else until we're born. Babies—babies cry no matter whether it's day or night. They don't cry just because it's dark. But then something happens. Night terrors. Creepy sounds maybe? I dunno. Is it two? Three? I wonder what's the age you figure out what darkness means—"

Book Three

XIV

From the beginning of hurricane season, Adam Finchem's name graced apartment lawns, traffic islands, the cement bases of Stop signs, and shop windows, along with innumerable footpaths throughout the city. ADAM FINCHEM FOR COUNCILMAN; ADAM FINCHEM FOR SCHOOL BOARD; ADAM FINCHEM FOR MAYOR; ADAM FINCHEM FOR JUDGE. The Finchem name leaned from not a few shopping carts piloted by the homeless downtown.

Medgar Coots had had the lawn signs printed. Had his minions plant the placards throughout the city, particularly near the courthouse and jail. Had destitute young black men approach the man familiarly in public. Spending the few hundred or so dollars was worth it. The intent was twofold: to harass Finchem, and to have his name percolating in the hearts and minds of the Johnsonville press and legal community. The *Times Union* had doggedly tracked down leads to a now defunct off-shore insurance company in the Bermudas. The company had, at one time, insured a good third of the poor blacks in the viatical debacle that had come to light—anonymous sources gave evidence that led to Dr. Finchem. The state's attorney had no alternative but to open the investigation, again. Medgar demonstratively and freely showed that he'd facilitated introductions between patients and Dr. Finchem, done on good faith, however. He presented to investigators the clinic log. There, somehow, a link was drawn between Dr. Finchem, the Smullian suicide, and Bayonne Burnett. "I'd known him—Smullian—through the HIV clinic," Medgar volunteered to investigators. "Well connected, probably could've gone anywhere, but I think he appreciated the anonymity the clinic provided. Morbidly obese, too. I suspect he suffered from that congenital disorder—gargantuan people with tiny hands and feet. Eat everything in sight. You have to chain the refrigerators closed. . . . And if I remember correctly, Mr. Smullian was rather promiscuous. Preferred black men. Young ones. There was one late night, I'd just closed the clinic—there he was in his Lexus under the parking light, burger in hand, and some head bobbing in front of the steering wheel."

He had no qualms about contaminating situations, one with the other. For Medgar let it be known that Bayonne may have introduced Finchem to Smullian—were they in cahoots in some scheme? More than a little alleged larceny may be at the root of things, Medgar would speculate to the various attorneys.

Medgar had finally gotten a hold of Toak the Elder's cemetery, too. Gummed instead of bitten—when he approached the old man again about the purchase there was little fight this time. Sold him some of his other properties, too. Just meekly insisted upon keeping the hospital, which Medgar didn't want anyway.

So, the final step in the acquisition of the graveyard was simply the old man's signature. Had to sit here and wait for Teo Toak, smack-dab in front of the evidence of an insignificant life: his bail bondsman's license, his certificate of appreciation from the Johnsonville NAACP, his 1978 letter of commendation from the Johnsonville Chamber of Commerce. And the photos: Teo and Ace Walker in a pretend spar, Teo and Jesse Jackson, Teo and mayors from 1976 to 1983. No photograph with his son, though. Of course this made sense—personal info and desperate circumstances were not a good mix. And typed, xeroxed, and framed:

True Friendship

1. When you are sad—I will hep you get drunk and plot revenge against the sorry bastard who made you sad.

2. When you are scared—I will rag on you about it every chance I get.
3. When you are worried—I willtell yo horrible stories about how much worse it could be until you quit whining.
4. When you are confused—I will use little words.
5. When you are sick—stay the hell away fro me untilyou are well again. I don't want whateveryou have.
6. When you fal—I will point and laugh at your clumsy ass.

This is my oath, Ipledge it to the end. "Why?" you may ask; "because you are my friend

Feddy narrowed his nose and pursed his lips before his first morning cup of black coffee, relished the bite, the bitterness. A quick pleasure but there you have it. Gentrification of the old neighborhood gave birth to the coffee shop, a little bohemian spot—twenty-year-olds with lip piercings, pioneering joggers with exercise strollers. Just down the street was the boarded-up residential hotel. Feddy crumpled a muffin, reshaped it into pellets, worried it into crumbs again.

Uncle Sam was a juggernaut when owed money. The garnish letters, the late-evening phone calls suggesting how one should comply. Threat-ridden. Persistently bad credit was like playing musical chairs, as Feddy saw it: at some point when the music stops there won't be anyplace left for him to sit. He once received a loan from a bank back in the 1980s. This he paid back in full. The loan officer was a wisecracking banking assistant who took a chance on him. Later indicted in a money-laundering scheme. Now—a bank would turn you down even if you just want to open a checking account.

He finally took a sip of his coffee. The brief pleasure sat squarely in the middle, between anticipation and satiation.

But overextension, dunning notices, living payday to payday— to be fucking broke! His $175 in checks circulated between three banks. They just had a newscast with a young woman being led away in plastic handcuffs for kiting less than that. For $175! For $175 he was courting an orange jumpsuit. And of the $536 paycheck advance from the check-cashing boutique? He calculated an interest rate of 28 percent.

Teo could help if he so chose. But when Feddy approached him with a systematic payment plan, Teo wouldn't even listen. Dumbed-down malice. He'd talk around and through the matter at hand. If pushed, Teo would offer jackass, off-the-fly solutions that no sensible person would take. All with a falsely stupid grin, as if he'd been the beacon of aid.

Feddy had asked Sharon to meet him at the coffee shop. By her behavior over the past few days he knew she would come indignant. She'd taken up smoking—again, she emphasized. Sharon had told Feddy that she had had enough of his shit, that she was tired of having to carry the brunt of their relationship, that he was a distant and cruel son of a bitch. Threw a bottle at Feddy that didn't break but ricocheted off him and was swallowed by an indoor plant. And that was it. The wad of her argument.

He saw her approach through the plate glass. A paisley yellow-and-green skirt that clung tightly about the hips seemed to exaggerate her thickness. A smallish red blouse rode up her midriff with each step as she stomped toward the coffee shop. And she wore her large, square glasses instead of her contacts. It was as if she were trying to show off that she could be ugly.

Sharon entered huffing. She didn't, at first, see Feddy in the chair, her glasses fogging from the air-conditioner chill, and for a minute, vacillated about going up to place an order before taking a seat in the corner easy chair.

Feddy walked to her. For a moment there played about her mouth a pleasure at seeing him, then a panic; finally, an anxious vindictiveness—the kind he had seen in women who, in coming to a decision about *their* heartbreak, attempt to jaggedly saw their pain into the targeted heart.

"What do you want, Feddy? This is one of the few mornings I have to myself."

"Thought I'd let you know I'm about to head down to St. Pete to see Father Clemons. He's dying in a hospice now. Dying." Feddy knew this was cheap. Pity—the emotion—he knew brought a certain pleasure to the person in whom it was invoked, disassembling. And manipulating pity as a tool—he'd try to beat her to the punch.

But the feint was seen, even anticipated, for she swooned into her panic: "You cocksuckers never fail," she said, almost in a normal voice. "You do dirt and now try to get me to feel sorry for you so you can slide by." She seemed to fish-pouch her cheeks deliberately, bulge her eyes. Feddy noticed she had on her old green rubber flip-flops, the ones that were worn to a slant at the heels. Wanted to demonstrate that she'd been left a cripple. "It's a wonder your son's not more fucked up than he is, though the motherfucker'll probably still end up in jail!"

Feddy's fingers dug into her shoulder, held. And she grew rigid in waiting, straining. As if that section of her upper arm could continue in dermal dialogue.

She began stroking his hand. Later—petting his fingers. He was at a loss. Then he felt coy, avid. And embarrassment was surfacing, for he felt himself getting hard and he was wearing only the sweatpants. Let himself occupy the thrill of ambivalence.

So she brought his middle finger to her open mouth and traced it around her lips. Heartache, anger, lust—flaring bursts. But fetid, too. Morning breath, greasy hair.

This wasn't one of his haunts, she wasn't known at the coffee shop. He let her fingers play about the elastic of his sweats.

She suddenly jerked them down and let it snap—the stretch band of the pants smacking his balls and exposing his dick. Feddy was still at half-mast.

He bent forward out of embarrassment and pain. Hiding and repositioning.

Sharon grinned maliciously. She got up from the chair and left the shop through the glass door—her ass stuck out, moving slowly and rhythmically through the wavy midmorning heat.

So. Not his most painful of breakups. But Feddy felt that whatever substance he took for a soul felt now like a leg that had fallen asleep.

Funny—a good three or four miles from the coffee shop he began to leak, ruminate. Several evenings ago she'd read both of Feddy's palms by moonlight. And was it last Saturday? While he was sleeping, she painted his toenails burnt orange.

XV

Feddy drove to St. Pete. Teo had hinted that he wanted to ride down with him.

"Still in the clutches of the old faggot?" It was Sunday. His father calling *him*. Feddy could hear Teo at the other end of the phone, rustling newspaper, pouring his coffee, muting the TV. He saw that he had phoned, twice, from his business—which was odd, for a Sunday. Sunday was the one day Teo would let himself pad about in his pajamas well into the afternoon, all day if he'd been entertaining a woman the night before. But then Feddy remembered that sometimes—on those rare Sundays when Teo extended his feelings of goodwill—Teo would come down to the business just to hang around Ernie. Did Teo feel sorry for him? Guilty? That Teo justified paying Ernie just above hourly wage for use of that back-room closet was criminal. Lonely, maybe? Ace and Teo were once such ace-boon-coons—maybe he was trying to recapture that old "back in the day" vibe. Feddy wondered. Usually during the summer—on those Sundays when pretending to be open for business—the door would be propped open, and an occasional muscular rattle of the venetian blinds would surge through the office, a ghost heralding some storm brewing off the coast. Teo's old Bakelite radio (acquired from a client—Teo didn't keep anything remotely worth stealing in sight) broadcasting the Sunday jazz venue on W-101 FM would compete with Ernie's television blaring wildlife and fishing shows from the back room. But today, when Teo called, he was by himself.

"He's in an old-folks' home in St. Pete, right? Dog pounds set up by evil and ungrateful kiddies. Never catch me in one of those sinkholes. Only things you ever see going in and out of those places are ambulances and Patty Hearses."

"No, Pop, he's not in a nursing home. I think I told you he'd been staying with another retired priest. Now, though, they've got him in hospice. The cancer's spread. Nothing else they can do now but control the pain."

"So you're going down to see him? To St. Pete? Been years since I've been down there." There was a pause. "St. Pete. Now just a few months ago I went somewhere on the west coast—Naples, I think it was—to see an old client that I'd bailed out more times than I'd care to keep track. Always showed up for his court dates, though. For his golden years, bought a glass-bottomed tour boat." Again the pause. "So, St. Pete?"

"Father Clemons is not doing well now, Pop. That's why they have him in hospice."

"That's a long ride to take in that piecy car."

Feddy had gently responded, "But this isn't gonna be a social visit. Nothing like that."

"No BFD to me, son. Just hate to think of you as one of those chumps all sweaty and doo-doo stank with car hoods up alongside the road, looking pathetic. But suit yourself. Just don't call me about a tow."

It worried Feddy how his father might have taken his rebuff. Admittedly selfish, the thought processes. Saw Teo trotting down to a lawyer, gleefully striking him from his will. And Feddy knew he had nothing else to fall back on after all his working years but his inheritance. Maybe he accumulated enough Social Security to get four or five hundred bucks a month—but where would he live as an old man? How would he eat? The nursing homes scattered around the neighborhood were pitiful. Wasn't the old-folks' home on LaSalle Street, for example, the one where fire ants swarmed through an open window, killing some bedridden old man?

Thus was Feddy's state of mind as he pulled into the parking lot of Father Clemons's hospice. It was heartening to see his friend in surroundings opposite his imaginings. At least by appearances. A soothing older Cuban woman led him to a comfortably appointed room looking out onto the Intracoastal. Lambent light—and Father Clemons didn't look like he was going to cash it in in the next minute or two. He looked comfortable, his legs under a Disney quilt on which Goofy surfed.

"How you feeling, Padre?"

"'Fair to middling'—always wanted to say that. Honestly, I think I'm taking up space. Don't think it's out of any sense of martyrdom because this is probably just the lull before the storm. But right now I feel like one of those jets queuing up at the airport, waiting for takeoff—and it's not very pleasant. Too lucid."

Feddy sat across from Father Clemons, on the twin of a chaise longue.

"You want to go somewhere?" Feddy asked. "I can take you somewhere if you like."

"No. I just need to appreciate the gift of being pain-free and awake.

"Remembering—memory—is too much a paradox, Feddy. There's the awful predicament of having to exclude in order to save. The mind can't hold everything as precious or worth keeping. It came to me a few days ago. I—remembered—how when I was teaching Palmer cursive (That's something lost now, the art of beautiful handwriting. Between e-mails and phones, no one cares about attractive script. Now my sister, brother, and I had wonderful, similar writing . . .), the kids, in correcting their mistakes, would trace over their script with erasers. Rubbing meticulously to where they leave behind a pink smudge mirroring what they wrote. That to me is memory. And memory is the mirror to suffering and pity.

"I was a chaplain over at County when the AIDS epidemic was peaking. I remember a couple, each loving and sincere with the other for years, and both of them were dying from AIDS. One of them—the 'healthier' one—was looking about his lover's face for a place to kiss. But even to brush his lips against his brow would have been too painful. So in lieu of a kiss, he would flutter his eyelash against his lover's lips."

Father Clemons got up went over to the water cooler. Feddy noticed he was wearing black dress shoes and black ribbed socks, brown plaid shorts, and a yellow island shirt screeching sunshine and leisure. "You look old-school," Feddy said. "Cool papa." Feddy paused. He ought not to poke Father Clemons with his worries but it was a compulsion. Of course it would be respectful if he kept his mouth shut and let the old man reminisce but he was alone here. Here being where, though? The land of the living? Feddy saw himself racing on the shoreline alongside some canoe carrying Father Clemons as it drifted farther and farther into open waters. When he'd visit Father Clemons when they were younger, the priest, whose room at the rectory was so spartan—a sagging twin bed with a black wool blanket, a splintery wood desk, and a kitchen chair—would go and sit upright on his bed and pull the desk toward him, as sign for Feddy to sit down in the chair. There, Feddy would "unburden." That was the word Father Clemons used. Feddy's Merlin. He'd lead him, made him think through his sentiment. He wanted the same cool comfort now. Besides, at the moment there was no ranting and raving. Maybe—selfishly, perhaps—the calm before the storm, but Feddy needed succor.

"You knew Ace Walker?"

"Asshole and bully."

"You remember he worked for my dad?"

"I knew him. It's a wonder your father wasn't ever sued just having him on the payroll."

"He died a few months ago. Same man that molested a friend of mine when she was a girl. He did boys, too. The weird thing—he saw himself as the savior in the community. Proud he helped a lot of the old folks in the neighborhood. Still a pitiful dick.

"It amazes me how people have these gaps and fill them in with crap. Crap spackling. And there's a man I think is worse than Ace because he's intelligent. A doc."

"I know. Dr. Coots."

The dark-skinned Cuban woman stuck her head in and asked Father Clemons if he needed anything. The priest asked if he could have some assistance back to his lounge chair. He'd been leaning on the table next to the cooler. Feddy embarrassingly stood up to help but the nurse shooed him away.

"You know, the thing is this," Feddy continued after Father Clemons settled back into the chaise, "I can't tell whether Coots behaves the way he does on purpose—that is, he intends to create the most damage possible—or just that he's damaged goods himself, with all these holes or misconnections."

"What does it matter to you?"

"Because he's messing with my son. At one time—though you can't actually say we were friends—we were at least partners. Business associates. Now, he knows I need my son back. Jesmond hasn't spoken to me for months. I've talked to Coots, and I'm sure playing shrink he's talked to Jesmond but I see him doing nothing but playing head games. Why? He seems to get a kick out of fucking up my son. And get a kick out of knowing that I see him doing it.

"That's why I ask you—what's the sense of it to him?"

He paused to watch the response of the priest. A boat towing a water-skier frothed the tributary coursing west. Father Clemons coughed politely, didn't say a word. Feddy knew he hadn't any right to feel hurt but he did, slighted. Feddy stared at him to see if a brow would raise—those white, wild, viny eyebrows against that beetle-black skin. Still Father Clemons didn't say or do anything. Let the silence become oppressive.

"Feddy, understand something." Father Clemons finally continued. "I'm not for long here so this is a major concern for me. And I'm awake right now. It's all too much—for anyone it would be too much. Like a flood and I'm drowning. The Crucifix, bobbing beside me, doesn't give much grip at the moment as a flotation device. The

fact that I will be leaving this life as I've known it for the past sev-
enty-odd years isn't sitting well with me right now. And all your
whining about Dr. Coots, your—philosophical—investigations
rolled into your bedside visit pisses me off."

There was a silence. The old priest cleared his throat. An insect
suddenly blew up outside and palped the glass, flew off.

"The bottom line is that you want me to tell you that your son
will be okay," Father Clemons muttered. "Fine then. Your Jesmond
will be fine. You have my blessing." He peevishly made a sign of the
cross.

"If you love your son, Feddy, you'll have to own up to the fact
that you were a poor excuse as a father. To him. Jesmond needs to
hear that from you because it's one of the few ways he'll see that the
way *you* behaved wasn't his fault. Coots doesn't matter. 'Feddy and
Jesmond' is all that matters. Go and get him back. You'll learn that,
sometimes, in being a parent, you abandon pride. So be a father.
Otherwise I don't want to hear about it."

Father Clemons stared at Feddy and sighed. "You and more than
ninety percent of the human population are afflicted with such
aches. Why? Because you couple. That's the one benefit derived
from my life choice—one of the few times I thank Christ for celi-
bacy. Mucking around as someone's lover or parent, you always find
yourself in a constantly shifting garden, either Eden or Gethsemane.
One or the other, Feddy, one or the other."

XVI

"Here are the results of the test. Look for yourself."

Medgar stood over Bayonne at the desk of his office downtown. The metal edge indented his duckish hips as he leaned over the young man, and Medgar's shadow shouldered out light as Bayonne bobbed about to read.

"That's a straightforward, qualitative test, either yes or no—the quantitative assay is something done when we want to know how big is the viral load you're carrying," Medgar said, darting his square finger over the paper. "And that there tells us that this one is a particularly virulent strain."

"I had an AIDS test before and it was negative."

"I know. I understand. You have to understand, though, that being HIV-negative at one point doesn't mean you're immune for life," Medgar softly replied.

"After Big Boy died, I took the test—he was positive, you know—and I was still negative. I don't understand."

"I know you don't." Medgar's fingers began drumming atop the desk. "Bayonne—I'm trying to decide if I should share this with you or not." He then minced over to the file cabinet, began rifling through the middle drawer. "You didn't know about this—I didn't know about it until recently." He plopped a manila envelope in front of Bayonne. "That's your insurance policy. Payable upon your death to fifty thousand dollars. You'd set that up with Finchem a while ago."

"Yeah. So? " Bayonne looked puzzled.

"Didn't Dr. Finchem do the examination, do up the papers for you?"

"And? *You* told me that that's a good idea, no matter what. 'Like having a little bank' is what you say."

"Yes. But I didn't expect you to cash it in so soon. Did you know that Finchem had you signing a viatical agreement at the same time? Look there, third paper from the top." Medgar stared at Bayonne. All the while, trembling. "Calm down, calm down. These are things, though, that need to be brought to light. I think he slipped the viaticals in there. Planned to backdate it when necessary. But that's not the worst of it, really." Medgar took to woolgathering, clicking a ballpoint against his chin.

"He infected you. Deliberately. I think the bastard—before he left us, our business—had planned you for a little cash reserve. This wouldn't be his first. I found out about some of his other patients as well." Then hurriedly explained inoculums and viral reservoirs, new and streamlined treatment regimens, side effects of Retrovir. "—And Finchem's back there, in all this, set up like a king. Pretty, brand-new house. Pretty, brand-new wife and tot. He's like a government witness—immune from prosecution. "

Bayonne was barely able to walk when he left. With each step, felt his legs shooting into his chest. Like squatting on an upward elevator.

Medgar peeked through the blinds, watched him stagger. If the mountain won't come to Mohammed, he reasoned.

XVII

A quiet Tuesday afternoon. Jesmond came upon Bayonne staring at the bricked-up fireplace, which had been painted black. Sprouted painted flames. Sarah and Ashley whimpered and growled, off in the garage office.

Bayonne was quiet, gently rocking. Lil' Monkey sat slumped and cross-legged on the mantelpiece, somberly picking nits from its little thigh, its little belly protruding like a middle-aged man's.

Jesmond lowered himself into a beanbag chair across from Bayonne.

"I'm got AIDS, man."

"You sure?"

"Yeah, I'm fuckin' sure!"

"Hold up, man. I mean how did you find out."

"I took the test. Coots told me."

"The skank's probably lying through his teeth." Outside, a singsong chirp penetrated the room.

"He showed me the test. Went over everything."

"Bayonne, he could have faked that as much as anything else."

"I've seen enough of those tests to know what it was. Anyway, he's got no reason to fuck with me like that." Bayonne took a pull from one of several beer bottles at his feet. "Shit," he sighed.

"Nowadays, man, it's not the death sentence it once was."

"Fine, dog. Let's just you and me switch places and you be the one with HIV."

"Bay, man—" Jesmond threw up his hands. He then pulled himself from the awkward squat he had settled into with the beanbag chair. He went to his room.

He would just add Bayonne's to the troubles on his list. They wouldn't be lost for company. Since the Bessie Coleman celebration he'd been doing his best to avoid any form of mood alteration—Jesmond had tried to explain to Peaches that he'd been high that day, that he was not actually predisposed to being a sissy or a coward. She wouldn't hear any of it, though. Jesmond had tried to call her several times, e-mailed, tracked down girlfriends as go-betweens—no response. Even though she was probably pregnant with his kid.

But Special Ed certainly was keeping tabs on him. Stalking—could describe it no other way. Either Peaches had given him up or he had ferreted it out someway, but he would call Jesmond on his cell phone to harass him. Most of the time he would just breathe. Though lately Special Ed had started extending invitations, "Just so we could get together. Talk about things." He had asked Jesmond just the other day to meet at Fresh Green Tomatoes, a health-food bistro, but common sense prevailed—Jesmond figured there was nothing to prevent Special Ed from having someone cut the brake line to his car while they were dining on tofu. And he knew where Jesmond stayed, too. There always seemed to be a Volvo prowling the periphery. Some poor attempt was made at poisoning the dogs—a lump of sirloin had been tied around a large pellet of d-CON. Jesmond found it on the patio in the backyard. "That's too bad," was Medgar's response when he told him about it. "This is what's known as collateral damage. Looks like you're going to have to find new furnishings. I'll give you a couple of weeks."

So, in addition to everything else, he now needed a place to stay.

It was a rainy summer. Yeasty rub of wet earth. Earthworm mounds—dirt blisters, he recalled a teacher saying. Jesmond stuck his head through the window space and looked up, mused at the trajectory needed to carry a ball of meat from the street over the roof and onto the concrete slab out back. Then the pang hit—Bayonne's plight settled upon him. Maybe. Maybe the blood samples were mislabeled. Or Medgar was lying. Or maybe all the worlds he knew were simply, slowly, coming to a raggedy end.

"JESMOND!" Bayonne shouted from the den. "Jesmond, man, help me out. I need to get my hands on a motherfuckin' gun!"

Feddy's bees—the largest shipment—were scheduled to arrive in one to two weeks. The best estimate. Haphazard weather patterns in the Caribbean led to unpredictable schedules. Two hurricanes brewing. One, by the looks of it, seemed poised to head into the Gulf of Mexico. The other, at the moment still off the coast of Africa, was more worrisome. The radar map showed feathery, delicate white bands gradually gathering into a ball of worsted yarn. It had the markings of the most ominous of the doomsday scenarios. And the computer models so gleefully televised by the local stations showed it making a bull's-eye right at the First Coast.

"Do the math!" Melan admonished Feddy. "I know you think I'm semiliterate after your years-plus of graduate education but, homeboy, I did at one point graduate from FAMU—almost in accounting, too! The bottom line is you ain't looking at any bottom line. The costs—and risks—you bring on sneaking this freaky-ass mess into the country . . . It's stupid, man. Not to mention that you put me at fuckin' risk. . . . Damn, Feddy. Why not bees that at least make some goddam honey! No, you get these little flesh-eating zombies that do what? Make shit?"

That Melan went off on something so tangential and inconsequential as his little project spoke volumes to Feddy. There were rumblings about moving government cargo up the coast to Kings Bay, Georgia, changing the status of the Johnsonville port. Besides the potential layoffs, a status change would mean less money in the city coffers, which, in turn, would mean that the city (and probably the state, too, since that meant money was leaving Florida) would be micromanaging day-to-day operations, since something had to be amiss to displease the feds. "After this one, I'm through then,"

Feddy answered. "I'd gladly close up shop now but the shipment's already on the way. And let me bite the bullet on the Used Clothes for Africa—I'll go ahead and shut that up, too."

Melan visibly relaxed, stubbing a cigarette around the soda-can hole. "I think it'll only be for a little while. Just till this stuff blows by about the feds withdrawing. Before you know it you'll be back out there pushing the Toak Fall Line," Melan grinned. "How's Jesmond?"

"Dunno. Haven't seen him for months."

"Grandpa yet?"

"Doubt it. Too early. Besides, my son screwing and knocking up a married woman isn't one of those things that make me walk around and hand out cigars. This Papa Richmond is supposed to be a psycho. The guys I work with say that he wants to, quote, take my son, gut and fillet him like a scum-sucking catfish, unquote."

"Times like this I wish my job had the clout that it had in the old days. You talk to the old cats. Then—say the word and the guy would've ended up in a crab trap somewhere in the St. Johns."

"Naw, man, that's not you."

"Not you either, Feddy."

"That's my son. Changes the whole complexion of things. You should be an animal for your kids, should be willing to steal, kill for your child. You've got a daughter, Melan."

"I'll be the first to tell you I ain't jack as a daddy, and that's with her not in trouble. All I can say to you is *Hasa Salama Lakem*, brother."

"You gone Malcolm on me?" Feddy winked.

"Naw, man—you. You."

"Can I help you, please?" The salesclerk studied her split ends while she spoke. Jesmond quietly observed the two while putting together a Plexiglas dining-room table near the entrance. The customer was a harried mother trying to herd three rambunctious chil-

dren, one of whom had managed to wedge behind the floor model of
a towering wall unit and entertainment center—black particleboard
pressed to resembled teak, marbled gold mirrors, ghastly and glowing large plastic lilies alternating between pink and chartreuse. The
child, a girl, somehow had gotten pinned between the butt-end of
a fifty-inch television—which, at the moment, thundered with the
qualifying rounds of the Pepsi 500—and a profusion of electrical
cords, water and air hoses feeding an eighty-gallon freshwater tank.
"Can I help you?" the young woman sullenly repeated, this time
rewarding the woman with eye contact.

"Can you help me?" The mother glared—then darted her eyes to
her daughter's face greenly illuminated alongside a gold carp.

"Cash!" the salesclerk immediately barked into a handset.

It was only after considerable wheedling that Cash had been able
to convince Skooch to hire his girlfriend. Of course, the fact that she
was his girlfriend was not even intimated. "But all the sudden it hit
me—if she ain't workin', I ain't gettin' paid. You know, with the rent
and all," Cash had explained it to Jesmond. "And it ain't like she's
got the king's ransom of pussy."

Cash, however, was speechless when confronted with the girl
trapped behind the wall unit; instinct and experience told him not to
trust children. Both now instructed him to defer to the two women
present. He thus assumed the most bored expression he could muster. "Well?" was his contribution to the situation.

"The kid there, Cash."

"I dunno. I guess call 911."

"Right. I *want* to see Skooch go ballistic after a rescue crew's
busted the fish tank and television."

The mother, whose long, olive face at first worried over her
child's predicament, became inflamed. "Look, I just came here to
see about a living-room set, not some TV. Not paying for some TV.
If anything happens it's not Jeanie's fault. It's the store's responsibility to make this place child-proof anyway." The mother, her
black-and-white hound's-tooth pants suit a smidgen too small, then

took it upon herself to grab at her daughter alongside the wall. A sleeve snagged on a protruding bolt and the wall unit began to rock. "Mom!" the girl shouted.

Cash, looking about for any help, got wind of the fact, suddenly, that Jesmond was watching.

"I'm glad to see you're making yourself useful. Don't let me interrupt," Cash snapped.

"Hey. You seem to be handling. Keep it real, though." Jesmond gave a Power to the People fist, waved a screwdriver, though he moseyed over to the conflagration.

The three of them (Jesmond, Cash, Cash's girlfriend) eventually pulled her out through a complicated system of over and under twists and flexings of child and attachments. The little girl made a considerable show of her disgust toward Cash's girlfriend, who repeatedly snuffled a runny nose against a forearm tattoo (green unicorn, rainbow). And the mother left huffing and threatening to sue, her brood trailing.

Cash's girlfriend working at Rent-to-Own left her son, Kobe, to his own devices. Initially he was parked atop a returned divan with Jelly Bellies, watching the Cartoon Network on the store's plasma screen TV, while his mother tried to look convincing crowing about the advantages of incremental purchases and foldout beds, scrunched-up apartment dryers. But in just a few days Skooch scooted the kid out, bellowing that he didn't run a day care. Jesmond watched as the boy retaliated by playing just a few feet from the store's entrance until his mother would chase him off, then coming back to play again. Jesmond bought him a nylon Batman wallet from the Dollar Store. In it he had put two dollars, a bubble-gum team card of the 2006 Tampa Bay Buccaneers, and a piece of paper with his cell phone number. He told the boy to call him anytime he got scared.

Right now, Jesmond caught sight of Kobe dipping into Pete's Pawn Emporium, scurrying right behind the woman's three kids. The boy would ping from one business to another—food joints,

auto parts, pawnshop, comic book store, martial arts academy—
until he'd tire or they got tired of him. Then Kobe would sit still on
a concrete curb across the way and stare at the store as if to catch a
glimpse of his mother. "He didn't like to be in the trailer all by himself," Jesmond would later recount to Feddy.

Pete's Pawn Emporium, the dark magnet. Bikers, drug heads,
ex-cons—the pawnshop, with its black wrought-iron windows and
silently prowling Belgian shepherd, attracted more than its share of
violent and unpredictable beings. Jesmond knew the ten-speed Kobe
wanted in there—the boy had pleaded with Jesmond to accompany
him more than once, "Just to look."

"I don't think that place is so cool for Kobe to be hanging out,"
Jesmond said to Cash, pointing to the shop.

"Enough with the fuckin' mother hen." Cash lately had started
to sport blond highlights, black sideburns. Also had a white fluffy
bandage over an infected piercing of his right eyebrow. "Listen,
man—I'm starting to think you're showing too much interest in that
kid. Makes me wonder if you're a perv or something. Those are just
the dudes that surf the Internet, all buddy-buddy. The next thing
you know, you see them showing up on *Dateline* as Mr. Perv, part of
some kiddy-porn sting."

"Man—fuck you. I'm just trying to educate your dumb ass that
there's too much weirdness in the place for a kid to hang around like
it's a Toys 'Я' Us. I'm gonna go get him." Wind bloused the plastic
sheets draping the sofas and wall units as he left.

Inside Pete's Pawn Emporium, the Belgian shepherd stopped
pacing back and forth between the display cases to stare down Jesmond. Pete's had few patrons of color and his dog was known for its
particular dislike of black people. The rumor circulating was that
Pete was a neo-Nazi or a Klansman, even though his wife was Filipino. He never gave Jesmond any trouble. He just didn't speak.

"Honcho, come here," Pete said. The dog went and begrudgingly
collapsed at his feet.

Kobe was sitting on the glass counter between Pete's assistant and a man in a leather jacket and mud-crusted jeans. They had him in a hockey mask, holding a snub-nose .38. The two men chortled as he swung the gun between them. "Pow," Kobe repeated.

"Come on, Kobe. Time to get," Jesmond called.

"You got a cool kid, here," the biker said aloud, though not in the direction of Jesmond. "Gimme five, little dude," he said, holding his hand up to be slapped, but Kobe slid off the glass, ran off. Left the hockey mask on a center island of army-surplus canteens.

Outside the pawnshop, Kobe dawdled and didn't cross through the parking lot but sat at his spot on the curb, concentrating, rubbing a bare heel back and forth against the black asphalt. "He thought you were my dad." Looking up to Jesmond.

Jesmond looked up at the sky. It had suddenly grayed. Fat raindrops began floating down through the now-quiet air. "Come on, little man. Looks like the storm's finally showed up."

"He thought you were my dad," the boy said again.

"I'm cool with it," Jesmond said, then smiled. "But listen, man. Make sure you understand this: don't ever, *ever* think you're as good-lookin' as me."

XVIII

The late June storm (in reality, only a tropical depression—much to the disappointment of the camera crews gawking skyward for the live feed) was Teo's new obsession. He had loaded his pantry and refrigerator with canned red salmon and root vegetables. Even called Feddy to his house. "Got plenty of batteries and flashlights. Need your help at Home Depot, though. Got to pick up a generator. You're not still thinking of going all the way out there to Louisiana now, right?"

"No, Pop. I'm staying right here," Feddy said. Hadn't been in his father's house for months. Surprised to see clothes upon clothes in the living and dining rooms, spare bedroom. "You got a sideline on eBay now selling clothes?" Feddy yelled from the back room.

"What? Naw, naw. Doing a favor for someone."

Feddy raised an eyebrow. "What you say?"

Teo drifted into the room. "An ex-tenant. Audrey's Consignments. Holding her stuff till she finds a new place or puts it in storage."

"So Coots gets the property from you—"

"Coots and his cocksucker, McKendree."

"—Then turns and kicks out your old tenants. Priceless. He's a real work of art, Pops. I don't know why you didn't go with what the lawyer outlined."

"After the initial consultation, figured I could do bad by myself. Had that shyster, Ybarra."

"You could've done better there, too—God knows you've got the money. But you'd rather sign up with a cat that hangs his shingle at a flea market."

"It all worked itself out. I figured that by the time I'd jump through their lawyer's hoops, my lawyer's hoops, the IRS—man, they even talked investigations of taxes on my titles—I figured it'd be easier to settle. Some cash, little property. Anyway, peanut, I'm tired, time to lighten things up. I'm telling you, getting old sucks, boy. Circles of pleasure get smaller and smaller."

Feddy rummaged through the clothing on top of a twin bed while his father hobbled about in ragged underwear in the front of the house.

"So you decided to give that Clemons fuck the old heave-ho, eh? What you do? Flush 'em?"

"No, Pop. Still sitting on the table." Father Clemons's ashes had arrived via Federal Express yesterday. There was an accompanying letter:

Dear Mr. Toak,

Thank you for being gracious enough to bear the burden of Jerry's (Father Clemons's) request. To refresh your memory, Jerry and I were priests in the same parish for more than a decade. Up until the time he went into hospice he'd been staying with my sister and me down here in Tampa. I said a funeral Mass for him after he died, followed by his cremation. It was a simple Mass with just a few local friends. Now, some distant family in Alexandria, Louisiana want to have a memorial service for him; the details and directions are enclosed. He requested that his ashes be spread upon the prison cemetery grounds at Angola State Prison, Louisiana. This is contrary to the teachings of The Church. Cremated remains are supposed to be buried or entombed. I had tried to talk him out of it. How are we to pray The Rite of Committal, for example? He has a cousin that's a priest. You can maybe work this out with him.

Parcel services are, understandably, squeamish about mailing cremated remains (cremains? Ha Ha).

In addition, I have enclosed Jerry's PhD dissertation and some old photograph of someone he said you'd know. He wanted you to have these as well. If there are any questions, please feel free to contact me.

Yours in Our Lord,
Fr. Mangalore, O.P.

"Hey!" Feddy hollered. "I want one of these shirts." His eye caught a Cuban guayabera with an old comic-book character, Hot Stuff, on the breast.

"Take it! Take 'em all if you want!" Teo barked from what sounded like the kitchen. "Because my son is here and isn't deserting his old dad in his time of need. Not gonna leave his old dad to dump some jackleg preacher's soot." Teo strutted into the room as Feddy was exchanging shirts. "Come on, peanut. Let's go pick up that shit and dump it off the Dane's Point Bridge. Tropical Storm Aretha can wash his charred ass back to Louisiana."

"Take it easy, Pop. The man's at a place where he's not gonna be a threat to you or anybody else." Feddy felt a little put off. It had not been the heartfelt, embracing farewell he'd envisioned. And now he was glued to promises and forced into steering ashes halfway across the country.

"The thing is—the thing is that each time I had to carry my carcass into that jail over there I'd thank God I was somehow able to keep you out of there. Yeah, you did your share of fucking up. But nothing to the point where we'd have to do that hand-against-the-hand-through-the-Plexiglas crap. Every parent's nightmare—prison or the morgue." His father was tearful.

So he would say the things that cut, tore. Why do children begrudge their parents' love? "I'll be going next week, Pop. I'll let the storm settle out, then I've got to get to Louisiana like I said I would."

"'Next week'? What sort of bullshit is that? 'Next week.' There's already a bigger storm sitting on the tail of this one."

"Sometimes I do what I say I'm gonna do. It was his last request."

"You decided at this motherfuckin' minute to be Mr. Goodbar." The old man stood in his shorts in the doorway with his hands on his hips and his ashy, thick, potato-heel knees akimbo, Yule Brenner in *The King and I*. Feddy had forgotten how short in stature his father was, how peevish-looking. Saw where his father, shaving, had missed the hair in the little cleft in his chin—had always spread and dug it out with a razor in the past. Feddy, looking now only at the corners of his mouth, pushed for the sulk, the frown.

"You feeling all right?" Feddy inquired.

"That's a good goddam question to ask me right now, don't you think? You ungrateful sonofabitch."

There was a lull in Storm Aretha. Wind pushed misty drizzle against the bedroom window in quick, washing pulses. His father cast about the room, seemingly for something to brain him with.

Teo repeatedly dapped a knuckle to a nostril. "Might as well take up with your priest buddy now, Frederick. Go. Get on, you dick spit. The flesh on my balls, the wool in my ass, my fart stains make up more man than you. Always saddled up with that old codger rather than me. You're a bitch, boy. Were you his bitch, Feddy? I asked you before—'cause we could of made a shitload of cash, here—

"Tell me that he was a daddy to you, boy. Really. Dad. Daddy.

"You know what I remember? This is funny, peanut, you'll get a kick out of this. But the day—you were about eight, nine—you knocked a jar of mustard on the floor and tracked footprints all through the house . . . I came in late; I think you were spending the night over at Seth's. They were Arthur Murray dance steps—I could trace your day. I thought about that as I mopped up following you. Lovely." Teo sighed. Caricature of maudlin.

Feddy tried to squeeze past Teo; the old man began clawing at him. A finger dug into his ear and a hand grabbed through his belt loop but Feddy pulled away. From experience Feddy was attuned to the pressure and depth Teo could press upon him. And like all parents—like himself—his father felt he had full license to suddenly expand and then compact upon his child as need be. But it was like watching someone scream under water, with all the facial contortion and jangly energy gently dissipated into a nest of bubbles and white noise.

Teo. His diminutive bulk. His thin shoulders heaved and he took to glaring accusingly at Feddy as Feddy solemnly picked up his windbreaker and overnight bag. Feddy opened the living-room door to a distant roll of thunder. The rain falling now was so small and fine that it at first appeared to have ceased; and there was a formlessness to the horizon, a monochromic roil of clouds, rearing trees. "Oh God," Teo said dully as Feddy walked to his car. The old man had fallen back into the living room. "Oh God," he repeated, though Feddy heard now a heart strain, a calling out, this expectation of a response.

XIX

Poverty and inspired idiocy led Bayonne to coordinate his murder-suicide with the public transportation system. He was broke. He didn't have a car. To compound matters, there wasn't a direct line that went out to Finchem's area. The Number 38 went to Regency Mall; there he would have to transfer to the Number 8 (Hart Plaza) or 15 (Regal) and ride for forty-five minutes to Hector Park. He would sit on a bench beside the St. Johns as it slopped its brackish water onto the park's concrete pilings. At this point the buses, paradoxically, became scarcer and more rundown—the inhabitants of the Ortega community didn't use them; the riders were primarily the domestics and work staff that would arrive on the 5:10 that morning and leave on the 6:15 or the 8:30 in the evening. So he would have to take the Number 52 or 70 (Ortega, Ortega Estates) and get off at the traffic island in front of an old-fashioned Rexall drugstore. He would then have to walk to Water Oak Plantation, a gated community that was a good mile from the bus stop.

Bayonne had been able to borrow a semiautomatic pistol. The owner was a fifteen-year-old girl with a paralytic arm who'd found the gun while scampering through a deserted house. Her younger brother had broadcast her find while playing on the city's basketball blacktop. Bayonne approached the boy, who took him to his sister, who loaned him the gun under the condition that he let her have his recent bootleg—a copy of the summer's blockbuster disaster movie.

Riding the Number 52, Bayonne again went over his plan: he intended to trudge through the marsh woods that came up to the

Water Oak community, walking right up to Finchem's westward lanais, entering through the back of the house. Medgar had given him Finchem's exact address, even showed him the home on Google Earth.

Why? Why do these things you know are wrong? He heard his father inside his head. And as he watched the shops and billboards float past the bus window the answers he'd prepared were unraveling—he found himself trying to pull together ends. There was his freedom-fighter–terrorist argument—Dr. Coots had him wait in his office while he talked with some Russian: one man's terrorist being another's freedom fighter and killing evil for some blah-blah in the future (Dr. Finchem infecting people with the AIDS virus was an evil). And too, he'd learned that *his* virus was some supermutant from San Francisco, one that attacked gay men in particular and would not respond to medicines—Dr. Coots showed him the articles about it alongside his lab results. If he wanted to keep Finchem from making any money off him with the policy, the one thing experience had taught him was that suicide made it null and void—all the crap he went through with Smullian. And since he was dying anyway—

The bus shelter while waiting for the Number 52 had provided very little in shielding him from Tropical Storm Aretha. The bus, as expected, was late; by the time he boarded he was drenched, though the gun remained dry since he had wrapped it up in a Publix grocery bag. And the air-conditioning blasted air cold enough to make him shiver. Still, the storm provided very good cover. He got off at the Rexall, crossed the rain-misted street to the copse of pines behind another housing development.

Jesmond hadn't been there for him this time. He had tried to discuss with him the ideas and plans rushing through his head but Jesmond only half listened.

There were quite a number of houses in the new development marked only by their cement foundations. From the rain, shallow scallops of water pooled in the uneven hollows. A scuffling sound emanated from a dark green Dumpster. Bayonne looked in. A water-logged raccoon had been trapped by the sloping metal sides and was frantically clawing to get out.

Bayonne approached Finchem's house from the back, tromping through a mist that hugged the marsh. He crossed the lawn in scant light. Bayonne stood staring into Finchem's family room. The floor was beige marble. There was a leather sofa. An enormous flat-screen television encompassed a wall. A golf tournament was on.

Bayonne patted his jean coat before finally studying the pocket. The plastic bag had become slick and part of it was stuck in the zipper. Beyond his feet he saw he was standing amid a fairy ring of toadstools.

Finchem was in profile and became aware of Bayonne's presence only slowly.

Bayonne shot the window without taking the gun out of the plastic bag. He then stepped through the space into the family room as an actor would pass from the stage into the audience, and he entered wiping his eyes with the heel of his hand. By the time he was able to open them clearly, Finchem was already on the phone. "You're a fucking murderer!" Bayonne shouted, "A destroyer!" He spoke without flourish but with an intensity that called upon his days in his father's church. "In motherfucking hell! You will see your white ass torn to pieces in motherfucking hell!"

Finchem stood panting. Bayonne shot him in the shin. The man buckled and fell, crashing through a glass coffee table. Like a drunk asleep on a counter, Finchem seemed to be resting placidly before finally lolling his head back. The maxilla was staved. A bright yellow orchid had fallen from the coffee table onto the marble floor.

The upstairs, the kitchen, and the living room were dark. Bayonne was never to learn that Finchem's wife had filed for separation. That she and their infant daughter had moved to her parents' summerhouse in Asheville, North Carolina; that Adam Finchem's only orbit had been a tight, small circle between the couch in the family room and the guest bathroom downstairs; that he ate always from the same Chinese takeout on the same leather sofa that served also as his bed.

Bayonne shot the doctor twice in the head.

Not long after, police sirens bawled up the circular driveway. Finchem had been able to punch 911. The silent alarm service also had been activated. A neighbor had heard the gunshots and had telephoned the police, who telephoned the house. Bayonne talked for a good twenty minutes to a special representative. Bayonne hung up with the promise that he would think hard about what they'd discussed, that he wouldn't do anything rash.

He had never smoked before. Cigarettes. That morning, from Publix, he purchased his first: a hard pack of mentholated Kools; and it was that evening he lit his first cigarette, which he held in a fist between his ring and middle finger. A policeman would hazily remember seeing the shadowy outline of Bayonne when he appeared in the dark living room at the front of the house, would remember the red scribble in the center of the room.

When Bayonne returned to the family room the golf tournament bothered him. It amplified his feelings of doom, for he could see Adam Finchem on those very greens teeing up for a shot. So he channel surfed, falling absently on the PBS station. It was a retrospective of Art Linkletter and his show, *Kids Say the Darndest Things*. A split screen showed a man next to himself as a kid of eight. Bayonne took the blanket, which had been neatly folded on the arm of the sofa, and covered up the corpse. He felt so hopeless.

By now a news truck had pushed into the line of police cars and emergency vehicles that had gathered. If he had been so inclined, Bayonne could have watched the whole thing unfold on the local Fox news, as his father was doing that very instant. Instead, he found himself trying to interpret sensations but they rushed by too fast—it was like trying to read billboards from a speeding train.

So the calmest thing to do was to face the end of the storm as it settled east. The horizon was a grayish yellow and extended well beyond the murky green expanse of the lawn. Bayonne hummed a whole chorus of a hymn before stepping through the front door, firing the gun rapidly and indiscriminately. Whereby he was fired upon.

Just at that moment the Number 52 rolled past the Rexall stop. The ceiling light had ignited the whole interior, and the riders' silhouettes jiggled to and fro in a haphazard way.

XX

Seth Burnett did nothing for the days that followed but sit before the television. Even when the storm disrupted the satellite feed and there'd be nothing but snow on the screen, he'd sit in his terry-cloth robe with his legs splayed across the bed, his skin ashy, staring. He was gassy. His small Afro was sleep dented and matted. His second ex, Martha, came upon him sprawled on his back across a bare mattress, watching a rodeo. "Come on, baby. Let's get you straightened up," and she led him to the bathroom and made him shower. When he came out he stood at his bedroom window while she put on sheets. He propped a foot on the sill and studied his toes. His son. Bayonne's feet—even as a baby—were shaped the same as his. Through a gap in the curtains Seth saw the movement on the avenue. His house was on a corner lot removed from the sidewalk by a Cyclone fence and one of the city's appeasements. Percy Herman, pushing his shopping cart full of cast-off clothes, black garbage bags, and an old Smith Corona electric typewriter, waved at Seth.

"'Suicide by SWAT' is what they say it was," Rachel relayed to Jesmond, huddling into him from her office couch. Understanding—she spoke softly and matter-of-factly, did not try to explain. Soothing, though. Jesmond had come by her office with Medgar issues, Bayonne issues, paternity issues, death threats. And soon he would be out on the streets—he had even stopped by Feddy's place but his father wasn't at home: the shades were drawn, flyers had accumulated in his door handle; an old dark woman in a housecoat had peered at him through the blinds of the adjacent apartment.

The drone of heavy equipment penetrated her office. It could be heard everywhere about the city after Aretha. There was a rush to get projects done before the next storm—Burt—hit. It had already rounded Cuba.

She got up from the sofa slowly, as if her knees hurt. Assured Jesmond that she was going to get some things checked out. She was going to see Medgar.

Bernard Irwin was at Toak's Bail Bonds with a small camera crew and a young man and woman who eerily resembled the Jackson boy and his mother. It was his intention to film Teo Toak reprising his role as Bobby Jackson's bail bondsman. The real Bobby Jackson slumped behind Bernard and his Bobby-double. The real Bobby Jackson had told Bernard several times that he did not like being the so-called technical adviser and that he felt he was being cheated of his chance to act.

Irwin was slightly miffed, too, when, after having gone to all the trouble to assemble the team before noon, he found Teo already engaged.

Medgar was sitting on the edge of Teo's desk.

Teo stared dully at a stack of papers adjacent to Medgar's ass. He lifted one or two documents, turned them back and forth, set them in a new pile. After a moment, he would pick up and do the same for another set.

"Ernie!" Teo shouted, though Ernest sat just a few feet from him at his desk. "Go and see what those motherfuckers want!" Lately, Ernie had come into a gimpy leg and grimaced as he pushed himself up from his seat.

"We're not open at the moment," Ernie said, not sure as to whom to direct the comment before settling on the Mother Jackson looka-like. His bulk blocked their passage into the office.

"Oh, Bernard Irwin!" Medgar greeted, coming up behind Ernie. "Look, Teo—Johnsonville's favorite native son! Lord knows I hope you haven't done something requiring bail." Medgar pushed Ernie behind him while motioning them in.

"No, of course not! No, man we're doing kind of a documentary about the Bobby Jackson case. See, Teo here—"

"Now what you need to make a movie about is that Bayonne Bur-nett fiasco. Twenty-something bullets riddled his body. The city is still dragging its feet."

XXI

A Mass was to be said by a nephew who was a distant cousin to Father Clemons. It was to take place at the old cathedral in Alexandria. Feddy's Gremlin did surprisingly well covering the six hundred miles from his home city up to Opelousas, at which point in time the little car had begun to seriously overheat. Feddy had forgotten his phone charger at one of the motels, either in Pemberton, Florida or Bicknell, Alabama—making a two-day trip out of what was normally sixteen hours. While waiting for a mechanic to replace his broken thermostat with a used one from the junkyard, Feddy found his first opportunity to touch base back in Johnsonville. A convenience store, a block or two from the overpass, had a sizable amount of Mexican foot traffic. Feddy stood in line behind several migrants in order to purchase a phone card. At the garage, he stood in line again for a phone booth. The booth listed against the outside wall of the garage. Decals advertising toll-free numbers for collect calls obliterated the metal post while a Wendy's coffee cup on the floor held a brown soup of cigarette butts. Feddy scooted the cup out and around the door with his foot.

"Hey, Melan. It's me. Hold your finger to the phone so I can smell where it's been."

"Your fuckin' bees are here, dog. And they're not, what you say—inconspicuous. And you sound pretty goddam cheery for an old buck making the cemetery stops. All I can say is you better hope your job's not gone when you're done. Those fuckin' bees are really pissing me off, Feddy."

Feddy decided to ignore the bee comments. "One old man's memorial. I'll be back before the first whistle Wednesday."

Melan was silent on the other end. Feddy heard, instead, faint ambient conversation from crossed lines, *So listen. Don't say nothing about me going to bingo, okay?* There was a scuffling of a chair and the click of a door closing. "So, Feddy. You don't know, dog, do you? About Seth's kid?"

"What? What's up, man?"

Father Clemons's cousin stood on the green corner lawn outside the rectory as Feddy's decrepit Gremlin puttered up to the curb. Feddy rolled down the passenger window in order to start speaking. He was still in a daze. For the past two hours he had tried unsuccessfully to reach Seth, pulling over at gas stations and rest stops along the way. Finally, he'd been able to get a hold of Rachel: they'd completed the police inquest and the body had been released; the service was to be at Seth's church this coming Thursday, Seth presiding.

He was a chubby young priest, midthirties. And in uniform: biretta, collar, and cassock. A hot nasty wind lifted and bloated the cassock—for a moment it looked to Feddy as if he were bare underneath. There was an ugly gray river—the Red River—that coursed part of its path in front of the cathedral. Feddy crossed it at several points on his way to the town. Squalid islands of foamy debris—sticks, dead fish, field carrion, sewage pulp—floated gently down the river. Funk also came from the paper mills along the river.

He had instructed Feddy to meet him outside. The young priest had previously informed Feddy that Father Clemons' search request to have his ashes spread on a prison graveyard was not acceptable—the family mausoleum (one of the few Creole mausoleums in that part of the state) had space set aside.

Feddy stuck his hand through the window to shake the priest's—he received, in turn, a meek grasp of forefingers.

"Father Thibodaux," the young priest reluctantly smiled. The radio squawked of the storm petering out after passing through the Gulf, but still delivering strong winds and rain.

"Feddy Toak. Come on in, Father. Sit down. Where'd you say you want to go?"

Father Thibodaux knocked his biretta askew squeezing through the car door. Rust and dents would allow the two-door to open only halfway.

"There's a Denny's not far from here. The rectory is being used in planning some big shindig for the bishop." In the span of the ten minutes it took for them to get from the cathedral to the diner's parking lot, he had let Feddy know that he was newly from Rome, and had studied canon law at the Vatican; that Father Clemons had come from a long line of distinguished Thibodauxs by way of his mother; and that there was no way in heaven his earthly remnants would decorate some criminal potter's field up at Angola.

"Where are the cremated remains?"

Feddy glanced over his shoulder at the large white cardboard box on the backseat. "Riding shotgun," Feddy grinned, but it was only weakly returned.

"So, what's with all this 'Ashes in the Wind' drama?" Father Thibodaux asked while spearing a fried egg onto his fork. Though it was close to three in the afternoon he'd ordered the Lumberjack Grand Slam Breakfast. Father Thibodaux thrust the whole egg with its runny yolk into his mouth.

That no one had ever visited Mike "Milk" Ashford (life for armed robbery) from the beginning of Father Clemons' twelve years as chaplain for the Louisiana State Penitentiary at Angola only reinforced the vast, melancholy emptiness of the clock. Milk had spent sixty-two of his eighty-three years on earth in a maximum-security prison. What really made Milk Ashford stand out in Father Clemons' mind, however, had been his request. In just his first few months at

Angola inmates had approached him for his help in pleading their innocence; several death-row prisoners solicited his aid in trying to get their sentences commuted. However, Milk's was his first—and, in looking back, only—plea to make tolerable the bramble and discomfort of eternity.

Since his seventy-fifth birthday he had been writing letters to anyone on the outside who might assist him in not being buried in prison soil. The one sister he had in Oklahoma had passed away. He hadn't had a visitor for the past thirty years. So he'd been soliciting strangers. A famous lawyer had written him back once. Another few times a nun.

Father Clemons had spoken to the warden about it. The warden wrote the priest a letter that was stapled to a mimeographed page from the prison law-and-regulation handbook—article something or another—dictating that prisoners without representative kin or previous and established dispositions were to buried, at the expense of the state, in prison ground. "I don't know what else to do," Father Clemons said. "Thank you," Milk responded. "You've been helpful. That, at least, sets my mind at rest."

He continued to write letters.

A half a year from Father Clemons' arrival Milk Ashford died. Number 79096 had listed Father Clemons as his primary contact. "This is my first prison burial," Father Clemons found himself telling the other chaplains. "May I do a small service?" he asked.

"That would be a wonderful thing," the Baptist chaplain said. He was a squat fireplug of a man who walked rolling from side to side like a cartoon of a sailor. This was because he had an artificial and hinged leg. "I'll be glad to accompany you if you like." They were standing outside, at one of the administrative facilities.

"Who else will be at the burial?" Father Clemons asked.

"The gravediggers. You. Me. One or two of the old-timers. There's one fella who'd been on death row, had his sentence commuted. However, if it makes you uncomfortable—"

"No no. That's fine. Milk was what, seventy-something?"

The Baptist chaplain laughed. "Actually, he was eighty-three. They get kind of vain here about their age the older they get."

The two of them rode out to the gravesite in an old ford pickup truck. The Baptist chaplain was driving. He reached across and turned on the radio. A piercing trill shot through the cab. "This only plays AM. Only get two stations out here, this hillbilly crap and some paranoid Baptist redneck rant outside of Homer. Drives the colored prisoners crazy." He then glanced over at the priest. "No offense."

"Would drive me crazy, too," Father Clemons said. "But I love me some Patsy Cline."

An identical truck with shovels and pickaxes awaited them when they arrived. There was a nice, shapely pit with smooth sides and even corners. One of four trustees walked slowly back and forth inside, meticulously examining the fresh space. The other three stood over him. Two guards stood under the shade of trees.

A black hearse soon could be seen trundling down the trace. When it pulled up to the gravesite, the driver, a sloppy rabbit-eyed officer, emerged snarling. "Come on hyer," he said to the trustees. "I need six of y'all for pallbearers.'

The trustees dusted themselves. There were only four of them, however. "Hell, I'll be a fifth," the driver said. Everyone then looked at the priest and the chaplain.

"Of course," Father Clemons said, "I'll be glad to."

What did he expect to happen? What did he expect to see? They carried the coffin, a plastic-surfaced pressed-board box, and rested it on three two-by-fours atop the grave. Someone had scrawled in black marker HEAD at one end. They all took positions around the coffin. The man who had been inspecting the space whispered to himself as to whether the grave was deep enough.

Father Clemons finished with the Twenty-third Psalm. Again the priest asked himself what did he expect to happen. The trustees, out of politeness, gazed at the priest, the wind gently curling the leaves of the Bible. When he caught his reflection in the windshield of the truck Father Clemons saw that he was still wearing his sunglasses. He quickly removed them.

The service was, of course, brief. The sun as if on cue disappeared into clouds. The prisoners lowered the coffin into the ground and then proceeded to spade the earth on top of it, the guards still standing under their respective cypresses, smoking.

This would be hell. The priest glanced around him. An eternity to limp about this prison world, spent as after a night of raging fever, the monochrome institutional blaze and asphalt, shadowing men without sound, despairing without sound, fear without sound. The sun would forever be hidden behind clouds, the day gray, the night just a shade darker, the shadows twinned as during an eclipse.

Father Clemons would bury eight more men in the potter's field in his tenure.

"So I think—I think he felt that they'd been left outside life. He didn't want to see them that way when they were dead. Spreading his ashes is a symbol for him."

Father Thibodaux raked a wedge of toast several times across the plate before fitting it into his mouth. He followed it with a large gulp of iced tea and sighed, "He's dead, his spirit has left the body. At that point you have to ask, 'Symbol for who? For what?' Scattering his remains goes against Church teaching, for by canon law there must be a reverent disposition. Besides, the whole thing smacks of vanity and pride—'Father Clemons watches over their souls.'"

Looking about the diner, Feddy happened to see an old man sitting with his adult daughter and his grandson. The grandson was enthusiastically recounting his day at a water park. The grandfather nodded gravely and appreciatively. Catching Feddy's eye, he gave him the subtlest of winks.

Feddy glanced at his watch. "Well, Father, if that's the case, let me go unpack at the motel and wash up a little. Then you call me when that business is done with the bishop, and I'll drop off the urn."

Feddy went to Target. At the motel Feddy emptied the contents of the urn into a brown paper bag. He then filled the urn with a mix of gray potting soil and landscaping pumice stone he purchased from Patio and Gardening, carefully wiping it down. Wind rocked the little car while rain, scouring the windshield, made the visible invisible, pelting Feddy all the way up to the rectory stoop. Father Thibodaux nodded hurriedly at his mumbled excuse as to why he couldn't stay for the service, and as Feddy sprinted back to the car, the priest gave a flippant wave goodbye and quickly closed the rectory door.

The old grandfather in the diner.

Feddy drove southeast to Angola with the old man's wink bringing tears to his eyes. It reminded him of Father Clemons. Not that Father Clemons ever winked at him. And it reminded him of Teo, though his father never winked at him either. He felt senseless and ashamed, weak in the knees at the thought of how much of his life had leaked away. A father's approval, an acknowledgment, just once in his life would have made him feel so protected. Even at his age he wanted to feel protected from the world, made to feel that there could be a second, a fourth chance in life.

He was not allowed onto the prison property. The Louisiana State Penitentiary at Angola was a fifteen-hundred-acre farming correctional facility with eight maximum-security buildings. The prison graveyard abutted another twelve acres of swamp, scrub bush, and stump trees.

Feddy left. The paper bag of Father Clemons' ashes bounced next to him in the passenger seat. Tossing the ashes at the prison fence would probably be the closest he would ever come to Father Clemons' request. He should have done it and recited the Lord's Prayer—hoped the wind would carry at least some of the dust to its intended destination.

XXII

The church keyboardist, Ronnie, had been a dear friend of Bayonne and was so distraught on the day of the service that he had to be escorted twice back to the organ from the vestibule. The whole affair was coming off slapdash due to the new storm, which had finally graduated to a hurricane. They had debated as to whether to proceed with the funeral (interring Bayonne, with a memorial service after the storm had passed)—but Seth had made up his mind to do it the right way. Though it would be a closed casket, he would bless his son as the Lord had intended him to do.

Hurricane Burt was on a direct course for Johnsonville. The seventy-two-hour evacuation notice had already been given. Some of the more nervous were leaving. The majority of people, particularly those in Reverend Burnett's congregation, simply filled up propane tanks with gas and bathtubs with water, bought candles and batteries and canned food and powdered milk, hunkered down inside their homes for the onslaught.

Seth Burnett blinked and regarded the prolapsed ceiling of his church from the pulpit. He was placing markers on scripture passages in his Bible, arranging the lighting and stand. The water-stained acoustic tile wouldn't stand another saturating rain. He directed Ronnie, who'd finally settled down, to play.

People were milling about the parking lot and the church foyer. Some cars were packed to evacuate after the service to relatives' homes in Brunswick or Augusta. Some were going as far inland as Atlanta. Pillows and evening blouses—still on hangers—were crammed into one back window. Another held stacks of framed photos.

The deacons steered folks to pews while Ronnie played "His Eye Is on the Sparrow." Reverend Burnett began to hum along, unconsciously, beneath the song. Reverend Purdy of Greater Timothy Baptist had come to assist. He was a Masonic brother to Seth, had known Bayonne as far back as when Bayonne was in diapers.

They were dressed, the two ministers. Reverend Purdy of Greater Timothy wore a rust-colored velour vest with a gold tie and a rhinestone tiepin; his rust-red bowler sat on the altar railing. Reverend Burnett, though—draped and resplendent in a pale and shiny lavender silk suit with cloth buttons; tan alligator shoes snuggled his feet. This was not to be a standard service. His deacons, his ex-wives, his children had tried to convince him that it would be best if Reverend Purdy alone performed the service—Purdy's face tried to show he was open to it; he had gently suggested that it would be best if Seth remained with his disconsolate family. Seth, though—his weight now serving him—let his girth speak unequivocally as he occupied his chair that he would not be moved from this decision.

There were four window-unit air conditioners that jutted from beneath the stained-glass windows; cooled, moist air smoked from the upper vents. "I think he really shouldn't have any say in the matter. His mind's too messed up with grief for him to think straight, anyway," one of the white linen church sisters mumbled loud enough in the back of the church to be heard all the way up to the prayer rail.

Seth—seemingly oblivious—noticed that the brown cardboard patch replacing the stained-glass panel in the front upper window needed itself to be replaced. The four-leaf-shaped watermark had gotten bigger. And the beetle-size bulb of the stand was too yellow, too weak a light.

He left for the quiet of the room to the side of the pulpit. There, he put on his vermillion robe and removed his cell from his pants pocket in order to silence it. Seth held the phone in his palm. It seemed to weigh a hundred pounds. In the voice mail there were two or three messages that'd been inadvertently saved from Bayonne. Like a lovesick soldier rationing out peeks for himself of a sweetheart when he is miles away from home, the Reverend Seth Burnett would let himself listen once, maybe twice a day, to Bayonne's excuse about being late meeting him for a job, or how he'd appreciate it if he'd talk to his younger brother about giving him back *his* Puma sneakers, Byron always took his stuff—

Instead, calls from Feddy. The first were condolences; the last, apologies on top of apologies—his car was smoking, his air conditioner, too, he had just pulled into a filling station so he was going to be late; though he just put in one new thing, he was stuck now in South Carolina getting a belt replaced on his piece-of-shit car. Seth silenced the phone and sighed. Leaving the little room, he snuck outside and around through the back to get to the pulpit antechamber.

Jesmond hurriedly squeezed in between Bethena and Bertrand. Agnes from Peebo's Cafeteria tried to pat his shoulder as he rushed by. The organist had begun "Just a Closer Walk with Thee," and the choir came in on the upbeat of the next chorus.

Bayonne's mother, Sadie, was in the front pew. "Lord. Lord. Please don't, Lord," Jesmond heard her say. She then wheezily took a breath, just like an asthmatic, and repeated the same.

When the congregation stood up, Jesmond craned about to see who was present. There was no Feddy. He caught himself gloating at his absence, but then he immediately felt guilty and embarrassed.

On the minister's dais, Seth sat next to Reverend Purdy. When Reverend Purdy got up to read the scriptural passage, the congregation flitted echoes of words and phrases.

The grief had been able to be contained, the disorder of sorrows held in check, up until the time three of the choir stepped out to the front and began, a cappella, "Savior, Pass Me Not." She gasped again, "Lord. Lord. Please don't, Lord." After a pause, Sadie Burnett began to scream.

The church sisters finally were able to calm her. But by now Jesmond's sorrow became quite clear to him and he had begun to silently weep. The organ had pulled into the breach left by the three-man group, thrashing and extracting grief from women and men.

It was silent when Seth went up to the pulpit to speak. He began with an orator's question—What did he, what does he—Seth Burnett—know of the vastness of God's plan?—but before he could answer, he blubbered. Howled his tears. And Reverend Purdy had to complete the eulogy, while Seth Burnett was guided to the front pew to sit next to his first ex-wife.

XXIII

Chaos met the Burnett funeral procession as evacuation traffic logjammed the northbound lane onto I-95. The highway patrolman, an anxious, thin-lipped boy of twenty-three or so, kept winnowing the cars, snarling traffic into a single lane that would inexplicably open again into three, just a half mile up.

Half the funeral party did not attend the burial due to either evacuation or misdirection. Jesmond was able to tailgate the black limousines all the way to the gravesite. The cars came to a rest and the people emerged. Bayonne's little niece, Bochelle, stood next to her mother, bowing in and out her belly while the wind pushed white azalea blossoms from the trees. Jesmond took his place, one among four pallbearers, carrying the casket from the car to the small patch of green plastic lawn that lined the hole.

At the church there were three lawn tables of fried chicken, potato salad, ham, pork ribs, sweetened iced tea, sherbet punch, broccoli and cheese salad, Coca-Cola cake, deviled eggs, macaroni and cheese, Publix sliced bread, collard greens, and an inspired creation of Rachel Ennis's mother, raspberry burritos.

The release of grief left people inflamed and ravenous. Jesmond, who had not eaten an actual meal in several weeks, pouted in his satiety. A couple in their fifties—the husband smiling pointedly to disarm people staring at them—were preparing paper plates to take home.

Jesmond stayed with Seth's sons to help clean and straighten up. The brothers told Bayonne jokes after their father had left, Bayonne the Rapper, Bayonne the Beat King. About how stupid Bayonne could sometimes be. Jesmond's was one of the few cars left in the dirt and gravel parking lot across the street. The Burnetts walked home. However, as he turned the key in the ignition the engine would not engage. Only click. Jesmond pumped the gas pedal and swore. And was startled, glancing into the rearview mirror, by a dark man in a double-breasted and horn-rim glasses, sprawled across the back-seat. "You enjoyed fucking my wife?"

He'd been at the funeral. Edward Richmond. Given the notoriety, even with the black weather looming, there were plenty of unfamiliar faces. Special Ed thumped the back of the driver's seat. "Did you enjoy fucking my wife?"

Jesmond's mouth was open and he panted a little, tasting sour breath. And the oppressive interior heat made sweat collect in the frayed little gap between his collar and his Adam's apple. He began fidgeting with the automatic window.

"You need this to do anything." Special Ed held up the distributor cap. "But I need to talk to you. I'm a daddy now. *I'm* a daddy. Got the blood test for my daughter and me to prove it."

Jesmond pulled his tie and the bead of sweat tracked down the exact center of his chest. His heart was like a wrecking ball, heaving in an arc through space—a hole of asystole—before completing the curve with a beat.

"I know you know I've been following you. But you still didn't tell me—did you enjoy fucking my wife?" Jesmond turned to face him. "DON'T LOOK AT ME!" the man shouted, banging the seat. "She left me. Left me with a six-week-old. Want you to know though, lover, that this isn't the first time. She ran off from a child up in Memphis when she was eighteen. Left it at a Bailey's Gym. Dropped it off at the child-care through one door, took off through the next. At the time she told me it sounded kind of sexy. Kinky. How old are you? I should fuckin' kill you through this seat."

Jesmond tensed to pull the door handle but Special Ed slammed his hand upon the lock point. "Don't. You're insulting me. I told you I want to talk to you. You know, I'm an officer in the military. If you were in the navy right now you'd be court-martialed and in the brig because adultery is a criminal offense. Not in civilian life but in the military. But she left a fifty-three-year-old man with a six-week-old baby and that's a criminal offense anywhere, right? Right now Ruth Martinez is watching her. Filipina. Filipinas are good with babies. They're supposed to be investigating my wife's disappearance but, personally, I think she went back up to Tennessee. The thing is, she's not in the military, just married into it, so what the fuck can you do?" Special Ed paused to stare out the window.

"You know, I thought of what it'd be like if one day, Baby One met Baby Two. That'd be a goddam comedy club. The Peaches-That-Sorry-Excuse-for-a-Mother-Deserted-Me Club. A good ha-ha." Special Ed then looked pensive. "I thought, for a moment, she'd track you down but now I see she really was through with your sorry ass," he said. He paused again, pulling thoughts. Then: "Maybe I'll marry the Filipina. 'Cause what the hell am I supposed to do with a baby?"

Teo got drunk. In the history of his existence, he had never surrendered so much for so little. Pride gone, too. Medgar Coots smiled while Teo signed away, moved the pen across the blank spaces. That he paid him pretty much market price for it wasn't the issue—it was that he felt old now and greedy for the collapse and the loss. He understood them now, the old whores: mole-ridden and gray-bushed trolling the boulevard under catcalls and insults, hustling with chin bristle, claws for nipples. Public display of their pubic defeat.

Medgar had evicted his Russian woman, Elena Koslov, from her little store and walk-up as soon as he purchased the property. Her short-tempered son tracked Medgar down and soon began shouting and threatening him. So Medgar had called security, and security called the police. As her son was already on probation, he was thrown into lock-up. She came to Teo, this time, not even for bail. Just dully asked his help—could he hold on to her inventory?

And Teo had called himself on stalking Medgar. Teo the Old Man. He crawled his Cadillac across Medgar's streets and haunts. He'd even gone to his clinic, just to sit there and nag at him like a conscience. But the joker instead put an arm about his shoulders and guided him through the facility. There were lots of young men simply lounging. He then settled Teo into the lobby while Medgar and the youngsters began to crack jokes about him: about his car, about his pocket kerchief and sport coat (it was summer weight!), his slight stoop. Rachel Ennis had even come in to see Coots. She glanced around before finally catching sight of Teo, shook her head. Teo finally gathered himself and left.

He woke up early the next day and began drinking. Asleep to the storm trackers. Woke up to the same: the hurricane looked to hit somewhere between Johnsonville and Savannah. Vodka and ruby red grapefruit juice that morning; Crown and Coke throughout the day. He didn't go to the Burnett kid's funeral—Teo's excuse was that it would look like he was trying to recoup his bond money. He tried puppying Medgar again. He meant the man to remember him, to even so much as say, *Yes, I swindled the hell out of you,* but the asshole just grinned. His big white grin with the little button of pink gum gapping the crest of his front teeth—and he hugged Teo, asked him what he could do for him. Teo muttered something about his stomach being upset and Dr. Coots reached into his inside breast pocket, withdrew a pad and pen and wrote him a prescription. "This will take care of things," he said and left Teo. And Teo dutifully went to Walgreens and received a bottle of some medicine they kept showing on television commercials, isn't that something.

The manager of his motel had come by to see him. "This doctor, your friend?" Teo shook his head. "He kick out Elena from the store and apartment. He made her son go to jail. I hear he take some your business, too.

"I did not particularly like you, Mr. Toak." His manager, Sergey Belikov, with the black-bronze circles under his eyes and nicotine-stained fingers, observed Teo while stretching out in Teo's La-Z-Boy—Teo wondered, briefly, how he had found his home. "But I do not like this Dr. Coots more. So I will make a proposition to you, Mr. Toak. I want to buy this motel of yours. I know this Coots wants to buy it, too. Sell it to me.

"You black American people are sad. Even your devils are small. Small demons. *Besovska.* Imps. Your kind can't even rule in hell. Instead of the battles where armies fight and worlds are destroyed— you are flies buzzing steaming piles of shit in the Four Horsemen's stable." He set the recliner upright and shifted to remove a large roll of money held together by a rubber band. "Here is ten thousand dollars. This is good-faith deposit. I do this for two things. First, to show you that, now, in this country, I have made considerable money; this means nothing to me. Second, to let you know that you should be afraid of me, not this Medgar Coots. I can teach both of you how to do bad magnificently. That I have no doubt that you will sell me motel or return money is what is important. As for Dr. Coots—I will address this situation."

His television had been playing continuously; sleeping again with it, never turning it off. A category 4 was what was predicted to make landfall in thirty-six hours. And his son had been burning up his telephone with calls Teo wouldn't answer.

Teo decided to evacuate. From the top of his closet he removed his green and tan suitcase, threw in (after a sniff) a musty oyster-colored pullover, a towel, a washcloth, his travel kit, two changes of underwear, painter's pants, tan slacks, and a white dress shirt that hadn't been opened and was still in its package. In the trunk of his car he loaded two wooden crates of canned foods and a shrink-wrapped case of Evian water. And on the passenger seat sat a little black-and-white television with a cigarette lighter adapter; he could watch shows and play DVDs. He took a couple of DVDs from his shelf but he didn't check to see what they were.

He was adrift in his melancholy, the moment stirring him with a false sense of progression, movement. It was a sensation similar to his experience sitting with his eyes closed on an airplane, being lulled by the shimmy and shudder of the craft into thinking he was in flight but upon opening eyes, finding they were immobile and still on the tarmac.

His gold Cadillac was, for a time, the wobbly caboose in a train of cars going to 95N in order to connect with the interstate heading for Atlanta.

"**The bees, Feddy,**" Melan said. He sat him in a low chair across from his desk. "That was it. The final straw, brother." In his long green army coat, hands in the pockets and arms spread open in a gesture of innocence, he pleaded that it was beyond the scope of what he could do—though he was the one who had put Feddy on the chopping block.

Listen. Let me be thankful that I let you screw me twice, Feddy wanted to say. Melan was both fervent and bored, already looking past him, all ready to shake his hand and push him out the door. But he took in a large breath and settled back into his chair.

"You told me all I needed to do was settle up current business," Feddy said.

"Unfortunately, this is not the time to be on the radar. And you've popped up quite a few times this year, Feddy."

"You've never said anything to me about it. All those times I've been in this office—all those times we've hung out together you've never said a word to me."

"Not too much talk was going on at the time, just a few squawks here and there so I didn't want to worry you."

Insurance. It came to Feddy as he sat across from Melan. He'd been held on to as the pop-up when they needed a sacrifice hit. Melan was probably involved with a bigger production, something that outweighed the relative chump change his little schemes brought in. And it would be stupid to threaten Melan with the fact that he'd profited from the ventures, too. Melan knew that. So—

"What are you giving me? Two weeks' notice?"

"The powers that be wanted you out of here as of now. They said they need to bring charges but I talked them out of it. Let's make it a week and you can quit on your own."

The dock's parking lot was mostly deserted. The Port Authority had, on paper at least, encouraged the workers to heed the evacuation notices. On the other hand, they did pay time and a half for those who, as they worded it, "by circumstance needed to remain."

Feddy had used again Caulder Shipping Line. Saw no need to improve on a good thing. The pod had come into port ahead of schedule because of the storm, arriving a couple of days ago. Feddy hadn't been able to work out any sort of delivery, coordinate any type of transportation *before* Melan's news—he took it now for what it was: this was to be a flat-out loss.

Leaving Melan's office, he was startled to see that it was nearly dusk. There were the usual light, blowing rains that heralded the major storms. Feddy walked through a prickly burst without any rain gear or hat. In a way he felt, for the moment at least, lighter. Unburdened. And strangely—wonderfully tired. The damaged refrigeration pod (same!) was in a different section, closer to the damaged Quonset hut.

On the ride after collecting the first shipment, one of the beekeepers, an old man from Arkansas, recounted the loss of his first hives after twenty-something years. His wife had died. He then went on to explain the ceremony in which the bees had to be informed of a death in the household. The telling of the bees. The ritual went back centuries. When a family member marries, the bees must be told or they'd leave, never to return. When the master or mistress of a household dies, a youngster must whisper it to the bees. Then there is several minutes of silence. If the hive resumes humming, the bees have consented to stay. This wasn't the case for the Arkansas beekeeper. The bees had upped and left.

The east storage bay was deserted. There were a few containers in this section, mostly single-item holders from infrequent shippers. Feddy's wet dress shirt clung to him. His jeans, too—even through the rain they felt clammy. He ran his hand across the pod's metal doors and found them slick. He then clanged back the doors and stared for a moment. The pod was empty. Feddy then walked away.

XXIV

There were four cars snarled in a fender bender in front of a strip mall just as bumper-to-bumper traffic entered a loop connecting Beach Boulevard to 9A. In the middle of their argument, one of the men—a thick man whose paunch rolled over his belt and who was, at most, only halfheartedly involved—suddenly turned to his teenage daughter, pointed to the strip mall, and sent her over to Cold Stone Creamery, where the light was on, they might still be open. "You can always rely on someone to profit on someone else during a time of misery, even for ice cream," a thin woman said, whose hair went every which way. "I bet you a cone goes for ten dollars. Some ice-crusted, freezer-burned crap like Eggnog Sprinkle." Traffic had been at a standstill for the past forty-eight minutes. People talked through windows and over cars and on cell phones to people several cars away. The man's daughter jogged back holding a small cold-storage bag and a spoon; there was loud speculation that it held more than a pint. She whispered something in his ear. The man simply shrugged and began eating straight from the bag.

None of the cars had shadows. None of the people waiting outside their cars had shadows. The sun had appeared during a lull and it was hot, and as it was noon, people were now fully awake and had begun questioning the necessity of leaving their homes. The storm loomed, gathered in distant and gloomy clouds on the far horizon like a dark celestial city.

Teo was a good thirty miles past the connector. He had had to retrace old real estate due to a misunderstanding earlier—he had thought there were documents he needed to retrieve from his safety deposit box, but he realized that the bank vaults were probably safer and more secure than his old car. He turned around and headed again north.

Two of the lanes had opened up and allowed their lucky occupants to surge ahead. A pickup truck had run out of gas and sat on the gravel pull-off; its driver and passengers looked despondent and envious gazing at the relatively fast-moving cars. For a moment, Teo felt happy and tooted his horn as he passed.

In front of him was a couple in an antique Oldsmobile convertible. They'd been arguing for the past thirty miles. Drinking, too. The passenger was a bare-shouldered middle-aged woman in square sunglasses. She was redheaded and loud. When the driver would pause to savor the impact of his argument, she would throw chips of ice at him. Two men in a BMW convertible drove alongside them, egging them on. It was when their speed picked up that their activity did as well: the men encouraged her to leave her partner and come with them. Encouraged her to jump. Teo watched her crouch, her high-heeled leg taut on the doorsill while her man tried grabbing at her. She leaped, sprawling into the backseat of the BMW. The men hee-hawed and the car then methodically weaved in and out of the slowly accelerating traffic before gradually pulling away.

The traffic stopped again with the radio stations nagging Teo—twenty hours to Atlanta, one and a half days to the middle of Alabama. The Cadillac was now bookended between an exhaust-belching tour bus and a semi with a Dixie flag in the grille. In two hours he'd just gotten to the airport exit ramp. It had started raining. Teo tried positioning the television so that the reception would improve but all he could pick up was a sputtering episode of *Bonanza* with Hoss zigzagging across the screen, looking like Fred Astaire.

Special Ed had Jesmond navigate his car with a drunk's precision to his house. "You know where I live, anyway. I don't need to give you instructions." At every traffic-light approach he had him slow to fifteen miles an hour, had him wait thirty seconds at stop signs. He also let it be known that he carried his semiautomatic, military-issue pistol.

A small Filipino woman sat in his family room in a kitchen chair next to a crib with a sleeping baby. "It's okay if you leave now, Ruth." When she left, Special Ed turned to Jesmond. "Really, you son of a bitch—I lied to you." There was a taxidermist's stuffed raccoon perched on the edge of the child's blanket. Special Ed picked it up and set it on the coffee table. "I was going to get her doll at some point from the Base Exchange," he muttered. He went on to explain to Jesmond that he had indeed undergone the paternity test, but the results showed that he wasn't her father with a 95 percent degree of certainty. "So my gift to you. Who knows who the hell the mother's been fuckin' but I give you Shirley." Shirley was the baby girl's name.

Jesmond sat on the mattress in his room at Medgar's house. The baby was asleep in a corner of the mattress. Jesmond Toak as daddy. He fell beside her, breathed her scalp. It smelled like condensed milk. Special Ed had giggled dropping him and the baby off at the car. "Hurricane coming, and you with the newbie. Priceless." Special Ed reattached the distributor cap. Left him with a car seat, bottles, diapers, and formula. Also the stuffed raccoon that Jesmond, in disgust, had thrown out the car window.

The dogs were quiet. Jesmond had put them in the garage office before carrying the baby in. They quietly followed his commands. He'd been told hurricanes did something to animals. The atmospheric pressure change seemed to have spooked them. Even Lil' Monkey seemed morose.

He hadn't seen Medgar since being given notice. Medgar hadn't been coming by the house and Jesmond took steps to avoid him. It had now been more than two weeks. But it would be just like Medgar to show up while he was at work, changing the locks and locking the windows, putting all of Jesmond's things to the curb.

Was this his child? How was he going to feed it? What was he to actually do with a baby? Should he evacuate? Jesmond closed and locked the bedroom door behind him, leaving the window ajar.

Jesmond entered the garage discreetly from the hall, opening the large door manually. The dogs and Jesmond stood next to the desk, facing the street. Jesmond squatted and brought to Ashley's snout a piece of beef jerky, which he then tossed onto the lawn. Ashley followed and sniffed, as did Sarah. The two then turned and stared at Jesmond for a good long while before finally trotting off in the drizzle.

He had called Teo, on both his house and his cell phone. The wind had picked up. Feddy drove to his father's home and began poking at doors, cupping his face against windows. The force of the wind had stripped the yard's magnolia tree of its green and brown leaves and pasted them against the white porch and front of the house—it resembled a child's version of a polka-dot home.

He entered through the front door; Teo had given him keys. It felt burgled more than deserted. The wind slammed open the door and leaped up the stairs, blistering the walls and wood floor and stairs with gobs of rain while Feddy, in the pandemonium, chased papers. Bills. Receipts. He then fought the door closed before finally going from room to room—leisurely objective, curious—as if he were a criminal investigator on a television show. He had never, in recent memory, spent so much time in his father's house by himself. There was a drawer of photographs; Teo was never much for collecting and sorting. Rifling through them, Feddy paused to wonder: in fleeing, what did he take? People often spoke of grabbing photo albums, wedding dresses, diplomas, heirlooms—things to anchor memory. And there was a lot of money in Teo's secret stash site, the third flour bin in the pantry: more than he'd ever seen nosing about as a boy. Left it alone. The clothes from his ex-tenant's shop were still strewn about the house.

As Teo figured it, it made no sense for him to continue driving north. He did the math. They were barely moving ahead at fifteen miles an hour, and that was during a good spell. The storm, from what he'd heard, was galloping across the Atlantic with the prognosticators predicting a tumble onto land between Savannah and Charleston. Thus, he would be stuck right in the middle of Hurricane Burt, having to pay triple rate for some fleabag motel off the interstate with sodden carpet and Spam sandwiches and dogs and children howling in the rooms, he'd seen last year's footage. He decided to head west for Gainesville.

However, in turning onto an unfamiliar county-road exit during a downpour, he became immediately confused and his new fears suddenly welled up again. His mind began constructing elaborate vignettes. For example, prisoners, using the hurricane as cover, would escape from the prison in Stark by weaving dental floss into ropes and bending forks into grappling hooks. They would come upon Teo in his car on some deserted back road, beat him senseless, and drive off with his car, leaving him to his death by the elements. Or Klansmen, in some dark conjunction of deed and nature, would have a stupendous cross burning, the fire orange and brilliant—and Teo's car would putter right into the open field below it.

So he was very happy when he found his way back to the James Point Bridge and heading toward the city. He could see the port where Feddy worked—Feddy had called at least a half a dozen times—and as he curled into the downtown he could still smell the coffee from the coffee-processing plant, all of which was reassuring. Still, his stomach was unsettled. He swallowed one of the pills Coots had prescribed. Hard, hard swallow—on a ball of saliva.

"Fuck Feddy," Teo said aloud to himself. Guilt was what made him call. Tit for tat Teo could say now, tit for tat. The neighborhoods were in a flurry with windows being boarded, and people scrambled through supermarket parking lots to buy up the last of water, candles, canned foods—the essentials.

A gas station was open with only three or four cars in line. But of course!—The price had been doubled from what it was the day before. Teo glanced down and saw he had only a quarter of a tank. He begrudgingly pulled behind a Jeep.

They would take only cash. "The machine doesn't work," the attendant said at the cash register. The man was Sikh. Teo knew he was lying but the man stared at a point beside Teo's ear instead of making eye contact as he counted out forty dollars.

He would be wise. It was too late to get someone to board up his windows. To stay downtown at the business with Ernie—one cot, one bathroom, sitting around without electricity, listening to him jerk off in the bathroom—

No. The storm was heading up the Eastern Seaboard to Georgia and the Carolinas. Teo decided he would beat traffic, find a cheap and comfortable motel while the rest of humanity slugged it out northward on the congested freeways. He would head to Orlando. Besides, it was inland.

XXV

The rains had come, along with the thunder and the sheet lightning, then just rain. Even with daylight there were no longer any boundaries—the horizon, like night, was limitless. Yellow and gray, the daylight; and the rain snowed, coming down in great near-white clots, a blizzard pasting waste upon transparent waste.

There were pockets of general merriment. The He Ain't Here was open for a select few: the brazen, the stupid, for the bar was a good foot or two below sea level. "This ain't shit! I'm from New Orleans!" yelled one patron.

And the shelters were already full. Some of the homeless found refuge in the generosity of a man who owned a storage facility—the constructs were cinder block and they were told it could easily withstand the assault of the storm, for it was only a category 3. Someone would tap on a designated door and it would roll up to reveal four or five men already on pallets of cardboard beside a bedside commode. One frightened man retreated and spread-eagled himself inside a Dumpster behind a Winn-Dixie.

Jesmond had been able to prop the car seat in the shopping cart as he made a last run to the supermarket, though he left Lil' Monkey in the car in Bayonne's pet carrier. The shelves were nearly empty. Shirley hollered throughout. He was able find four cans of goat's milk on the infant aisle. "It's actually better for them than formula," the clerk tried to assure him. Jesmond draped her with a black plastic bag, then repositioned his backpack before running out to his car. Loading the car, with a wailing child, under billowing and snapping awnings, he implored a teenage girl who was passing by to take Lil' Monkey, and she, bewildered, did.

He found space in a shelter that was a high school gymnasium. The floor had been divided into designated squares by masking tape and priority was given to those with children. Because of Shirley, he was given an army cot and blanket. Shirley had again begun wailing. But there were other crying babies, shouting children, weeping adults.

There were families in the designated squares. A white woman, wearing only a bathing suit bottom and an orange halter top, was corralling about close to six children. One of the officials told her she had to wear more suitable attire. Her husband was stretched out on the olive-green cot, his head propped up with a blanket. He was playing a Game Boy. There were two ancient black women, one of whom was in a wheelchair, the other with a Parkinson's dodder. They'd been given a spot somewhat removed from the tumult, right next to Jesmond and the baby. The one motioned the other to wheel her over to Shirley, who'd lapsed into a gasping squawk. Jesmond fumbled with pouring formula into a bottle when they introduced themselves. "I'm Sister Mildred and this is my sister, Sister Lawrence. What a lovely chil'. How old is she?" Jesmond did not feel like explaining the situation, said she was his six-week-old newborn, that the mother had run off. "Well, we've had our share of dealing with children. We'll help out any way we can. Between the three of us it'll be fine."

The dogs, Sarah and Ashley, huddled in the entrance to Medgar's house, looking forlorn and miserable. They had loped about the neighborhood, but when the rains and winds began tilting trees and blowing over trashcans they scurried back to the house to find the garage door shut. There they howled.

Feddy watched the mayhem from his second-floor-apartment window. Couldn't help but hear it. It was like a freight train had been redirected into his living room. Down below, the bushes were strewn with newspaper, Styrofoam take-out containers, a pair of yellow sweatpants. Two young men were trying to negotiate a tarp-covered shopping cart full of what appeared to be electronic appliances. They plowed against a headwind, down the center of the brown water that made for the street, trying to avoid the deeper and faster-moving tributaries of the ditches. Marching with a heavy foot, lifting through the water. Then an unfortunate event: an unseen manhole (though Feddy thought they should have noticed the brown geyser) swallowed the cart front, tipping it and the men over and into the wash, sending the two a good twenty or so feet back down the street.

Teo's cell must not have been working. While he was sitting at the window, Feddy repeatedly punched numbers—he had spoken to Ernie at the office ("I ain't leaving. Got enough canned tuna to last me a month"); called County Hospital and the morgue. Either he got a busy tone or nobody was picking up.

He settled back in his chair and finally decided to call Jesmond. Feddy noticed he'd begun sweating, that his palms were itching. He got Jesmond's answering machine but left a message. "This is your dad. Checking up on you, seeing how you're making it through this mess. Give me a call when you get a chance. Dad. Oh, my number is—"

The first thing he'd do when he got back to civilization would be to have a good going over at one of the hospitals—not County, Teo said to himself, they'd just as soon zip you up in a bag after one of their botched experiments as rut a cat. His insides needed the once-over. He had already taken two of the pills Coots had prescribed and, if anything, his gut was worse. He needed a drive-through with one of those scopes once he got back. Really, though, a bathroom was what he needed now. He'd hit both rest stops between here and Palm Coast. And on the drive to Daytona he realized how alone he was. Visibility was five feet and gray. The rain made a cocoon.

There'd been a Volkswagen Beetle that had hugged his path. They had their interior lights on and at one point Teo saw them vigorously gesturing, arguing. Teo and the Volkswagen drove a tandem fifteen, twenty miles an hour. Coming alongside them into Palm Coast sped a motorcycle, but winds blew it down and bike and rider slid sideways, disappearing into the gloom.

Now, even the Volkswagen had peeled away. He was on some track of beach freeway. The radio made him nervous—he'd miscalculated, the hurricane had made landfall somewhere before Verona Beach. So for the past hour he'd been playing a DVD of *Sanford and Son*. There was something calming and reassuring in the black-and-white familiar chattering alongside him.

There was an exit he had missed, he was sure of it. However, the key thing was to keep calm—at the first off ramp lodging sign he'd be there in a heartbeat. Sleep in a latrine if he had to. Until then he would calm his nerves explicating the evils of Coots.

The motherfucker raped the dead and dying. He hoped the deal he'd made with Belikov would begin to bring him unending pain. Ernie attributed Coots's behavior to his being queer but the actual truth of the matter was that he was worse: he pretended to be queer. Pranced about with his tail in the air with a wink for his little faggots—then did his best to screw them out of anything that made life worth living.

The anger did bring him to a youthful place.

But the hurricane slapped and skidded the car about the road. Made the steering wheel sweat-slick. Made his stomach his heart's trampoline.

Jesmond had been able to quiet Shirley with a feeding, and he was quite comfortable on the cot. The infant was held in between his knees as he sat Indian-style, the bottle propped on his wrist while he listened to music from his iPOD. He'd periodically pull out his cell phone to see who'd called: Cash's number appeared, as well as Skooch's from the store. But his daddy had left a message. He ignored it for now.

Four men were playing an exuberant game of dominoes in a corner behind him. After winning, one of the participants stood up and began strutting, then took to scraping the gym floor with his foot as if clawing for grain.

Jesmond's phone shook in his pocket. It was a number he did not recognize. It made him feel very helpless and small—this not knowing who called. Because it spoke of so many things he did not know. "Yeah," Jesmond answered.

It was Kobe.

His mother had left.

Cash and the woman had started out arguing about moving the trailer. She had wanted him to hitch it to a truck and move them from the ditch to at least the vacant lot across the road. Cash replied that they were not in a ditch, that in fact the trailer was in a good location, the brace of trees providing a good windscreen. Anyway, he couldn't park in somebody else's lot, plus he didn't have his truck anymore. She then proceeded to let it go. She yelled, threw things, wept incessantly—all the time apologizing that her behavior was due to stress over the imminent catastrophe of Hurricane Burt as well as her AADD—Adult Attention Deficit Disorder. Cash stood and watched her carry on for a good long while. "You're one crazy bitch—I don't need the aggravation," he finally said and left. Kobe's mother was beside herself in heartbreak. She got drunk on the old Morgan and David that'd been sitting on the counter for several months and began calling Cash incessantly. He'd disconnect and she'd call again. When she finally got through she blubbered an apology, said she wasn't equal to the ground he walked on, would he please come back? "You come to me," he said, loud voices in the background. "Lemme see your love. I'm down here at Cap'n Shaw's for a hurricane party. You walk on down here, sweetheart. Heaven's just a few blocks away." So she tucked up in a parka, tightening the hood about her head, shot on lipstick. "I'm sorry, baby. I'm sorry but this is love. This is what love will make you do. I'll be right back after I talk to him. You just hold tight."

Jesmond explained the situation to the two nuns. Another child, he said. A boy this time, but again the mother left. They cooed and reassured him. No problem, they said. We'll look after Shirley. You go get the boy.

His stomach. His lower intestines, in particular. Teo caught himself scanning for where he might be able to stop. "What the hell am I going to do?" he asked—of no one of course except for the talking head beside him, but he had muted Redd Foxx several miles back.

He had become delicate. Shamefully, he had soiled himself. Teo fumed that it would be like Coots to give him something to make his bowels act up.

Twixt light and dark outside: more a murky yellow glow that his headlights ghosted. Teo's reason brought up the painter's pants in the suitcase. There was no one else to see him—he could strip; the rain would wash him off; he'd be no less for wear but for the injuries of humiliation and weather. He drove close to a mile, mapping what he thought was the shoulder of the beach road before the car came to a stop on its own. The wheels threw sand.

Teo hadn't the faintest clue as to where, submerged in the chaos of the planet, he had stopped. The rearview mirror fluttered an Armageddon that was nipping his tail; and fear, like suddenly opening a drawer of knives, was something that now rested in his lap. He tried contacting Feddy—it made him angry that the call wouldn't go through, that there was no signal. Teo was angry with his son for having called him and not, somehow, making him pick up, answer.

The noise outside bothered him the most. Teo released the sound on the television so that a laugh track washed through the space. Fred lampooning Lamont.

The car moved. The wind nudging his big car, ever so gently. He reached between the seat divider for his suitcase in the back and was about to exit before ruminating the logic of his stupidity. Smirked at his reflection. And grew more frightened—for he knew he did not want to be the old man found fouled in excrement.

So he decided to leave his clean pants out in the front seat. And he decided to leave the engine running. But turned off the television.

Water sluiced into the Cadillac as soon as he opened the car door. This, Teo could already see, had been a mistake. He had stepped out and the wind had pushed the door closed and then pushed him farther onto the beach, then into a newly formed sand gully.

He made it back to the car, breathless. He fought the wind trying to open the car door and he eventually won—not without a gash to his forehead. Drenched, he decided to remove his trousers while crouched in the driver's seat, threw the soiled pair into a wad on the floor before he realized that the other pair was soaked. So he sat there in his boxers, shivering, bleating the steering horn, incessantly gauging the chance that any new activity on his horizon might be hope of rescue.

XXVI

You can't leave the shelter.

"My son's out there."

"You didn't say anything about another child."

"His mother. Something happened to his mother and my son's by himself."

"Then you'd be leaving an infant untended. Somebody from EMS will go get him. Or the fire department."

"Will they go now?"

"I have no way of knowing that."

"Her aunts will watch her while I'm gone."

"Who?"

"Her aunts. Those are her aunts."

What he did not know was that the majority of Bayport was becoming submerged. The rain was now mostly a fine spray but the storm surge had already washed into the coastal section of the low-lying area. Jesmond nodded and agreed with the shelter supervisor that he should stay. However, when she was distracted with an argument across the gym, he simply left from the exit next to the bathroom.

Jesmond planned to drive with his headlights dark until he reached the bridge. It was about ten at night but there was enough ambient light to navigate, and, too, there were the distant pulses of heat lightning. Police cruisers prowled the neighborhood, and there was a cadre of gleeful youth testing doors with the weakening of the storm. Crouched next to a Hispanic store selling religious paraphernalia, Jesmond watched from afar their movements change into a foot pursuit. The runt of the group slipped and fell. He was immediately leaped upon by the pursuing officers and pummeled.

Though there was a curfew, the Hart Bridge did not have a police car blocking the entrance and Jesmond drove alone all the way to the Bayport exit ramp. A billboard ad proclaimed upon his descent: DRESSLER PALMS, A GATED LUXURY COMMUNITY. HAVE YOUR SAY IN THE PLANNING STAGES. INQUIRIES AT 223-9760.

The wheels of his little Toyota sank perilously low in the water. He drove in the middle of the street but he could still feel the surge trying to pull him, first in one direction, then another. He was afraid that if he hit a drop that was too deep his engine would cut off and he would float away.

The parking lot of the shopping center a good mile from the trailer was already under water. The comic-book shop's mascot, a five-foot urethane replica of The Hulk, was bobbing on its side, chained to a post. A small tree was rolling end over end, caught in a drainage depression wash.

A skiff came across the murky expanse of the parking lot. In it were two men. One was black and the other was older, Filipino. "Say, man. You can't go past here. The whole area down there's flooded." They explained that they'd spent the past several hours rescuing people trapped in houses and cars.

"Did you pick up anybody out there in a trailer near Turtle Creek Drive, over near the base's east entrance?" Jesmond asked. "A little boy? My boy's out there." They asked what he looked like. Then shook their heads no after Jesmond's description. "Nobody left out there anyway, that ain't accounted for," the black man said. The Filipino sat blinking at him.

"I've got to get out there. He's alone. He's by himself." The Filipino continued to blink at Jesmond. Then: "Look, Russell. You and him go on and take the boat. I just can't do, amigo. Too tired. God bless, though." And the Filipino said nothing else, simply hauled himself over the bow of the skiff and sloshed through the murk to what Jesmond imagined was some semblance of home.

"Yo, man, don't worry—we'll find your kid. He's gonna be all right." The man took the till of the outboard and guided them to the deeper waters of a runoff.

There were so many drowned trees and cars and planks and sheds. Swollen geography. A refrigerator floated by. A ripple of shadows coursed through the water ahead of them. "Suspect those are moccasins," the man said. He uncovered a shotgun he had next to him. Jesmond thought for a moment of the possibility of the man having a dual role—Jesmond could be found dead, the victim of some elaborate robbery scheme. His father had called him. He wanted to call his father.

"Hey, Pop." Jesmond made sure that he was heard speaking to another man. "I need your help." He quickly explained that his granddaughter was in a hurricane shelter but now he was about to go and pick up his grandson, who was stranded out here in Bayport. He would call him as soon as they reached him. Jesmond then closed his phone.

They puttered down a crooked new channel, the hump of a car roof as an island. The man paused beside it, shining a light onto the neck of a street sign poking up through the pearl water. Pearson and Larson Road. It was the cross street before Cash's rental trailer. "Caint go down there with the boat. Too dark, too low. And too much stuff floating I caint see." They moored the boat to a truck on a rising crest of road and waded forward.

They slogged past a small apartment complex, ten or so units. It had stopped raining. People were clustered on the second floor, dangling from the wrought-iron railing to escape the heat since they were without electricity. Beams from flashlights whipped about Jesmond and the man. "How you all holding out?" the man asked. Then: "Any of you got a boy—what's his name, man?—Kobe up there with you?" With the negative they plowed ahead.

The trailer surprisingly rested a little above the flood line, a hillock in the depressed lot. The rotten fence was a broken xylophone. The kudzu had been spun and draped black about the trailer in the weak light, and a pendulous figure-eight loosely slid and flopped from the branches of a collapsed tree into the muck with a smack. It was then that Jesmond thought to phone Kobe.

"Another dad-gum cottonmouth," the man said. "They're one mean-as-hell snake. And I left the shotgun in the boat. Just as soon fight you, you cross their path."

Jesmond's cell call would not go through. "Kobe!" Jesmond then yelled.

"I'm going back to the boat to get my gun."

"Kobe!" he yelled again.

From the trailer he heard a small, swallowed reply—more like a mew. Jesmond plodded to the trailer. The water came to his thigh. He thought enough to move his cell phone to the inner pocket of his windbreaker.

The trailer was at lean from a large tree limb elbowing into its left panel. Jesmond scouted his light about the handle and the edges before prying open the door.

Like stepping into the cabin of a ship run aground—the floor at a funhouse tilt, the windows a watery, cataract blue (his reflected light). Another limb (probably the same tree) had stabbed through a back room, branching into the dinette. "Jesmond"—he heard the mewling voice behind him—"my leg hurts but I don't think I broke anythin.'" The boy lay in the wedge of a heaved countertop. Black stink gobbled up from the floor drain. And the floor—ropy and slick and pasty—moved in segments. He called him again—"Oh, Dad. Please. Please. I need your help."

XXVII

This is what you are to do if your child is in desperate need. You first determine how much of your heart you will allow to be ripped from you. A quarter? A third? Of course, you say *all*, but that is not feasible and you are not presented with that option. You then briefly perseverate over the verb *to do*—What am I to do, what am I to do, what am I to do? Then you are to get in your car and drive because it is an action. The needful situation also requires action. You know that the little Gremlin, the little car that you have carrying a flashlight, a cooler, a first-aid kit, a tarp, an ax, and flares, may not be feasible transport to the situation that confronts your child. An amphibious assault vehicle would be best. You briefly dream of commandeering one of those vehicles from the naval base, guns ablaze—but you quickly sink like a stone to the reality of how best the little car can deliver you to your child. The best you are to hope is that all you planned will stay afloat.

The best Feddy hoped was that the car would get him through the natural and police blockades to at least the vicinity of Jesmond. There, if need be, he'd drive the car till it floated, float the car till it sank. At that point he'd say it tanked because of the storm and then wait to see what the insurance company would say. Short of the four hundred or so dollar's worth of repairs recently, the car wasn't worth five hundred.

He understood now that the boy was not his grandson, but that he had been abandoned by his ma and had been hurt somehow by the storm and flood. And there were snakes. A plenitude. And that the man assisting him had not yet come back.

It was now close to five in the morning. Still dark, but a faint yellow-red cast of dawn ichor. When Feddy got to the crest of street where Jesmond's car was parked he came upon the man he sensed had initially accompanied Jesmond. People were huddled about the skiff and several were looking up, watching behind Feddy. For the man had been bitten, several times in fact.

Feddy recognized him. His pain had not yet translated the man into anonymity. Feddy knew him from County Hospital; the man had been an orderly. He was a regular guy but had a vicious stutter whenever he was around women. "I think he was with my son rescuing my grandson," Feddy volunteered.

"Yeah? Well he ain't helping 'em now. Got bit at least twiced by a cottonmouth," a woman tending to him said. She looked past Feddy to flag an approaching rescue van.

Feddy told them that he understood that they were tied up but that he could not wait for Fire and Rescue, those were his children. He felt embarrassed and conspicuous in his explanation.

The woman had pointed out to him a special access road that was a high ridge coursing behind properties. Part of it went onto military grounds, which was why there had been a padlocked gate.

Feddy drove nimbly atop the gravel trace. Jesmond's cell phone had died out, so he navigated by anxiety as well as the few landmarks suggested. By vicarious desperation, too. Jesmond had told him about the submerged Larson Road, and coming upon it from the back allowed Feddy to drive almost halfway into the field behind the trailer before his wheels began sinking.

The waters shimmered vaguely yellow with sunrise, holding the trailer like a moat. Feddy sloshed beside the car, and from the trunk, put everything but the ax into the large cooler. (He had actually stolen the ax from a neighbor's shed.) He draped the ax over his shoulder like a lumberjack, dragging the cooler behind him. As the water came to his knees, the cooler began to float.

He'd been told that water moccasins could strike while in the water; though Feddy had also heard that they preferred swinging from an overhang and hitting with the momentum. He took to holding the ax over his head as he approached the trailer.

The tarp. Feddy had Jesmond position Kobe on top of the tarp and they carried the boy in a sling between them. But the brown car had sunk deeper into the mire and the engine turned only briefly before gasping to a stop. So they positioned the boy on top of the cooler and floated him between them, toward Pearson and Larson.

"I wouldn't put your hand there," Feddy said to his son. They were pressing through bramble, fallen trees, floating debris. Jesmond was about to push against the V of a fallen water oak. It was wrapped with a snake the circumference and color of a grapefruit. Feddy plodded through the water into the spray of something he had felt but had barely seen—gnats? noseeums? a spiderweb remnant? (It would come to him a year or so later, barelegged in the kitchen as the dust from the vacuum-cleaner bag flew—an odd thing to remember. What was it?)

After they had surrendered the boy to the EMS truck, meeting them in the parking lot of the apartment complex, Jesmond fell onto his father—this large mass of man atop Feddy—and began shuddering with tears.

XXVIII

S ometime in the 1950s an old Irish priest, a Father Mahoney, had been sent by the archdiocese of St. Augustine to tend to the affairs of the very same parish in Johnsonville that Father Clemons was to administrate a decade or so later. Father Mahoney was a drunk and a deadbeat—Church officials had sent him there essentially to separate him from his misdeeds in Boston. When Hurricane Dora hit in '53 (landing as a category 4, by all accounts) things were already not going well—Father Mahoney disliked immensely his charges, blatantly addressing the congregation as pickanninies from the pulpit and would openly get drunk on communion wine during confessions. Dora flooded the low-lying areas of the north and west side—the black areas—and people sought refuge in the relatively higher ground of the church's interior. Father Mahoney, however, had chained the church doors closed. Seventeen people ended up dying in flood-related deaths. At the inquest, Father Mahoney stated that he'd feared that the sanctuary would be looted.

Hurricane Burt reproduced certain aspects of the previous catastrophe. Fifteen people suffered death by drowning in the low-lying areas; a king-size bed floated down Martin Luther King Boulevard with a dead elderly black woman; Mahout Zagreb, the owner of Gator Cabs, was to be indicted for extortion and negligent homicide—he had instructed his cabbies to carry people to shelters only if they had a hundred dollars in cash or something of equal value, a wheelchair-bound man died as a consequence; looters ransacked the zoo claiming hunger, but several rare gazelles and a zebra sustained serious and festering arrow wounds from a bow hunter gone awry, and the mate of the black swan had been removed—its partner was so heartbroken; there were shootings with deaths; there were suicides; while foolishly cavorting in the Atlantic, Irwin's cameraman filmed his own drowning during a storm surge; the attorney general of the state of Florida broke down on national television and weepingly confessed to his infidelity; a middle-aged man in camouflage was arrested for shooting stray dogs, dogs that he claimed were carrying the rabies virus, if anyone was astute enough to check; there was a boat from Cuba disguised as a car—or a car disguised as a boat—that was blown off course, all the way within twelve miles of Ponte Azul, the wealthy neighbor of Johnsonville, but the coast guard picked them up and towed them (twenty men and women) all the way back to Miami to be deported back to Cuba; also there were two sightings—bizarre, disturbing reports—of swarms of bees landing upon and apparently consuming the cadaverous remains of drowned livestock; prisoners from the Stark, Medium Security Penitentiary did indeed try to escape under the distraction of the hurricane, but by tunneling east with spoons, inspired by the movie, *The Shawshank Redemption*—they had barely gotten five feet from the prison grounds, however, before they were arrested, for their guards were waiting for them; and even more intriguing was a man, spurred by the candor of the attorney general (this man was a retired newsman, both a print and television correspondent who had traveled throughout Asia, South and Central America, the Middle East), who confessed on his grandson's blog his life's story—how he'd been an executive for a major television network with a sizable retirement package, but then his wife developed cancer, dying a year later, depleting him of his retirement nest egg of close to a half a million, forcing him now to live in an in-law cottage in his son's backyard in Ortega, "I was a bad man but I'm recovering now"—for he used to drink, he used to drink because at close to the beginning of the last century, when he was three years old, he had drunk from a Mason jar he found sitting on a rock near a river in Montana, drunk a mouthful of lye that nearly dissolved completely his esoph-agus: "I was supposed to have died"—his father then beseeched *his* father for help (he was a preacher in good financial stead, his grand-father), but his grandfather told his father, the retired television and print correspondent's father, that it was to be God's will; and his father went bankrupt saving his life. And so it was that after dinner, his father, the retired television and print correspondent's father, would pull out the Bible and have them each read from it, and they would then take turns providing rational refutations of scripture passages.

The Cadillac was found buried headfirst in a cleft where the beach had suddenly given way. The driver's side door was wide open—wet brown-black sand obliterated the floorboards and portions of the seats and steering wheel. There was nobody inside.

Police and volunteers combed the beach in a quincunx pattern, stepping two feet forward in unison, poking a stick a foot or more into the sand in a half-moon pattern, then another two feet forward, repeating the same. "Something our chief there learned in his half-day seminar," one of the sergeants smirked. However, on only the fourth advancement somebody hit something. They uncovered the body of a light-skinned elderly black man, about five feet six inches, clad in white painter's pants and a T-shirt, barefoot.

XXIX

The weather was hot but the skies were clear. There were still parts of the city without electricity and at night reporters would show live aerial footage of black empty swatches against the constellation of city lights. "At least for those of you that can see this," one reporter quipped.

Feddy sat watching the news in what had been Teo's living room. Feddy had left Rachel's office earlier that day. "Congratulations, Feddy"—they had spent the past few hours excavating ledgers and leases and deeds and portfolio and bank statements—"you've just moved into my neighborhood," Rachel Ennis remarked. "But most of this shit's too convoluted and complicated for a simple trial law-yer like me to sort out completely. I'm gonna put you in touch with a friend of mine who deals with estate issues." They talked as well about his granddaughter. "Now you've got to follow me here. For Jesmond to get custody of Shirley we have to make sure that Peaches did formally abandon the child. Then we still have to walk the tight-rope regarding Edward Richmond—now I'm sure he's not stupid enough to just leave *his* child with the party in an adultery case, so I bet you the paternity stuff is true. The question before the courts will be, though, whether Jesmond is actually the father. Once that's established we're home free."

Kobe was another matter.

His medical evaluation revealed old fractures, bruises in odd places; it also demonstrated that he was well below his percentile for height and weight. And Kobe's mother had yet to make an appearance; for that matter, Jesmond hadn't seen or heard anything from Cash. "Maybe they ran off and got married," he joked. They found a grandmother in South Carolina. That he was half black she ascribed to God's punishment. He was soon bundled off with the old woman in a station wagon held together by duct tape.

When Teo Toak lay in state, Feddy took the keys from his own pocket and studied the safety-deposit-box key. Teo had given it to him years back. Hinted at what it hoarded. Feddy followed to the letter Teo's burial plan.

The key now rested in a saucer on the coffee table. Whatever belonged to the past or the future he decided didn't exist except in memory or in anticipation. One of Teo's business partners was to come by this evening to talk over a project that was never completed. He said his father was about to sell him his motel and that he'd given him money as a deposit.

"Don't know about that one, Feddy," Rachel had mused, "See what contract was drawn up. Of course, don't sign anything yet. Just play it by ear."

When the time came—they'd agreed upon ten that evening—Feddy had already decided to go through with the sale, if the man was on the up-and-up. He knew the man a little: some Russian who'd already been the motel's manager. And Feddy had done the homework and checked with the tax assessor's office as well as appropriate websites. A fair offer would be close to five hundred thousand dollars. At some point he would need a CPA. His cousin, Paul, was a CPA. Maybe—

At five after ten a stooped, sallow man with bags under his eyes stood before the peephole. He looked weary, stooping into the living room, but he smiled at Feddy as he introduced himself. "Sergey Belikov. I'm sorry about the death of your father. I understand there was no funeral?"

"I did what he asked. Readings at the gravesite. That's all he wanted."

They chatted about property and the suspected boon areas of the city, about the possible closure of the naval base and what impact it would have on the collective pocketbook. Then: "I will be direct with you, Mr. Toak. I had given your father money, as I have told you, as holding payment for the motel. Of course, with his death there is no way to verify that transaction. It is only my word. But I can tell you are a perceptive man. And I am prepared to pay you four hundred and eighty-five thousand dollars for the hotel, not counting this ten thousand."

Feddy briefly studied Belikov. "That will be fine," he finally said.

"You do not want to check around as to whether I give you a fair price?"

"I've looked into it. The only thing I don't really know is what your ledgers show. What the monthly net is, for example, how much is the Country Hearth Inn's net take."

"It barely breaks even on month-to-month. But understand, I do not want the motel for the pleasure of running a short-stay motel. It will help me in other ways. But I would like to ask you—do you know a Medgar Coots?"

"Yeah." Feddy again studied him. "You must have dealings with Medgar."

"He has done a major injury to someone I know well and take care of. He cheated your father, too. There are properties Medgar Coots pushed him into selling so much below their value. My friend tells me he made your father into a very unhappy man and that he tries to hurt your son. Did you know Melan is my friend?"

"No."

"Yes. A business associate. I am close to my father as you were, Mr. Toak. In fact he lives with me. I would like to ask a favor of you, Mr. Toak." He played a cigarette between his fingers. Yellowed. Calloused. Spoon-shaped nails. "May I smoke? Of course, I will make sure that you are duly compensated. I would like you to have Medgar Coots meet with you at your father's hospital. The closed hospital next to the cemetery property that Mr. Coots swindled from your father. The cemetery that is to be part of the airport expansion. But I will talk to Mr. Coots."

XXX

J esmond sat at a Waffle House on Emerson and Beach, awkwardly displayed as a new father—a car seat holding his daughter faced him on the tabletop. He found himself lately thinking quite a bit about Peaches. It amazed him how easy it was to become obsessed. He wasn't even sure that he could call what he felt love—he suspected it was really boredom. Ecstatic boredom. These were all things he would have to adjust to.

While Shirley slept he pulled out sections of the paper, halving the halves quietly so as she wouldn't awaken. It was the metro section that caught his attention. There was Kobe's mother. She was in jail.

Jesmond stared at the picture. After a while he read the piece. Her name was Peggy Haledon. She'd been arrested in Pensacola for possession of a kilo of cocaine with intent to distribute. Her accomplice was not named but was remarked to be the thirty-two-year-old male Caucasian passenger in her rental car. In the mug shot she demonstrated a fierce squint.

When Feddy called Medgar, he agreed to meet with him on the property about said property. Yes, Medgar said, he would be interested in possibly taking the hospital off Feddy's hands. Too. For he had helped Teo out with that white elephant, that derelict Negro graveyard—the city was pushing for maintenance and upkeep, particularly since that eyesore might well become some designated landmark, and access to it was cut off by the airport—how in the world was he ever to move such a piece of property? No, he agreed, there would be no need for attorneys right now, though did he use that woman—What's her name? Rachel Ennis?—for his property and tax issues as well. *We're practically brothers, Jesmond is like a son to me—let me give you the name of a good real estate attorney I know. And don't worry, there won't be any conflict of interest.*

The pictures in the hospital foyer. The picture glass all dull with dust. Feddy craned and stooped to study all the black-and-white photographs of the nursing classes, all the black-and-white photographs of the medical house staff; then a Christmas party in the sunroom with all the patients dated 1948, and three of the nursery with children dated 1952, '54, and '55; then two color photographs: an aerial view of the hospital, and the hospital foyer with the self-same photos.

Feddy felt eerie and despondent—as if Teo, smudged and hidden somewhere in all these pictures, had been betrayed by him; that all he needed was to be recognized and revealed by Feddy but for Feddy being too inept.

As it was two in the afternoon, the light from recessed corridor windows bled stark noonish light that made the windowless areas even darker. Feddy settled down in a plastic bucket chair in the lobby to stare at the double glass door with the little hexagon wires.

Sergey arrived with two companions. When he stepped into the lobby, he pointed ahead and the two men who accompanied him followed as directed. "When Medgar comes, bring him to the second floor. Tell him that there is something odd that you want him to see." Sergey seemed to grin sheepishly at Feddy before disappearing into the dark of the stairs.

Medgar appeared, waving.

Almost girlishly ebullient—Medgar waddled from photo to photo, placing a finger onto this glass, then the next. "Come on,"

Feddy said, "Let's go upstairs. There's something I want you to see."

At the stairs, both took a first step, then stepped back for the other. "Shall we dance?" Medgar joked. "You know what this reminds me of?" he continued. *Shirley Temple Theater*? Bill 'Bojangles' Robinson in *The Little Colonel*—tapping number up and down the stairs"—Medgar then proceeded with a little tap-dancing exhibition. Feddy silently watched.

Medgar smiled as Feddy directed his attention to the hospital grounds below through the clouded wintry glass. Winked. Feddy thought it was at first to his reflection, then realized it was to the trio mirrored behind them.

"I am afraid you will not be happy man, Medgar Coots," Sergey finally said. Medgar still hadn't turned around. Instead, addressed Sergey's reflection—"Hmmm. I suspect you're here because of the incident with the little Russian waif."

Feddy surveyed Medgar. A thin crown of sweat. But he was not fearful, not sad, not anxious. Instead, contentedly opaque—Feddy couldn't see a single thought move across his face.

"The son of Elena Koslov was made a woman in jail because of you. In the jail he was robbed of being a man and he sought out and killed the thief. Now he will spend more years in prison than he has being a man. So I will make you suffer for what has happened to the mother and son. And you will suffer like this: I will tell you now, very slowly, so that you may understand, that you will soon be unable to move below your chin, Dr. Coots. I was a special soldier, a colonel in Chechnya; I know that anticipation is the best form of pain. That is why you are not to blind prisoners—you would deprive them of the ability to anticipate. You will not be able to move because you will be pithed. You are a doctor, you know what pithing is." Sergey softly stroked the nape of Medgar's neck.

Medgar was to be swaddled in the Used Clothes for Africa: he was to be smuggled out in a shipping container headed for a port in Tanzania. For the voyage, a long thin hose connected to a large water bottle would be pinned to his cheek; there would be a bucket of kibble at his side. And all identifying items would be stripped from him; instead, he would be dressed in clothes from the container that was to be his sarcophagus.

"—Your tomb. Whether Ivan will paralyze you so you will be able to feed yourself depends on chance and anatomy. Usually there is enough movement to allow you to breathe, not to yell. You will not be able to yell. And to move your hands enough to bring food to your mouth? That will depend upon chance, too. May you survive the voyage and experience a foreigner's kindness to a cripple.

"But I will take your glasses. I was a myopic, so I understand how painful it is to see the world so blurred."

XXXI

Feddy left quickly, before the cascade of events. Belikov was clever—he had to give him his due. That evening, with its smoked-glass windows, Medgar's car would be driven to one of Belikov's chop shops and his Mercedes would be broken down and the parts dispersed throughout the states through all his Russian connections. Melan, of course, used him—his cars that he had to move quickly that weren't on import manifests. Feddy felt he was now forever bound to the man: complicit in knowledge if not in action. Belikov wouldn't have to say a word if their paths crossed in the future and Feddy would respond as if it was a debt owed, such was the nature of complicity.

"Hey, Pops." Jesmond was sitting on the stoop of Teo's house as he parked his car. His Gremlin. After the water had receded and the mud had hardened the car was able to be backed out, just like that. For grins, Feddy decided to hang on to it for a while longer. He had been presented with the bill for Teo's Cadillac. They had removed it from the beach and towed it back to the house. Jesmond said he wanted the car but the verdict was still out as to whether it was worth repairing.

"Where's my grandbaby?"

"She's with Ma."

He was about to say something, about whether that was a good idea to have his ex-wife watch the child, but held his tongue.

"You know, Pop, I really think I loved her. Peaches." And the boy then went on to elaborate his litany of sorrows, his interior chorus of grief and love's reasons.

"As I see it—I, Medgar Coots, did a good thing not telling the boy, not telling Feddy, the possibility of their maladroit parentage, the potential misparentage. I wonder if current genetic testing could really sort this mess out, sort out the father from the grandfather from the son? Sort out who was what to whom? Anyway, I did good.

"As of now I remember . . . I remember in Stockholm, Sweden, a public toilet: the outside was a mirror, as you'd walk around it you'd see everything reflected, the surfaces were all mirrors. But inside? Inside you looked out on the world. It was a one-way mirror. Sitting vulnerable on the crapper you felt the world was watching you but the world is really oblivious. That, to a tee, represents Kierkegaard's man with a transparent soul."

The animal-control officers were silently patrolling the neighborhoods. Newly feral dogs—abandoned, remote, hungry dogs—trotted through lawns and porches, climbed through open windows even of occupied homes; a pack made up of a boxer, two pit bulls, a poodle, and a terrier mutt had fanned through a supermarket and held it at bay.

"The shelter's getting full. I hate to think of what they gonna do," Jesmond commented on the local news rattling through the screen. He was again on the stoop while his father gently rocked in the porch swing, thumping. Jesmond stood up and stretched, looking through the screen at the clock on the mantel. "Almost eleven thirty, Pops. I'm going over to Ma's place. Why don't you walk with me?" He stared at the mantel. "You ever gonna send those ashes?" A vase holding Father Clemons sat next to the clock over the fireplace.

"Dunno. I'm trying to decide whether I should just go ahead and send them to his cousin with a little note apologizing or try to get back up there around Angola and do what he wanted. We'll see."

They talked about Shirley as they walked; they talked about whether they would go ahead and keep the bail bond business—"It really could be Toak and Son"—keeping Ernie as a partner, or just closing it outright.

They were passing through a neighborhood where the power still hadn't been restored; there were no streetlamps, only moonlight. Creatures seemed to fasten on to objects—leaves, stoops, branches, car hoods—betraying nothing of their existence until a leap or a beating of wings or a yawp. Then they would startle.

In front of them, on a front porch, two canine forms could be made out. They studied Feddy and Jesmond—by their stillness. Then one dog turned to press its weight against the front door, whereupon it opened and the dog entered. The other stood watch awhile longer before trotting behind it. "I know those dogs. Those are Coots' old Dobermans," Jesmond said, walking up to the porch.

"Man, get your ass down here! You're liable to get yourself shot," Feddy half shouted.

"Come on, Dad. You know this woman. Miss Pinch, right? Old woman been living by herself for years? I have no idea what those fuckin' dogs might do."

Candle remnants guttered from Blue Willow saucers. They listened for other sounds in the house, listened through the asynchronous ticking of her clocks, walked onto the dampening runner in her hallway, listened to the tandem clicking of Ashley and Sarah upon the hardwood floors. When the dogs caught sense of Jesmond they made their way to where he stood, and they followed his lead to the front door and quietly left. And Jesmond returned to see his father standing over the recumbent, sleeping form of the octogenarian Miss Pinch. She had gathered her arms about an old doll in lace with a large celluloid head. And Feddy, stooping over and arranging the white bonnet on the doll, looked to his son for what they should do next.

S locum Consolidated Enterprises had purchased, in succession, four mortuaries, three in Florida and one in Georgia. In addition, there fell onto them a crematorium in Georgia that was, for want of a better term, a steal. The volume was relatively modest but steady. The former proprietors, a blind man and his nephew, made arrangements to continue supervising the unit for a nominal fee but with a sizable stock-option package.

The facility was deep in the pinewoods bordering northern Florida. One man, a sixty-six-year-old Vietnam War vet, operated all the kilns, solo. He suffered from emphysema, and his reconnaissance movements during the war had left him hazed and dark and derelict. As time progressed his moods became darker, and as he felt, in addition, cheated, he took to simply tossing the bodies into the woods, unburied. He would return urns filled with quicklime and gravel. When his activities were finally brought to light, a number of families affected expressed their outrage and disappointment by filing a class action suit against SCE. SCE, in turn, was outraged and embarrassed and charges were brought against both the supervisors and the Vietnam vet. "Please remember that those motherfuckers gave me not one goddam thing I wanted," the vet said before a live television interview at the site. With that, the wind unpinned the loosely tied trench coat and he sat cross-legged before the camera, naked as an egg.

Hundreds of bodies were removed from the woods. And a year later, a young boy hunting rabbit scuffed up a tendril of root piercing a vertebra.

About the Author

Solon Timothy Woodward was born in Jackson, Tennessee, and grew up in Northern California. He attended Harvard University, where he studied biology and philosophy and was the fiction editor for the college literary magazine *The Harvard Advocate*. He then studied medicine at the Mayo Clinic College of Medicine and the University of Virginia, where he worked on his fiction writing with the novelist John Casey during his spare time. His short fiction has appeared in *The Gettysburg Review, The Indiana Review, Shenandoah, Fiction International, The African-American Review* and others. He has been the David R. Sokolov Scholar in fiction at Breadloaf, and the Tennessee Williams Scholar at Sewanee, which chose his story "A Touch of Lubitsch" as their entry for Harcourt's Best New American Voices 2007. He has twice been a finalist for the Pushcart Prize. He lives and practices medicine in Jacksonville, Florida.